FICTION TITLES BY IAN A. O'CONNOR

The Wrong Road Home

Point Option

The Pegasus Directive

The Twilight of the Day

The Barbarossa Covenant

The Seventh Seal

NON-FICTION TITLES BY IAN A. O'CONNOR

With Howard C. "Scrappy" Johnson

SCRAPPY: Memoir of a U. S. Fighter Pilot in Korea and Vietnam

What readers are saying about

THE SEVENTH SEAL

"If you want a book you can't put down, you've come to the right place!" *–David Rosenstein*

"Great book for anyone who likes thrillers with many twists and turns. You will continually change your mind about who the bad guys are." *–Terry Everett*

"This is a story David Baldacci or Daniel Silva would have loved to have." *–Rick Vair*

The Seventh Seal is the best I've found in the recent spate of releases calling themselves "thrillers". *–Kae Bender*

"Exciting action through to the end and will keep you guessing all the way." *–John Siniscal*

"Very good book. I had a hard time putting it down." *–Deborah R. Graham*

"Fantastic!! Loved it ..... Can't wait for the next one. The author writes such great stories that feel so real." *– Chris White*

A Justin Scott Thriller

THE SEVENTH SEAL

VATICAN'S AMBASSADOR IS CHARGED WITH MURDER IN POLITICAL THRILLER

IAN A. O'CONNOR

Pegasus Publishing & Entertainment Group

LIBRARY OF CONGRESS CATALOGUING-IN-PUBLICATION DATA
Library of Congress Control Number: 2025918731
Pegasus Publishing and Entertainment Group – USA.

O'Connor, Ian A., 1944-

THE SEVENTH SEAL -
File
Fiction - Novel
Thriller – Murder –Political – Mystery – International Intrigue

ISBN – 978-1-7374229-8-3 Hardback
ISBN – 978-1-7374229-9-0 Paperback
ISBN – 979-8-9997861-0-4 ebook

First Edition – First printing: ©May 2004

Second Edition - First printing: ©May 2015

Third Edition - First printing: © September 2025

Cover and Interior Design by Glen M. Edelstein, Hudson Valley Book Design.

Visit Ian at: www.ianaoconnor.com
This is a work of fiction
Printed in the United States of America
LSC-C 1 2 3 4 5 6 7 8 9 10

CONTENTS

To my wife Candice Myers O'Connor
My forever compass.

THE SEVENTH SEAL

CHAPTER 1

"Speak," Justin Scott commanded, his tone tense, angry, barely civil. Twice in the last ten minutes his dinner had been interrupted by in-your-face salesmen hawking junk, and in all likelihood this intrusion would make it three despite his number being on the national do-not-call list. He stood ready to sever the connection with a curt, I'm not interested.

"Mr. Justin Scott?" The voice was tentative, polite, formal.

"Who's this?" he challenged.

"My name is Monsignor Capelletti," the voice replied. "I'm the chief of staff for the papal nuncio, Francis Cardinal Kettering. Your name was given to me as someone to be trusted, someone who can help. And I very much need your help."

Justin took note of the caller's accent and rhythmic ebb and flow of his words. *Sure sounds Italian,* he allowed, anger fading fast. *And calling on behalf of the Vatican's ambassador, no less. Easy,* he immediately cautioned, *you more than most know this town's an asylum without walls which means the caller could be nothing more than a talented prankster.*

Inquisitiveness, however, won over the moment, and nudged aside the last vestige of his anger. "What kind of help?" he asked in his most noncommittal voice.

The question was ignored. "I have a car en route to your home as we speak, Mr. Scott. My driver's been instructed to take you back to the embassy."

"Whoa, not so fast," Justin replied, his newfound inquisitiveness giving way to a skepticism honed by over twenty-five years of FBI training. Though retired from government service, he was now self-employed as a private investigator, his skills eagerly sought by the city's coterie of rich and powerful trial lawyers. "This old fool has no intention of climbing into any car simply because an unknown voice over the phone asks him to. What did you say your name was?"

"Monsignor Capelletti," the voice replied.

Well, you sure have the accent down, Capelletti, or whoever you are. It was time to see where this conversation was really going. "Hang up," he abruptly commanded.

"But why?" The puzzlement was genuine.

"So that when I dial the Vatican Embassy and you come back on the line I'll know that you're legit, that's why," he replied in a voice a tad more sarcastic than he'd intended.

Justin broke the connection, counted to three, and called directory assistance. A minute later he dialed the embassy and was immediately put through to Capelletti. His manner mellowed considerably upon hearing the familiar voice. "So, what can I do for you, Monsignor?"

"It's really Cardinal Kettering who has need of your services, Mr. Scott," Capelletti said, using the diplomat's ecclesiastical rank as a hook. "He begs you come as soon as possible," he added, in a voice trailing off to a whisper.

"Why, has your cardinal murdered somebody?" Justin asked with a deliberate lightheartedness meant to convey to Capelletti that his use of dramatics was really not necessary.

"That's exactly what's happened, Mr. Scott," the priest said, his words now barely audible.

The enormity of Capelletti's acknowledgment caught Justin by surprise. *Did I hear what I think I heard?* It took him a long moment to conclude that indeed he had. "Well, you've certainly piqued my curiosity," he managed. "Who did you say recommended me?"

"I didn't, Mr. Scott, but it was Jack O'Bryan. He called from Rome less than an hour ago and said you'd remember him. I don't want to say anything more because I'm no longer sure this line is secure."

Justin knew O'Bryan. He was a priest; no, a monsignor, he corrected himself. But more importantly, Jack O'Bryan was a man who passed muster.

Capelletti's use of his friend's name worked its intended magic. "I'll see you just as soon as your driver can get me to your embassy."

* * *

For twenty minutes Justin sat and listened as Capelletti recounted a tale as strange as any he had heard over a lifetime of strange tales. Through it all he kept thinking it more than just a little peculiar that Cardinal Kettering had remained conspicuously absent. Especially in light of the fact that he had supposedly begged for this meeting.

"Would you ask the ambassador to join us," Justin said when Capelletti had finished. "I'd like to hear what he has to say about the murder last night." Something's definitely not kosher here, he found himself thinking with a sense of foreboding.

Capelletti shook his head. "I'm sorry, Mr. Scott, the ambassador will neither be seeing nor speaking to anyone. At least not for now.

Those orders came from the Holy See only minutes before you arrived."

Justin stared at Capelletti, willing himself to believe the man. His inner voice warned that he was probably being used—if not by this priest—then by someone in Rome. But he couldn't figure out why. And, yet, he reasoned quickly, if Capelletti was indeed telling the truth, then he had to assume that the wall of silence was already up and this man was merely the messenger. Which meant someone far up the ecclesiastical ladder was firmly in charge.

Justin only had to look at Capelletti to know the man was under enormous pressure. His sense of unease blossomed. It was time to leave. He rose and Capelletti followed suit. The priest led the way to the front door.

"I'll speak with the police first thing in the morning," Justin said, his voice deliberately cold as he stood on the top step and offered his hand. "I'll need to hear what their homicide folks have to say before I decide whether or not to take on your case. I'll be in touch, Monsignor. Goodnight."

Capelletti shook the proffered hand, nodded a silent good-bye and slipped back inside his embassy.

Justin had made no promises. He hoped Capelletti realized that what little he had agreed to do was only because of his friendship with O'Bryan.

Homeward bound in the luxury of the embassy's limousine, he summarized what he knew and what he suspected. None of it was good.

Tell you one thing, he thought, as the car whizzed past the floodlit Capitol, there are folks in Washington and folks in Rome who're now in some serious trouble because of the stunt the Pope's ambassador apparently pulled last night.

and he mouthed a prayer that his friend O'Bryan wouldn't be counted among the soon-to-come casualties.

CHAPTER 2

Justin trailed a busload of Japanese tourists through the massive front doors of the Washington D.C. metro police headquarters. It was nine o'clock, Tuesday morning, and already the temperature was crowding the eighty-degree mark.

He maneuvered past the suddenly-stalled group and made for the sign-in desk. Once cleared, he headed for the elevators and the second floor office of Commander Valerie Tobias, Chief of Homicide and boss to scores of detectives spread among the city's seven districts. Everybody addressed her as Inspector rather than by her official rank of Commander. He had phoned at seven-thirty and she had said, sure, come on over.

Memories stirred as he allowed his thoughts to linger on Valerie Tobias. He'd first met her more than a dozen years ago when she had been a newly minted detective named Valerie Covington. She'd been so cocksure of herself, even then, he remembered, taking to the drudgery of the job as easily as slipping into a fashionable suit. She seemed to possess a natural gift for solving murders—a woman's intuition she would always insist with a self-deprecating shrug of her shoulders—knowing full well that was utter nonsense. The truth was far more mundane. It was the result of her being thorough to a fault in every facet of investigative procedure. That singular trait was her forte.

They had met while working a case involving the murder of a congressman. They'd clicked, and became an item. So much so that Justin asked her to marry him a scant three months later. He now blushed at the remembrance.

Valerie proved to be the smart one and said no. She had sensed it wouldn't work—a woman's intuition, and for real this time—and for all the right reasons. Difference in age, difference in religion, differences about differences. Except sex. On that score she'd always agreed they were in the groove, a seamless one every night the sun went down. She had readily admitted that she loved him, but in the end she could not bring herself to believe that he was truly over his recently estranged wife, and her woman's intuition whispered a siren's song to her passionate heart that he never would.

She severed the relationship then held her ground. She refused to return his calls, refused to answer the door, refused his flowers, letters, or telegrams.

Justin was devastated. Months later he heard that she'd married an engineer named Dan Tobias. He also learned that they had a daughter.

Because of the nature of their jobs, their paths had crossed several times over the intervening years, but long ago they'd settled into just being friends.

Where had the years gone? He was overcome with a sense of loneliness as he rode the car up a floor. He had reconciled with his wife just as Valerie had predicted, but they'd drifted apart again after several years of trying. They, too, had remained friends, but no longer was there any talk of another reconciliation. "Old dogs, old tricks," he sighed through the haze of nostalgia as he made his way down the freshly painted corridor toward a rendezvous with love lost.

As he came to Valerie's open door he spotted her standing with her back to him, and her phone pressed close to her ear. She had changed so little.

Valerie Tobias was a perfect five-seven and boasted of having carried the same one hundred and twenty-four pounds since her sophomore year. She was a firm believer in exercise and diet, but was no fanatic. She wore her black hair to her collar, always quick to describe it as her best asset whenever complimented. She was considered to be very attractive by both men and women, and the one lesson she had learned and retained from her interlude with Justin was the importance of clothes. At work she always wore tailored, size eight suits, unless, of course, the occasion called for her to be in uniform.

He couldn't help but overhear as he continued to gaze.

"But it's our case, Chief, and they know it. We have sole jurisdiction in the District."

The voice at the other end cut her off. Justin couldn't make out the words, but he saw her stiffen as she listened to her boss. At one point she eased the phone away, but only far enough to unsnap a small earring and toss it angrily on her desk.

She took a deep breath. "Very well, I understand." She slowly placed the receiver into its cradle, then immediately slammed her fist down on the desk. Everything danced. "Dammit!"

"Bad timing on my part, I see," Justin said, as he rapped on her doorframe.

She wheeled, saw who it was and her face immediately softened. She made a brave attempt at a smile, but didn't quite pull it off. *He's still a heart-stopper*, she thought, as she studied Justin's strong, lean, no-nonsense face and stylishly cut graying hair.

"A little bird cooed to me that you were seen at the Papal Embassy last night. Could that be true?" she asked, trying, yet failing miserably in her attempt to sound indifferent.

Justin chuckled. "Good news still travels fast, I see. So tell me, Val, was it a canary, or maybe a stool pigeon, that sang his little aria in your ear?" He came all the way in and stood next to her. "Doesn't really matter which, but yeah, it's true, and that's the reason I'm here. Means you've already got the place under surveillance. Figures."

Valerie's mouth tightened. She walked around him, shut the door, returned to her desk and plunked herself down in her leather swivel chair. Motioning him to do the same, she waited until he was comfortable, then asked, "What can I do for you, Justin?" Her tone said it all. She was still ticked.

"Tell me whatever you can about the Kettering affair," he said, crossing his legs, making himself comfortable. "I'm not looking for anything classified, but I'd like to compare your take on what happened with what I was told last night."

* * *

It was seven o'clock in the evening, the last Monday in August, and the first day of the new school term. Valerie Tobias was at Georgetown, preparing to enroll in the graduate arts program. She was seated in the library, hunched over a desk, filling out her course schedule when her beeper chirped. She frowned, dug the electronic annoyance from her purse, then arched an eyebrow in an unconscious show of surprise as she studied its display. She retrieved an iPhone from her bag and punched up the numbers from the pager as she made her way into the hallway.

The call had come from the Chief of Police, and Matthew Tuchmann answered on the first ring.

"Inspector Tobias, returning your call, sir."

"Where're you, Inspector?"

"Georgetown. The campus."

"Official business?"

A look of exasperation flitted like a butterfly across her face. "No, Chief, I'm enrolling in a graduate course in seventeenth century French literature. I was just getting ready to walk over to the registrar's office."

"You driving a marked unit?"

"Negative. I'm off duty, so I'm using my own car."

"I want you here at the Daly Building on the double. I'll have the campus police send over a patrol car to save time. We'll run you back for your car later. Where exactly are you?"

"The library." Matthew Tuchmann had been on the job for three weeks, coming to the department from the number two position in Chicago. He was still feeling his way, and in the process had ticked off more than a few of the ranking officers in the department. He had developed the annoying habit of calling members of the senior staff or even his advisory council at all hours, more often than not with demands that the person being called drop whatever he was doing and haul ass to his office. And it was invariably over something picayune. Tuchmann was fast getting the rep of a nit-picking micro manager. But some inner voice told her this wasn't one of those times.

The chief must have been a mind reader. "Relax, Tobias," the electronic voice in her right ear counseled. "We have a Red Flag in progress, and I need you, pronto. Be outside the library in five."

"What gives?"

"You on a landline?"

"Cellular; encrypted," she replied.

"No, it'll have to wait till you get here. The ether still has ears, if you get my drift."

She did. There were police groupies, police wannabes, and just plain old members of the fourth estate who monitored police radios with scanners in constant search of a breaking story. Illegal though it was, some enterprising souls could even intercept encrypted cellular conversations. "I'm on my way. Tobias, out."

She reached the entrance of the library just as the university police car drove up. The rain which had threatened all day finally made good on its promise, and she zigzagged in a mad dash of several yards to the car, getting soaked in the process. She yanked open the right rear door and threw herself in.

"Hold it right there, missy. This look like a frigging taxi? Get your butt outta here. Of all the goddamn nerve!" The officer's half-turned face was flushed with anger.

"I'm Inspector Tobias," she replied in an even tone, holding aloft her gold and blue shield. "I think you were sent for me."

"Ah, jeez, I apologize. I was expecting—"

"Someone with *cojones*?"

He laughed. All was forgiven. "Where to, Inspector?"

"Police Headquarters. I authorize using your light bar and siren, just don't get us killed, okay?"

"Right on."

She spent the next few minutes drying herself off as best she could. Then she checked her makeup and hair, trying to bring some modicum of respectability to her appearance, loathing the thought that she would soon appear before the chief dressed in blue jeans and a sweatshirt. *Damn*! Oh, well, she quickly rationalized, it *is* my day off.

The car came to a stop under the portico entrance of the District of Columbia Metropolitan Police Headquarters at 300 Indiana Avenue Northwest. She thanked the driver, and double-timed her way into the building, beelining toward the bank of elevators. She flashed her badge at the sergeant-receptionist, and without breaking her stride, entered a waiting car. She rode it up to the third floor, the sanctum of official police power in the nation's capital.

Another ID check awaited her before she was allowed into the chief's suite. The duty secretary smiled brightly from behind a huge mahogany desk, but before either woman had a chance to exchange greetings, the door to the inner office opened and out stepped Commander Leon Baldridge, aide-de-camp, or, more appropriately, *factotum* to the man himself.

Baldridge was an office cop. He had risen to the heights of power by playing politics from the day he had graduated the academy some twelve years earlier. Every district commander in the city feared him, and he reveled in that knowledge.

"You could have come dressed more appropriately, Tobias," he hissed through clenched teeth.

"Stuff it, you prissy little dandy."

"Is that Tobias out there?" a voice called. "Send her in."

Valerie entered the office of Chief Matthew Tuchmann without a backward glance. She missed the smile of satisfaction spreading over the secretary's face, and the look of apoplexy on Baldridge's.

"Sit. Thanks for coming on such short notice." The chief glanced up as his assistant entered and proceeded to close the door.

"No. Please wait outside, Leon."

"Very good, sir," replied Baldridge, all fawning and servility.

"I mentioned a Red Flag on the phone," the chief said, eyes averted, fingers busy rifling a file before him. "We meet in the main conference room in ten minutes with the Director of the FBI, the Deputy Secretary of State, the Counselor to the President, plus about a half dozen other muckamucks who have titles longer than rolls of toilet paper. Meanwhile, I want to use this time to bring you up to speed."

"I see." Valerie repositioned herself noisily in the leather chair, acutely conscious of her casual appearance, but the chief was obviously too preoccupied to notice.

"We have a murder on our hands, Tobias. It's our worst nightmare come to life. Well, close to it."

She shuddered involuntarily. In a town that experienced at least two murders every twenty-four hours—and that was on a slow day—for the top cop to summon her to his office spoke volumes.

"Someone in government?" Apparently something big had gone down, and here she was, the last to know. Where were all her detectives hiding? At least one of the three hundred and eighty-four members of her command could have picked up a phone.

The chief let out a bark of a laugh. "Would that we be so lucky. I could handle that standing on my head. A lot more serious, I'm afraid."

Her blood ran to ice. The Number One? Number Two? God in Heaven! But, no. *That* would have been all over the airwaves in seconds.

"Who's the victim?" The voice was certainly hers, yet to her ears it seemed somehow totally disembodied.

"We haven't a clue who the victim is, and probably won't have a positive ID for at least a couple of days. But what we do have is the body of a Caucasian female found stuffed in the trunk of a car. You'll hear the whole story in just a few minutes. It's not the victim that's giving us trouble; it's the suspect."

Valerie sat mute, but maintained a steady gaze into the chief's eyes.

Tuchmann stared back. "Our suspect is none other than the Papal Nuncio. To put it in terms that every man on the street will understand, I'm saying, Tobias, our *numero uno* suspect is the Vatican's Ambassador to the United States; His Eminence, Francis Cardinal Kettering."

"Impossible!" The words were out of her mouth before she could stop them.

"Wish it weren't so, but it is." Tuchmann rose from behind his desk, still holding the file. He glanced down at it as he began pacing. "This is your folder, Tobias. I had it sent up from personnel right after I called. Like it or not, because you're the top homicide detective in the city, you're going to find yourself on the hot seat right alongside me. I wanted to get a better feel for who you are, what makes you tick."

"Forget my folder for a moment, sir, and fill me in on what we've got. I'm shocked, and more than a little peeved that I wasn't given a heads up by my staff. Needless to say, this is the first I've heard about it."

"Chill out, Tobias, okay? You were deliberately not informed on my orders. I made a decision to put a tight wrap on all information until we could verify what little we had. None of us on duty knew where this thing was taking us until only a short while ago. Up to then all we had was a John Doe pulled in on a drunk driving charge."

"How about giving it to me from the top?"

Tuchmann studied his Rolex, using the moment to gather his thoughts. He had his own agenda and wasn't about to be sidetracked.

"Says here you've been a cop for thirteen years, but promoted only two months ago to your present assignment and rank. You could be considered something of a fast burner." He paused to study her over the top of his reading glasses. "Could it be a gender thing, Tobias? Or could it just be that you're really that good?"

This guy didn't mince words. "I'd like to think it's a competency thing, sir," she answered quietly.

"Well, I hope you're right, because the spotlight is sure going to shine on you for the next however long it takes us to clean up this nasty mess."

Tuchmann returned to his chair and sat heavily. "Okay, here's what we've got."

* * *

In the conference room, she heard it all again, only this time in detail. There were twelve people gathered, and once the doors had closed, a guard was stationed on the outside, standing two paces from the electronic signboard that read:

RED FLAG BRIEFING IN PROGRESS.
NO ADMITTANCE.

Being the only woman present she felt as though every eye in the room was on her. She was acutely aware of the image she must be presenting. Her inspector's shield was now draped around her neck on a standard issue chain, so all were aware of her position. Still, it rankled to have been summoned from on high so totally unprepared.

Starting with Tuchmann and followed by the Executive Assistant Chief, each in turn introduced himself, everyone seeming to know everyone else. Except her. She spied a still angry look on Baldridge's face as he cast his onyx eyes in her direction. He sat perched on the edge of his chair to the left of his sovereign. Ever vigilant, ever protective.

Tuchmann spoke. "Lieutenant Braddock will brief us on what's gone down, then we'll put our heads together and hopefully come up with a plan as to how we're going to handle this." He nodded to Braddock.

"I was the duty commander last night," Braddock began, eyes steady on Valerie. "At 2:20 a.m., Monday morning, Patrolman Winston Singleterry informed central dispatch that he had just come across a single car accident at Seventeenth and Fuller. Before exiting his unit, he read the license plate numbers to dispatch and asked for a make. He observed there was a lone male leaning against the hood and bumper of the vehicle, and advised he'd be on his portable."

Braddock halted long enough to flip to the next page of his notes and continued his recitation in a dry, even tone. "It had been raining, and the pavement was still wet. The subject had apparently lost control and slammed into a tree. Singleterry approached and asked if he was hurt. The man appeared disoriented, and with his flashlight the officer observed a large cut over the man's right eye. It was pretty deep, and still bleeding.

"When asked his name and directed to produce identification, the subject did not, or could not, respond. He did, however, turn and face the officer, and it was then that Singleterry detected a strong smell of alcohol. He repeated his request for identification, at which point the subject took one step forward, stumbled, fell to the ground and couldn't get back up. Singleterry got on his radio and called for an ambulance and a tow truck.

"Both were dispatched to the scene at 2:27 a.m. At 2:30 a.m., central came back to Singleterry and informed him that the vehicle was registered to an owner in Gaithersburg, Maryland.

"While waiting for the ambulance, Singleterry looked inside the car and observed no other occupants. He then checked the glove box, but found nothing to identify the individual now in custody. At this point all we had was a drunk driver, and a single car accident."

"How was the ambassador dressed?" This from Judge anderson MacAllister, the FBI Director.

"Regular street clothes, sir," replied Braddock. "Lightweight dark blue windbreaker over a white shirt and black pants. Black socks, black shoes. Typical gear for late August nights. But nothing to indicate he was a priest."

"Go on."

"The ambulance arrived at 2:44 a.m. The John Doe was placed on a stretcher and transported to the hospital prison ward and not to central booking. The tow truck showed up as the ambulance was leaving and took the car to the police pound. Everything was back to normal by 3:00 a.m. Singleterry cleared with dispatch and continued his patrol."

"Please describe the subject," the director said.

Braddock passed around a series of photographs. As the group studied the pictures, he continued his briefing. "These were taken at the hospital. The subject was booked, photographed and fingerprinted, then placed into the prison ward after being treated in Emergency. He had been put on an I.V., but only after blood had been drawn for testing. He's Caucasian, five-foot-eleven, one hundred and fifty pounds, late fifties early sixties, white hair, blue eyes, no visible scars, birthmarks, or tattoos. He barely responded to questions from the doctor who treated him, but did say enough that it was noted in the medical work-up that the subject spoke precise, grammatical English, but with a pronounced German accent."

This time Tuchmann broke in. "Nothing required further attention in this matter until some four hours later, at seven in the morning. Braddock, who was just going off duty, was summoned by the honcho at the police pound to shag over there, pronto. That sound about right, Loo?"

"It is, Chief. I arrived at the pound at seven thirty-three a.m., and was taken to the car seized by Singleterry. Seems the shift supervisor had opened the trunk and discovered the body wrapped in a blanket. That's when he got on the horn to me. I unwrapped the blanket far enough to identify the victim as a white female, a woman I'd guess to be in her early thirties. She appeared to have suffered blunt trauma to the left side of her head. The trunk also contained what looked like a candlestick wrapped in a towel. At that point I declared a crime scene and secured the area. The mobile crime team and the medical examiner arrived some fourteen minutes later."

Valerie shot a quick smile at Braddock as he stood by his seat. It was a silent tribute, and Braddock correctly read her face and nodded that he understood.

He continued. "The prints and photos we'd taken of our John Doe in the Emergency Room were faxed to the FBI, and we also wired a package to the Gaithersburg P.D. along with a request that they contact the registered owner of the vehicle. That's where we ran into problems."

As if on cue, the group leaned forward, all eyes and ears riveted on Braddock.

"The car's owner was home when the police arrived, and he showed them his car which was still in his garage. Claimed he hadn't had any reason to have moved it for the past two days, and sure, sometimes he parked it on the street. So what? Well, they immediately spotted that the tag was missing, and, no, the owner stated that he hadn't noticed it gone. But the kicker was the car was identical to the one we had in the pound. And I mean identical. This year's model Crown Victoria ; deep blue in color, same interior, damn near identical mileage. The only difference was a single digit in the vehicle identification number. That's why no one suspected anything at the time. We had a match through the tag, so no one went the extra step and compared the VIN of the vehicle in the accident to the one registered in Maryland. It just looked right. Sloppy procedure on our part, yes, but understandable. That screw-up cost us a couple of hours, though."

"Okay, Lieutenant, forget the *mea culpa*," the FBI director said. "What did you get back from us?"

"No match. No prints on record. Ditto from Maryland. So now it was back again to the FBI, this time for a run on the impounded car's VIN. That took a couple more hours, but that's when we knew we had the makings of a real problem on our hands. The car was registered to the Apostolic Nunciature to the United States, more commonly known as the Vatican Embassy. But it wasn't in the official fleet, which meant it didn't have diplomatic tags. The car's a brown bag. Every agency represented here has a few. It's used when the embassy folks don't want to draw attention. As you all know, any cursory run through state computers or NCIC on any such car will give the asking party false information as to ownership. And that's what we had in this instance. It said the car was titled to an off-shore corporation, but further digging revealed the true owner."

"Please continue," said Tuchmann.

"Now we have to involve the State Department. I mean, I can't just go waltzing off on my own to the embassy, so I coordinate with a liaison officer and make an appointment for two o'clock to speak to someone there." Braddock glanced quickly at his notes. "A

Monsignor Capelletti met with us, and confirmed that the car in question was indeed a privately tagged vehicle. We informed him of the accident, that the driver was suspected of being drunk, and that we'd discovered a murdered woman's body in the trunk. I then showed him a photo of the subject at which point he became quite alarmed. He wanted to know if something had happened to the cardinal. Excuse me, I asked, what Cardinal?

"Cardinal Kettering," he replied, "the nuncio to the United States." He looked at me as if I'd just landed from Mars. He demanded to know where the cardinal was, and Mr. Channing Wilson, he's the liaison from State, assured the monsignor that the cardinal was okay, but that he was in the hospital."

"Did you tell this monsignor why his cardinal was in the hospital?" Tuchmann asked.

Braddock shook his head. "Not in so many words, sir, but I'm sure he put the puzzle together real fast. In fact, we did, too, so we excused ourselves and returned to our cars where we each called our respective offices because we both concluded that we had a possible Red Flag. As called for by procedure in such cases, I spoke directly to you, and Wilson relayed the information to the secretary of state. That took about a half-hour."

"Go on."

"We returned to the embassy. The monsignor informed us that he had already called for a private ambulance to transport the ambassador back to the residence. I have no idea how he knew which hospital, but he sure had to have pulled some diplomatic strings to just whisk the ambassador home like he did."

"Too right," said the representative from State, scanning the room as he spoke. "So you all see the problem?"

Eleven heads nodded as one.

"Seems we have a murder on our hands," he said, "and our prime suspect, wild as it sounds, is none other than a Prince of the Church. A prince, I might add, who also happens to enjoy diplomatic immunity. So, if for some unholy reason the man is indeed guilty, he gets to walk, just like that Libyan diplomat did who shot and killed the female cop in London back in the mid-eighties. This is going to cause a ruckus heard round the world once it breaks in the press, so it'll be our priority to see that our government doesn't get sucked into a political free-for-all."

* * *

"Now you know everything I know, Justin," Valerie said, hooking a thumb toward the phone. "That was Tuchmann informing me that we'll be taking a back seat to the FBI on this. Seems the feds have been given the ball, courtesy of the White House and the Justice Department. I objected, as you no doubt heard, but the chief let me know that the order for us to disappear came right from the Attorney General herself. The FBI's been given complete charge of the investigation as of this morning, and they've wasted no time moving the body from the city morgue over to theirs. Tuchmann also let me know they'll be conducting the autopsy, and there'll be no outsiders allowed in to observe. Then he has the balls to tell me we're still considered to be working the case should anyone ask." She let loose a mirthless laugh. "Am I the only one thinking this ain't going to pass the smell test?"

Still brimming with suppressed anger, she picked up a pencil and began drumming on her calendar pad. "Tuchmann actually sounded pleased that he wasn't going to be responsible for this hot potato, and when I reminded him it was illegal for the feds to step in, he primly told me to chill out. 'The guy's got diplomatic immunity,' " she mimicked wickedly. " 'We went over this yesterday. You *dig* what that means, Tobias?' " She threw the pencil down. "I *dig* what the hell it means. It means Kettering will have hotfooted it out of the country before the autopsy report's even been typed. But Tuchmann assured me he was promised by the AG that we'd be kept informed at every step of the investigation. *Not!*" She turned her guns on Justin. "So what were you doing at the embassy last night? Did you meet up with the murderer? Has he hired you to spin some BS alibi for the press to swallow?"

Justin ignored her questions but posed one of his own. "Do you have a make on the victim?"

Valerie jumped out of her seat and began to stalk. She shook her head and waved her hand. "You tell me, because we don't have an inkling as to who the hell she is. Or was."

"When can I talk to Braddock?"

She shook her head angrily. "Are you deaf? Answer *my* questions first, dammit!"

"Relax, Val, I'm not your enemy. Look, the chief of staff at the embassy, Monsignor Capelletti, asked me to poke around. The cardinal wasn't available for questioning last night, but according to Capelletti he insists he draws a blank about everything that happened to him Sunday night, Monday morning." Justin held up his hand to cut her off. "And, yeah, I think the guy's full of it. I told Capelletti the same thing your chief just told you. Kettering's got diplomatic immunity. March him the hell out of the country because the man can't be tried for anything, not even murder."

"Great advice, G-man," she said, her voice heavy with sarcasm. "So when's he leaving?"

Justin shook his head. "Seems Kettering's playing mind games with the Vatican. Supposedly he's threatening to stay and fight if a charge of murder is brought against him. But Capelletti let me know with both barrels blazing the Vatican will not be a party to that nonsense. Fact is, Rome wants him gone, like yesterday, because all the vibes I'm receiving tell me just one thing; the crowd over there in Italy really believes Kettering offed the woman in the trunk."

"At least they got that one right," Valerie Tobias answered moodily. She stood, then smoothed her skirt with both hands. "Look, I've got to get some coffee in me before I start to scream. Tag along to the commissary, I want to propose a deal. I'm mad as the devil at the feds, and I think I can see my way to helping you as long as you promise to help me." She smiled. "Tit for tat."

Justin rose. "What kind of a deal?"

"Tell you downstairs." She opened the door and guided him into the corridor with the palm of an impatient left hand placed squarely on his back.

Justin felt an involuntary rush. He tried to ignore the feeling. "I'd give anything to be a little fly on the wall in the Vatican this morning," he said, "sitting there hearing everything the Pope has to say about his man in Washington. I bet His Holiness is some kind of steamed about now."

"You think he might've said a no-no?" Valerie rejoined, her hand flying to her mouth in a display of mock horror. Then she laughed loudly at the very idea.

Justin grinned. "Novel concept, Val. All I can say is: One never knows now, do one?"

He fell into step, pleased to see that her anger had vanished.

CHAPTER 3

The New York Times broke the story before sunup the following morning. The usual 'unnamed sources' were quoted to lend credence, but in general the narrative was a legitimate first cousin to the facts. As always, everybody 'in the know' vehemently denied being the 'unnamed' conduit. But the damage had been done. By eight o'clock the satellites linking the continents had spread the gossip to the far corners of the globe. Print and electronic editors everywhere scrambled to include this explosive exposé in their afternoon editions. The piranhas of the fourth estate were about to partake in a feeding frenzy.

The Holy Father was given the news by phone in the early evening by Rafael Cardinal Miglianico, the Vatican's secretary of state. The pontiff was at his summer residence at *Castel Gondolfo,* but returned to Vatican City within two hours of being summoned. He met with a small clique of advisors in his private quarters at ten o'clock that evening.

"That's everything as of a half-hour ago, Holy Father," Cardinal Miglianico said, summarizing the day's events. "Monsignor

Capelletti at our embassy in Washington has been in constant communication with my office from the moment he first learned of this matter. I commanded him to go to bed after our last conversation. The man's been working with very little sleep since Monday, and was starting to sound like a punch-drunk prize fighter." Cardinal Miglianico, pushing seventy-nine, tall and lean as a whippet, took great pride in his own stamina. Men half his age couldn't keep up, and his staff referred to him in private as the MiG-41, a sly comparison of the man to one of Russia's latest sleek jet fighters. Miglianico was aware of the appellation and loved it.

"Where is Francis now?" The Pope was dressed in a white shirt and black trousers, with soft bedroom slippers hugging tired, aching feet. His personal suite within the palace was Spartan, in stark contrast to the many rooms of this ancient edifice all crammed with priceless treasures.

"In the embassy, Holy Father," Miglianico replied. "He has said absolutely nothing of this matter to a soul. I spoke with him briefly several hours ago, and my only advice was for him to remain sequestered and make no comments to the media. I also advised Vatican Radio that my office would be releasing an official statement shortly."

"Who was the woman, Rafael?"

Miglianico shook his head, a genuinely sad expression crossing his face. "No one seems to know. A total mystery."

Monsignor Jack O'Bryan, a member of the cardinal's inner staff, and an American Jesuit holding a Ph.D. in political science from Georgetown University cleared his throat. O'Bryan was a rarity among Jesuits in that he had been elevated by this Pope to a rank not usually bestowed on members of the Society of Jesus.

"I spoke with my liaison at the American state department late this afternoon, our time," O'Bryan began, "and he informed me that the FBI had been directed by the White House to conduct the autopsy. He suggested this will not sit well with either the police department or the local medical examiner's office, but he feels there's not much either can do except grumble. The pressure being felt by official Washington has become intense, and because the cardinal enjoys diplomatic immunity, everybody's looking to us to see what steps we're going to take."

The Pope absently twirled his papal ring. He had followed the rapid conversation in Italian with ease. As a man with a fluency in four languages—and a working knowledge of a half-dozen more—there was not much in the way of linguistic nuance that escaped him.

"Which brings us to the crux of the matter. Do we voluntarily recall Francis, or do we wait until the President declares him *persona non grata*, and publicly expels him?"

Again, O'Bryan spoke up. "Such a course of action wouldn't be imminent, Holy Father. Cardinal Kettering has not been formally accused of any crime. Note that I use the word, accused, not, charged. There's a big difference, and it's not merely one of semantics. As an ambassador, he cannot be charged with anything, even murder. But, before it could ever come to that, there would have to be a finding of what's called, probable cause. Until then, His Eminence is guilty of nothing."

"Then maybe we should recall Francis for consultations," the pontiff said.

O'Bryan shook his head. "I strongly advise against that course of action, Holy Father. At least for now. The American press would portray the ambassador as scurrying to seek sanctuary inside the Vatican. Rightly or wrongly, it would be interpreted as an admission of guilt. Recalling him now would do irreparable harm to the Holy See. I counsel we wait."

"Rafael, how about you? Do you agree with our young friend?"

"He makes a strong case, and in light of what we know, I think the right one. So, yes, I agree. We should do nothing, at least for the time being."

The Pope turned and faced the only other person present, a man who had not uttered a single word: Monsignor Ignacio Caffarone. He was the Holy Father's private secretary, and as such wielded enormous power within the confines of the Vatican, the surrounding Eternal City, and beyond. Because of his proximity to the Pope, he was treated with the same deference accorded the members of the College of Cardinals. All wanted to be his friend; none his enemy.

"Ignacio?"

Caffarone had been busy scribbling notes of the proceedings in shorthand. With his gold pen poised midair, he uttered a sigh, a sound of despair, and shook his head.

"Forgive me, Holy Father. My heart is filled to overflowing with sorrow for His Eminence. I fear my judgment or opinion would be of no value to you at this moment. I must say, however, that I am sure there will soon come to light a perfectly good explanation for what seems to have occurred, and I am confident that our brother in Christ will be fully exonerated."

O'Bryan couldn't believe his ears. He had formed a dislike for the man the moment he'd met him nine months earlier, and try as he might, he could not bring himself to harbor any feeling of Christian brotherhood he knew he should feel toward a fellow priest. Now he simply saw Caffarone as an oily, fat weasel; a man already positioning himself on the fence, waiting to see which way the wind would blow. O'Bryan found himself disgusted by the blatant display of false compassion. He saw Caffarone as nothing but a toady; a charlatan trying desperately to hide a bloated, running-to-fat figure beneath an expensively tailored silk cassock bordered to perfection with the purple piping of his honorary ecclesiastical rank. He hated the pathetic vanity the man displayed with the laughable attempt to hide an almost bald pate with carefully arranged wisps of tinted hair plastered from one side of his skull to the other. And he silently laughed at the thought of the ridiculous, often talked about, two-inch elevators hidden inside his high-priced Swiss shoes.

O'Bryan knew that Kettering and Caffarone were anything but friends. But what had surprised everyone, himself included, was that when it had been decided to send a cardinal to the United States as the new ambassador, Caffarone had wholeheartedly endorsed Kettering's appointment. That had been six months ago, and it had been an appointment of historic proportions. Cardinals were Princes of the Church, a rank far elevated above that occupied by mere ambassadors. But the Pope had had his reasons, and even O'Bryan had agreed those reasons were sound. The Roman Catholic Church in America was an institution teetering on the precipice, and the Vatican was genuinely alarmed at what the future might bring. A troubling number of the laity had seemingly lost confidence in its ecclesiastical leadership, fueled by a lingering—and still-growing—discontent with the liturgical changes instituted by the Vatican II Council under the pontificate of John XXIII. To say nothing of the uncovering of sexual misconduct on the part of many in the clergy. This misconduct was not limited to the rank and file. Bishops and archbishops had also been shown to have had feet of clay. Indeed, even a cardinal had been accused of homosexual activity by a former seminarian. Thankfully, he was soon proven to be guiltless. But his reputation had been besmirched, and there were those who would not believe in his innocence, no matter what evidence had been brought forth to corroborate such findings. Over the past decade untold tens of millions of dollars had been paid by the Church to those it had wronged. The Catholic Church in America was an institution in crisis. Some even whispered that its very survival was at risk.

So, to salvage the Church of Peter in the New World ,this Pope took a bold, imaginative step in dispatching someone of Kettering's stature to Washington. He was, in essence, sending a message for all to heed. Things were about to change.

To label Francis Kettering a conservative would be the understatement of the year. In certain circles of the *Curia* he was referred to as "that Nazi" behind his back, a moniker meant to define his unbending nature; a verbal reinforcement of his unyielding position on matters of faith and morals. Kettering was an authoritarian of the first order, and his Teutonic Viennese roots were glaringly evident. Quite simply, he had been the right choice at the right time. And now this.

"I understand, Ignacio," the Pope smiled as he responded. The man saw nothing but good in every person. Guile was foreign to his nature, thus he was slow to spot it in others.

He addressed them all. "There's not much more we can do tonight. Please, go to bed, but remember to say a prayer for our brother Francis before you retire."

The meeting was over.

* * *

Cardinal Miglianico steered O'Bryan towards his suite of rooms. It was a few minutes past eleven.

"Jack, I need to go over some things that are troubling me. I promise not to keep you up much longer. Can I maybe bribe you with a small brandy?" Miglianico had switched to English, a language he enjoyed.

O'Bryan laughed. "Twist my arms, turn the screws, I'll gladly succumb."

Miglianico beamed. "Good man."

Five minutes later they were seated in a comfortable study, the promised elixir generously poured and sinfully enjoyed. Miglianico turned serious. "Jack, I fear the worst. In my heart I pray that I'm wrong, but I must be prepared to face what you often call the worst case scenario."

O'Bryan nodded. "This is truly a no-win situation. If Cardinal Kettering is accused, and subsequently expelled, then the damage done to Holy Mother Church will be incalculable. But if he is exonerated, then there are those who will see it as nothing more than politics. A whitewash. A deal crafted between two governments. The only way Kettering could clear his good name would be in an open trial such as he is suggesting, but, that, of course, is impossible. Assuming that he is indeed presumed guilty, I hasten to add."

"Do you think he might be guilty, Jack? Could Francis be capable of such terrible misconduct?"

"My honest opinion, Your Eminence?" O'Bryan didn't wait for a response. "Who knows what any of us are truly capable of? Even Jesus showed righteous anger and indignation with the money changers in the temple. So, yes. In a fit of anger, all things are possible. Even murder. Correction. Especially murder."

Miglianico took a small sip of brandy, cradling the snifter in both hands while slowly rotating the glass. He seemed mesmerized by the amber liquid. He finally spoke, eyes still on the brandy. "I agree. And that is why I asked you for a few minutes of your time. I need answers in order to do my job. Answers as to how I might best serve the interests of my Pope and my Church. Those answers are to be found only in America. So, here's what I propose. I want you to go to Washington and become my eyes and ears. Find out what's really going on."

Miglianico peered at O'Bryan. "You mentioned earlier that you had Monsignor Capelletti contact a private investigator you know there, a Mr. Justin Scott, I seem to recall? Who exactly is this Mr. Scott, and can he be trusted?"

"Justin's a retired FBI agent," O'Bryan replied. "We became friends while I was at Georgetown getting my doctorate. He taught a course in international terrorism. I also had the good fortune to see him in action firsthand. He helped the Church manage a very delicate situation involving the kidnapping of a priest and three children. There was a ransom demand and death threats implied if we alerted the authorities. I approached Justin with the full approval of the Archbishop, and he took charge. No one was hurt; the hostages were freed; and the two kidnappers went to prison for life, with no hope of parole. Justin is simply the best, Your Eminence, and we're going to have to learn to rely on his advice, *if* he's willing to help, that is," O'Bryan said.

"I see." Miglianico suddenly looked tired, his face reflecting every one of his years. "What if Cardinal Kettering should stand trial?" he suddenly asked. "What if it was then proven in an American court that Francis was guilty of nothing? Tell me, young man, what would that accomplish?"

O'Bryan smiled at the thought of a trial that could never be. "Everything, Your Eminence. It would show the world that Mother

Church practices what She preaches. It would show that we refused to hide behind a technicality of international law. We all subscribe to the theory that ambassadors must be free from any-and-all possible persecution by a host nation. Because without that inviolable, universal guarantee, discourse amongst states would be almost impossible. The world would be in a constant state of war."

"Aptly put. But if it should come to pass that the Vatican decides it to be in our best interest for Francis to stand trial, then I want you to quietly approach the best law firms in the United States and see if any would consider representing Francis. I'm sure your Justin Scott could be a big help to you there."

"You mean you'd actually consider revoking Kettering's credentials?" O'Bryan was flabbergasted at the prospect, and its attendant myriad ramifications. Such a course of action had never been taken before; at least not to his knowledge.

"Jack, when you spoke to the Holy Father earlier, you said there was a profound distinction between being charged with a crime and being accused of one. It's not just a matter of semantics, you said. So, to use semantics, I was thinking in terms of suspending his credentials, not revoking them."

That's why you're the secretary of state, O'Bryan thought. But in a voice so soft that Cardinal Miglianico had to strain just to hear, he said, "and by doing that you'd still leave open an escape route just in case Kettering was found guilty."

"Yes. It would save Francis, but quite possibly destroy the American Church in the process. I just don't know, Jack. It's only a thought, nothing more at this point. But it is something to be considered. We must study all our options, even those we find most distasteful."

"You know of course, such a defense would cost the Church millions."

Miglianico looked glum. "I've heard that justice in America comes at a high price. But there's much at stake, and that's why I want you in Washington. I'll inform Monsignor Capelletti of your coming, and let him know that you're my personal representative. He'll understand that you speak for me in any and all things pertaining to the matter at hand. You also have my permission to approach Cardinal Kettering, but I suspect he won't have anything to say. At least not yet. He must be in a terrible state of depression." Miglianico started to take another sip of brandy then changed his mind. He looked up at O'Bryan, noticing that a strange look had suddenly crossed his face.

"What are you thinking, young man?" he challenged.

O'Bryan shook his head, trying to dispel a thought. It wouldn't leave. He repeated the gesture, then said, "I'm thinking that I know who we should approach to defend Cardinal Kettering if matters should come to that. I'm thinking of someone who is a recognized authority in the field of criminal law, a lawyer fully conversant in both civil law and canon law. A lawyer who could successfully defend the cardinal."

Miglianico shot out of his chair. His fingers involuntarily squeezed the fragile glass still clutched between them, shattering it, splashing the brandy over the front of his clothes and down onto the Persian carpet at his feet. "*No!* Say no more. I forbid you to even mention the man's name!"

O'Bryan was on his feet in a flash. "Are you all right, Your Eminence? Have you cut yourself? Are you bleeding?" He whipped out a sparkling white handkerchief. "Here, take this."

An angry Miglianico brushed aside the proffered hand. "I cannot believe you would even entertain such an idea. How in the name of God could you dare to think of that man?" he shouted his rebuke.

"Because I'm doing my job," O'Bryan shouted back. "I get paid to give advice, whether it's what you want to hear or not. And you of all people know that he's got the best mind you've ever crossed. And if your scenario plays out, then Sean MacMillan is the lawyer we need in our corner. Case closed."

O'Bryan suddenly realized that he had been shouting, and he was mortified. "I apologize, Your Eminence. I'm truly sorry. Please forgive me."

Miglianico sat back down heavily. He waved his right hand in a feeble gesture, exorcising unseen demons. "You have nothing to apologize for, Jack. You're right, of course. He definitely is the one man who could see this thing through to a satisfactory conclusion, *if* such a conclusion were possible. But, no matter what I think, Francis Kettering would rather die first than be defended by your friend MacMillan. Believe me, I know Francis."

"Well, we don't have to make any such decision right now, but I would like your permission to at least approach him if and when the time comes, and see if he would consider taking the case. He could just as easily tell us to go pound sand."

"Did I hear you correctly? Pound sand?"

O'Bryan laughed at the expression on Miglianico's face. "It's American slang, Your Eminence. It means, take a hike, get lost."

"Pound sand."

"Yeah. Sean MacMillan could certainly tell us to do just that, and frankly, I wouldn't blame him."

Miglianico sighed, then yawned deeply. It was now only moments away from midnight and O'Bryan could see the man was genuinely exhausted. "You have my permission to talk to Sean if it should come to that. Of course you do. But not a word of any of this to Cardinal Kettering. He would never agree to such a thing, but if we're forced into that position to save the credibility of Holy Mother Church, then His Holiness might have to command Francis to acquiesce. We'll see."

O'Bryan got up. "I'll leave for America just as fast as I can, Your Eminence." He glanced at his watch. "I should be out of here by tomorrow, Friday at the latest. I'll not stay in our embassy though. That way I'll be free to move about at will. Before I go to bed I'll telephone Justin Scott and let him know I'm coming. So, with your permission, Your Eminence, I'll say goodnight."

"Goodnight, Jack. Have a safe trip, and thanks for putting up with a cantankerous old man. Keep giving me advice, even that which you fear I don't want to hear. God bless you." Miglianico made the sign of the cross in the air a couple of feet from O'Bryan's head.

O'Bryan was halfway to the door when Miglianico called out. "One last thing, Jack."

O'Bryan turned.

"Pound sand!" Miglianico was grinning from ear to ear. All was forgiven.

CHAPTER 4

Valerie was returning to her office with Braddock after wolfing down lunch on the run when central dispatch called. It was Friday, an eternity having passed since the Monday night meeting with the chief. Everyone in the department was keenly aware of being forced to take a back seat to the FBI with this case, and each knew that the orders had come from the President. The bureau had marched over and had seized control of all the physical evidence. It rankled.

She was riding shotgun, staring out the window and quietly feeling sorry for herself when the speakerphone came alive with her call sign.

"Central to Echo Seven."

"This is Echo Seven. Go, Dispatch."

"You have a call from the FBI, Inspector. You want a patch?"

"Roger."

A moment later a male voice came over the air. "Special Agent Sams, Inspector. I have something for you whenever it's convenient for you to drop by. Monday's fine if you can't make it today."

She glanced out the window for a quick look-see to pinpoint her location. H Street at the Convention Center. She keyed her mike. "I'm three minutes away, Mr. Sams. Let's meet in the lobby in ten minutes."

"Copy that. See you in ten."

She turned to Braddock and grinned. "See how good things come to those who wait, Tom? You heard the man. Step on it. It's showtime!"

Fifteen minutes later they were escorted by Sams to a small conference room on the fourth floor of the J. Edgar Hoover Building. Both declined the offered coffee, and Sams wasted no time placing a videocassette in a VCR and punching the start button. A second later, there she was. Braddock involuntarily sucked in a huge gulp of air. My God, it was her!

The woman on the screen pirouetted several times, smiling, pouting, then smiling again as she sashayed down a long ramp, her body undulating with an easy sexuality as she moved. Multiple cameras zoomed in on her face in rapid succession, and caught her image from various angles. She was dazzling.

"You found out who she is!" Braddock's eyes never left the monitor. "Damn good work."

"Ah, not so fast, Lieutenant. Fact is what you're seeing is a computer-generated image of the lady." Sams froze a full frontal headshot on the screen. "Before the autopsy we had a beautician fix up her face and hair, then we took multiple photographs from every angle. We knew that her eyes were blue and her teeth were perfect, so we assembled all that information and fed it into our computer. This is the result. Once again she's a living, breathing beauty. Not bad, huh?"

"And you have stock footage in your computer of various sized women, or men, as the case may be. You superimpose the head on a body of like height, weight, color, et cetera, et cetera, and, *voilà*! The computer can make her smile, laugh, cry, stick out her tongue, or even shoot you the bird. Whatever Lola wants, Lola gets," Valerie said.

"There you go, Inspector."

"I'm impressed." and she truly was.

"So you still don't know who she is?" Braddock's disappointed look revealed that he already knew the answer.

Sams shook his head. "Not yet. However, I can tell you that the autopsy is complete, and we should be able to release a copy of the report to you within a day or two."

Valerie glanced at Braddock as Sams rose to switch on the lights. Her look said it all. We get to see it when they're good and ready, and not a minute before. And it's strictly a courtesy thing, because we're off the case anyway.

Braddock nodded. Understood.

"Can you tell us anything about her? Any sort of preliminary heads up?" Valerie asked.

Sams mulled the request for a moment or two, then smiled. "Of course, Inspector." He didn't refer to any notes. "As you saw, she was a hell of a looker. Early thirties, five-nine, one hundred and twenty-eight pounds, and, as I mentioned, blue eyes and perfect teeth. Death was caused by a single blow to the head, pretty well instantaneous. There was no sign of a struggle; no other marks on her body. She was definitely caught from behind, and totally unaware of what was about to happen."

"You obviously have no match on file for prints. How about Interpol? No word back from them yet?"

"Not yet, Inspector. Should be a reply any time now. They've had the prints for almost a day and a half."

"So you called us here just to see a video?" She kept her voice calm, but there was no mistaking the edge to her tone.

"No, Inspector. Not just to see it. This is your copy. I know you want to stay abreast of the investigation. With this tape you can make dupes, color stills, black and whites, or what have you. It's yours." He waited a full five seconds, then added, "But, I can't release it to you until the judge says okay, which should be shortly. A day, maybe two at the most."

Valerie stood. "I see. Thank you, Mr. Sams."

"You're welcome, Inspector." He offered his hand. "Of course, if you come across any information you will let us know right away?" A big, genuine smile creased his preppy face.

So that's what this meeting's all about, she reasoned, not returning the smile. The bureau needs help, only they're too proud to ask for it. "Of course. Just like we know we can expect the same from the bureau. Good day, Agent Sams." Her jaw was visibly clenched as she opened the door and led the two men into the hall. She addressed Braddock. "Let's go, Lieutenant. These are busy people. Mustn't waste any more of their time."

Back in the car, Valerie decided to drive, hoping the activity would help calm her.

"You're thinking what I'm thinking, Val. Those dicks have no intention of giving us the full autopsy report. They're going to sanitize the shit out of it, and feed us only what they want us to know. And we'll get the video about the same time as I get my twenty in to retire. That your read on the situation?"

"Go to the head of the class, Tom." She stared straight ahead, weaving in and out of the heavy, noisy traffic. Her hands gripped the wheel as if she wanted to strangle it, her jaw still rigid with anger. "They discovered something big during the autopsy, Tom.

I could smell it the way Mister Bureau Man patronized us as if we were a couple of hayseeds who'd just blown into town from Podunk, Arkansas. I feel it all the way down to my toes."

"Me too, boss."

"Damn them all!" She banged ferociously on the steering wheel.

"My sentiments, exactly. You sure got a way with words, Val."

* * *

O'Bryan was beat. It was now Friday evening in America, and he'd been in the air for the past eight hours, save for a forty-minute stopover at Kennedy. On the long, transatlantic flight he had read the latest news magazines on board, all hastily put out with Kettering's photo on the covers, their common story line strongly suggesting a sexual link between Kettering and the still unknown victim. It was depressing.

He had grabbed the seven o'clock shuttle to Ronald Reagan National Airport, and as he trudged out of the refrigerated terminal he was greeted by a stale blast of Sahara-like air which forced him to stagger backward as though he'd been physically assaulted.

"Well, aren't you a sight for these worn-out old peepers," a voice mocked, then belly laughed, somewhere behind him. He turned to see Justin's grinning face. The older man held out his hand. "Been a while, Jack. Hear you're now one of the movers and shakers in that big village on the Tiber. Congrats."

O'Bryan grabbed the proffered hand. "You haven't changed; still as ugly as ever," he replied, returning the grin, the weariness disappearing from his face.

"And you're still a cheeky snot, I see," Justin parried, then slapped O'Bryan on the back. "Welcome to Washington, *Padre,* I only wish the circumstances were different. I'll tell you all I know as we drive. You mentioned on the phone that you didn't want to stay at the embassy so I've got you a place at the Watergate. It's a condo. Belongs to one of my friends who's away for the summer. I live two floors down, so it'll work out fine. Consider it yours until he comes back."

Justin briefed O'Bryan as he drove in the post rush-hour evening traffic, ending with the news that the autopsy had been completed. Valerie had told Justin of her visit to the bureau, and was still fuming three hours later when she'd suggested to him that the feds were withholding a ton of information. She also noted that the FBI still hadn't a clue who the victim was.

"So I called one of my pals in the FBI morgue," Justin continued, "but the guy wouldn't tell me diddly. Said I'd have to wait until the director gave everyone the nod. And this from a chum I'd worked with for twenty years." He shook his head in the rapidly fading light. "Jack, there's some super heavyweights calling the shots on this one, people way above the director level, and my instinct tells me they're fast putting together an airtight case against your Cardinal Kettering. Got to be honest. It doesn't look good."

O'Bryan stared impassively into the oncoming headlights. Without turning he asked, "Regardless of what everybody in the bureau's saying, will you still help?" He turned full-face toward Justin. "As soon as I was told what had happened that night, I immediately thought of you. It's imperative that the Church uncover the truth, no matter what that truth may turn out to be." He held up a hand to parry the protest he knew was coming. "I know the kind of help I'm asking for doesn't come cheap, so I'm authorized to pay whatever your price. There'll be no quibbling when it comes to your fee; it's that important to Rome."

Justin was taken aback. Money was the last thing on his mind. "Jack, you embarrass me with your confidence in my assumed abilities, but I must tell you something right off. I believe Kettering did it. The evidence is solid—at least that which I've seen to date, along with other stuff I'm told exists. So if you were to ask me for my advice, I'd tell you to run away as fast and as far as you could. There's only going to be losers, and then more losers connected with this mess." He glanced over to O'Bryan. "I'm sorry, Jack, I really am." He waited a second or two then added, "But if Kettering really insists on waiving his immunity and standing trial, then it's a lawyer he needs, not an old worn-out gumshoe named Justin Scott."

O'Bryan had to smile in spite of the seriousness of the moment. "Spare me the worn-out gumshoe moniker, you crock." He rubbed his face to hide a yawn then asked, "You're a lawyer, right? I mean, all you agents had to be lawyers back in the dark ages when you joined the bureau. So let me hire you to be Kettering's lawyer and not just his investigator. You be the one to defend him in court. Who'd be in a better position than you? You'd know all the facts."

"Jeez, surely you jest? Haven't you been listening to a word I've said?" Justin couldn't see O'Bryan's face to tell if his friend was kidding or not. *Lord, maybe he was for real with that misguided, off-the-wall, absolutely insane suggestion. Better set him straight right now.* "Look, Jack, sure I graduated law school decades ago and I've kept up my membership in the bar, but that's it. I've never practiced law. *Never*. You dig?" He shook his head. "Don't even think such thoughts. There are dozens of lawyers out there who'd love to be top dog on this case, and I'll gladly help you pick the right one."

"Only kidding," O'Bryan said, yet not quite sounding sincere. "We have in mind asking a Harvard professor named Sean MacMillan to help us when and if the time comes. But till then, just find out what really happened last Sunday night, even if you have to come back and tell me Kettering's guilty, okay?"

Justin let loose a small sigh as he wheeled into the parking garage of The Watergate. The tires on his new Jaguar saloon squealed on the hot, dry pavement. "All right, for old-time sake I promise to sleep on it. I'll give you my final answer in the morning." He spoke as diplomatically as he knew how, knowing he would find a good reason to bow-out gracefully after sunup. "Now, go to bed, Jack," he commanded quietly, "you're all done in."

At four-fifteen Justin was awakened by his bedside phone's ringing.

"Scott," he answered, sleepily.

"Mr. Scott, please listen carefully. The Cardinal Kettering affair is none of your business. Tell that priest in the morning that you will not be helping him. And, yes, I know you're not one to be intimidated by threats made in the middle of the night, but believe me when I tell you this: people will most assuredly die if you persist in this folly. That, my dear fellow, is something you can take to the bank. There'll be no further warnings. Good night."

Justin pursed his lips as he put the phone back into its cradle. He sat up stiffly, then banged a fist into his pillow several times to reshape it, and settled back down. *Polite bastard*, he thought, *even if he had sounded slightly tipsy.*

Sleep eluded him. The more he thought about the call, the angrier he became. "You've pissed me off," he finally said aloud. "Bad move," he added, his hackles rising. He was now wide-awake.

Justin rolled out of bed knowing in that instant he was going to tell O'Bryan to count him in. He went to his desk, took a yellow legal pad from the top drawer and began to write rapidly, filling page after page with all he knew about the case. He worked past daybreak.

And all the while his thoughts kept returning to something O'Bryan had said.

CHAPTER 5

Justin caught a fluttering image of Kettering out of the corner of his eye. He picked up the TV remote and keyed the button to bring up the sound. It was three minutes past seven.

"The grand jury convenes sometime early today," the weekend announcer was saying, "and according to a credible source close to the investigation at the FBI, the evidence against Cardinal Kettering is damning. It's conceivable that the grand jury could come back with a finding as early as this morning. Let's go to Steve Miller who's standing by with the latest from Vatican City."

The screen faded to a sea of colored dots, but only for the second or two it took the satellite to downlink its information to New York. "Good morning, Steve."

"Joan, it's now afternoon here in Rome and, as you can imagine, this story is getting bigger with each passing hour. Just moments ago the Vatican Press Office released a statement which said that Cardinal Miglianico—he's the papal secretary of state for those viewers who aren't familiar with the name—has already left for Washington to meet with his counterpart. He should arrive sometime later today. The theory given the most play here is that should Cardinal Kettering be indicted, he'll be declared *persona non grata* by the President and immediately escorted home by the Vatican's top diplomat. Joan?"

"Any word as to the Pope's reaction to what's been happening in Washington?"

"The Holy Father hasn't made any public statement, Joan, but reliable sources say that he's been devastated by the news. It's even been suggested that although the two men were not all that close, the pontiff had regarded Cardinal Kettering as one whose counsel he trusted. And he always considered him to be above reproach. Maybe what we're really hearing is that the pontiff is already distancing himself from his man in Washington. In any event, this has to have come as a heavy blow, especially since it's no secret that the Church has recently been under fire, so to speak, and on so many fronts. Joan, Cardinal Kettering hasn't been formally accused of anything, so this drama will play out to the end. It's the waiting, the not knowing, which has everyone here in Vatican City on edge."

"Thanks, Steve. I know we can expect to hear from you regularly in the coming days."

The feed from Europe was replaced with a tight headshot of the New York anchor wearing a bright, cheerful smile. "Stay with us for the rest of today's headlines after this station break and a message from—"

Justin dispatched the woman into electronic oblivion. He stood in the center of the room, his brain digesting this latest development. He guessed that O'Bryan hadn't been informed of Miglianico's travel plans, unless of course the two had talked during the night. Maybe the folks in Rome had already abandoned the far-fetched notion of Kettering standing trial. Maybe Miglianico had spoken to

Kettering in the wee hours and the man had confessed. Maybe this was bigtime damage control. Maybe, maybe, maybe. He picked up the phone. It was time to call O'Bryan.

* * *

Justin swung his Jaguar into the thin line of late Saturday morning traffic in front of the Watergate, and headed for the Vatican Embassy. O'Bryan sat beside him.

"I've decided to help," Justin announced without preamble, his eyes glued to the road but hidden behind aviator sunglasses. "I still think there's one hell of a good chance your man's guilty," he went on, "but I promise I'll carefully weigh the evidence as it becomes known. Despite what you might think, I'm not a pigheaded old duffer, at least not yet. Facts can persuade me to change my opinion if they prove me wrong. And therein lies a perfect world. Sound okay by you, Jack?"

O'Bryan was elated. "I can't ask for more than that. But maybe after our meeting with Miglianico you won't need to go further." O'Bryan stole a glance at his watch and frowned. "I had no idea he was coming. There wasn't a peep about it when I left Rome yesterday. My guess is it means the decision's been made to whisk Kettering out of here, and all the talk about his staying to stand trial was just that. Talk."

"Could be, we'll know soon enough." Justin fiddled with the radio as he spoke, tuning in an all-news station. Satisfied, he then lowered the volume so as not to disrupt normal conversation.

* * *

Justin and O'Bryan rose in unison as Cardinal Miglianico entered the drawing room.

During the drive to the embassy they had learned from a news bulletin that the grand jury had handed up a rare, weekend decision. Based on the evidence there had been a finding of probable cause implicating one Francis Cardinal Kettering in the murder of one Jane Doe. The die had been cast.

"Cardinal Kettering will see you now," Miglianico announced. "I've told him how you've graciously agreed to help us, Mr. Scott."

Miglianico continued. "Cardinal Kettering has assured me several times that he had absolutely nothing to do with the young woman's death, and he's painfully aware of the trying times ahead. But he insists he wants to clear his name. He's even volunteered to shoulder the expense and not burden the Church, but I told him we would worry about that later."

Justin raised an eyebrow. "Are you saying that the Church guarantees the costs, Cardinal? Remember, we're going to start to rack up some rather sizable expenditures in the next few weeks, especially if we have to prepare for a trial."

"I understand, and yes, the Church guarantees the money will be there."

Justin picked up his briefcase and motioned with his head. "Shall we, gentlemen?"

Cardinal Kettering was standing with his back to the window as the trio entered. He was dressed in a simple black cassock with a Roman collar, and O'Bryan gasped involuntarily at the man's appearance. Kettering was an old man. The once proud, ramrod posture had given way to a distinct stoop, and he actually shuffled as he came forward. He held out his hand to O'Bryan. It was like ice.

"Thank you for coming, Monsignor."

"Your Eminence," O'Bryan acknowledged the ambassador with those two words and a nod.

Kettering turned to face Justin. He pulled himself to a more erect position and stared in momentary silence at the taller man. Then he announced in a firm voice, "I did not kill the woman, Mr. Scott."

"Cardinal Kettering, before either of us says another word, I want to hear it from you that you are acting of your own free will in having me here, and not because you've been so ordered by Cardinal Miglianico or the Pope."

Kettering's eyes registered genuine surprise. "I assure you, Mister Scott, I'm exercising my free will in this matter. The Holy Father ordered nothing, and neither has Cardinal Miglianico."

"Good. That's what I needed to hear." Justin gestured that they should all sit. They were in the ambassador's private office; a spacious, high-ceilinged room, now flooded with bright, late summer sunshine. The day had been a repeat of yesterday; another Washington scorcher.

They took seats grouped around a low marble table. Justin placed his scuffed and scarred leather case on the polished surface, but did not open it. "May I speak freely, Your Eminence?" he asked, addressing Cardinal Miglianico. "I don't mean just for the present, but I mean from this point forward." He glanced over at Kettering, then back to Miglianico. "Last night, Monsignor O'Bryan asked me in jest if I would consider becoming the cardinal's lawyer in addition to being hired as an investigator. I told him that I didn't feel qualified, even though I'm a member of the bar in good standing. But something compelled me to give it more serious thought later, and the more I did, the more I realized that just maybe Jack was onto something. You see, by following his suggestion, I can come to the table as both lawyer and investigator—at least as far as the authorities are concerned, and that bestows upon us the lawyer-client privilege of silence. As merely an investigator, I could possibly be subpoenaed as a hostile witness and forced to testify, but no one can touch me if I'm the cardinal's lawyer." He looked at all three, taking special note of the look on O'Bryan's face. *Got you there*, he thought.

"So, if I'm to be Cardinal Kettering's lawyer," he continued, "I must warn you that I will not be swayed or intimidated by rank." He spoke slowly and deliberately so there would be no misunderstanding. "I am to be the man in command, and my word on all legal matters will be final." His eyes turned to the accused. "You're certainly free to fire me at any time, Cardinal Kettering, and if you do, I'll leave quietly. But understand this; there'll be no persuasion that will bring me back. Ever. Are we clear on this, gentlemen?"

All three mumbled that they were.

With those words Justin had seized control.

"Then let's get started." Justin snapped open his case and extracted a yellow legal pad. As he rapidly flipped through a dozen or so pages, it was evident he had been busy. He found what he was looking for, and placed his thumb on the dog-eared page to mark it. "Okay, here's where we stand. Cardinal Kettering has been indicted by the grand jury as of late this morning." He shot a look to Kettering then to Miglianico and saw in their expressions they already knew. "But," he continued, "because the ambassador enjoys diplomatic immunity, that action really is meaningless. He's bulletproof. But before the government of the United States declares him *persona non grata,* it is the will of the ambassador to freely turn himself over to the authorities, and if necessary, stand trial in a court of law in the United States to prove his innocence." He glanced at Kettering. "Is that an accurate summation, Cardinal?"

"That is correct, sir. I'm innocent of the charges, and wish to clear my good name."

Justin held up his hand. "That's just fine and dandy, but let's take this one step at a time." He turned to Miglianico. "Please inform the American secretary of state that as of this moment the Vatican is voluntarily suspending diplomatic immunity for its ambassador, but not revoking it. I'm not fully convinced this is the step I'd take, but I understand you've already alerted the authorities to this possibility, so I'll learn to live with it. However, there will be absolutely no talk of the ambassador being taken to jail, or even leaving the embassy grounds to attend a bond hearing. Bond would be denied, and Cardinal Kettering would be handcuffed in front of the media, if only for a minute. That won't do. So, Cardinal Miglianico, you will give your personal guarantee to the government of the United States that if this matter should come to trial, then Francis Kettering will appear for his day in court. Until then, the cardinal will remain at the embassy, and he will not leave unless for a medical emergency. Understood?"

"Yes," said an obviously subdued Miglianico.

"That announcement's sure going to blindside the press," O'Bryan said. "I guarantee you, they've been betting that Cardinal Kettering would be leaving on the first train out of Dodge."

Justin made no comment, instead he continued with his instructions. "Cardinal Miglianico, as of now, I want Monsignor O'Bryan working for me. I need someone I can trust, and someone who can communicate with you on a moment's notice." Justin allowed a hint of a smile to cross his face. "Jack's not a lawyer, but as a priest, he, too, can invoke that special privilege of confessor to Cardinal Kettering, and as such he can't be subpoenaed by the prosecution. I'm not saying they would try to subpoena him, mind you, but I want to be in a position to stop them cold in case they should."

It was obvious to the assembled clerics that Justin had done his homework. They were impressed.

"He's yours for as long as you need him, Counselor."

O'Bryan flashed a smile at his friend.

"And, lastly, we come to the matter of my fee. I will want a retainer of $500,000. That is a low figure for a high profile case such as this. If I prove the cardinal innocent before going to trial, or he decides to cut a deal and skip town, then that money is to be considered fully earned. If, on the other hand we go to trial, I'll need help, and my fee doubles. Win, lose, or draw. And if we lose, we appeal. Rest assured it *will* go all the way to the Supreme Court for a definitive ruling. This case is unique, and its ramifications are staggering."

He paused long enough to glance at his notes. "Next, I want Jack to open a special bank account for us so that we can begin immediately to draw on it for expenses. They are separate from any fee I might earn. I suggest $200,000 for starters." As he spoke, he placed the yellow pad in his case and snapped it shut. "I'll have the necessary legal papers drawn up for signing before I make a press announcement." For the first time since entering the room, Justin visibly relaxed. He flashed a humorless smile. "Any questions?" As he looked from one to another he knew that the speech regarding the fee would be the test to see whether or not they were serious about wanting to prove Kettering's innocence, or were merely posturing for his benefit.

Miglianico actually managed a small chuckle. "Jack reminded me a day or so ago that legal action in this country would be expensive, but I must confess, I had no idea just how expensive.

One million dollars is a lot of money, Mr. Scott. We can talk more about that later."

"No, Cardinal Miglianico, we cannot talk about it later. It's not a topic open to negotiation. That's my fee. And I should remind you that figure doesn't include the salaries of the other lawyers I'm sure I'll have to hire to help me prepare the case. The $200,000 account Jack's opening on Monday will be drawn down to hire additional staff, engage other private detectives if necessary, forensic experts, et cetera. The money will go fast, I assure you. This is only the tip of the iceberg. Any other law firm would charge you at least double the figure I just quoted. The prosecution is the whole U.S. Government. It has unlimited resources at its disposal, and the justice department will spend whatever it takes to get a conviction. Like it or not, in the eyes of the public this ranks as one of the crimes of the century. Not just here in America, but everywhere. And it's going to get the same attention as the trials of those terrorists responsible for attacking New York and Washington. Now, gentlemen, if I'm indeed hired, then I'd like a few minutes alone with my client."

Nobody called his bluff. He was in.

* * *

An hour later Justin and O'Bryan were driving back to the Watergate.

"So, is he guilty?" O'Bryan wanted to know. "I'm sure that was the first question you asked. I know it would've been mine."

Justin kept his eyes on the busy road. "Wrong. I'll let you in on a secret, Jack. I don't know of any lawyer worth his salt who'd come out and point-blank ask his client that question. You see, you assume once you're hired that your client is telling the truth when he professes his innocence, and all personal opinions at that point be damned. That way you can honestly devote your best effort to mounting the strongest possible defense. Think about it. If you knew your client was guilty, would you really do the best job? Or would the knowledge that you were defending a guilty man make you do less than your best just in case you were so damn good that a guilty man got away with murder?"

"Well, since you put it that way, I see your point."

"But I did ask him who the woman was."

"And?"

"And he denied any knowledge of who she was, or how she got to be in the trunk. We didn't get into why he was in the car at that time of night, but he reminded me that the police still haven't released her identity yet. He also claims he doesn't know how the murder weapon just happened to have only his prints plastered all over it. I then asked if he had an idea as to who the woman *might* be. I was getting exasperated; I felt he was sparring with me."

"And?"

Justin gave a sad little shake of his head. "Jack, the man broke down and started to cry. It was downright chilling to watch. I have a hunch he knows a whole lot more than he's telling." He slammed on his brakes to avoid rear-ending a taxi that had stopped short. "We've got our work cut out for us, Monsignor," he said in a formal voice, "and I do believe this is going to get very, very nasty before it's over."

"No more run away as fast as you can, Jack?"

Justin managed a laugh. "Nah. That was yesterday's news, *Padre.*" He eased the car forward.

"I hear you, Justin. Thanks for coming on board."

CHAPTER 6

"Val, come here. Quick, honey, look at this!"

Three days had passed.

"I can't Danny, I'm dressing Dania."

"*Valerie*! It's the FBI. They're about to announce the identity of the woman in your murder case."

She dropped her child's shoe. "Mommy'll be right back, sweetheart." She rushed towards her bedroom and the television set. The phone began to ring. She stood beside her husband, eyes transfixed to the screen. She picked up the receiver and immediately placed it back in the cradle, breaking the connection. No way was she going to be disturbed.

In front of her stood FBI Director Judge Anderson MacAllister. He began to read. "I have a brief statement to make. When I'm finished, I will not be fielding any questions." He paused long enough for the press to comprehend the rules of engagement. "The young woman whose murdered body found nine days ago in the trunk of a sedan belonging to the Vatican's Embassy has been positively identified. The victim had no criminal record in this country, and thus had no prints on file with the FBI. Likewise, she was not known to the Royal Canadian Mounted Police, or the Mexican Federal Police. She was not a fugitive in any sense of the word. Her prints were sent to Interpol, but a negative response came back from that organization. However, working on a tip from Europe, the Federal Bureau of Investigation has positively identified the woman as one Maritha von Snellenberger, of Gagny, Switzerland. She is ... ah, *was* the wife of a prominent Swiss banker. The husband has not yet been located or notified, so out of respect for the family we are not making any more details public at this time. There is no record with Immigration that this woman entered the United States using a passport in her own name. That, and a number of other factors, made it difficult for us to identify her before now. As soon as we can release further information, we will do so. There will be a photograph of the victim distributed to the press after this briefing. That is the end of my statement. Thank you." Judge anderson MacAllister walked away from the podium without a backward glance.

"So, what does it mean, Val?"

She shot a sideways glance at her husband. "It means that the bureau has just screwed me again. They were supposed to relay any information to me before going public with it."

The phone began to ring. Danny picked it up, listened, then wordlessly handed it to his wife.

"Valerie, it's Braddock. You'll be pleased to know the bureau delivered the tape just as their main man began his dog-and-pony show. They really are a bunch of shits."

"Forget it, Tom. Listen. I have to drop Dania off at school, then I'll be right in. We need to brainstorm our next move. See you in an hour. Bye." She replaced the receiver, and turned to speak to her husband.

Danny Tobias held up his hand. "Val, I can drop Dania off. You go on. Really, it's okay."

She reached over and stroked her husband's cheek. "Thanks, that'd be a big help."

Dania was their twelve-year-old daughter. Because the child had been born with severe Down's syndrome, she would never mature beyond the mental age of four, five tops. But she was the sweetest child either could have ever hoped for, and she was the light of both their lives. Sadly, she probably would not live to celebrate her twentieth birthday.

* * *

Valerie strode into her office thirty-five minutes later. Braddock was already there, slouched in a *faux* leather chair and reading *The Washington Post.*

"You know, Val, I'm getting more information on this case from the frigging press than from anywhere else. We may as well be the janitors here because we know squat about what's going down. So much for all that ballyhoo about being kept in the loop. You and I aren't going to be told bubkis." He tossed the paper aside in disgust.

Valerie threw her purse on the desk. "Don't remind me." She took a deep breath, then exhaled slowly. "Well, I for one am through being out of the loop and I don't care what the feds are saying or doing. As of now things are about to change. Here's my first order. Who's your best sergeant? Peter Delaney? Tony Prichard?"

"Neither. Maria Delgado, hands down. Why?"

Valerie shook her head. "Not Maria. She's too valuable to me on the street. Pick one of the other two to act as your shift commander until further notice. I want you with me full-time on this."

Braddock wore a doubtful look. "You could find yourself in a world of shit with the chief, Val," he cautioned. "The guy clearly said, hands off, it's no longer our case."

"Tom, let me worry about the chief, okay? I take the fall if it backfires, fair enough?"

"You're the boss. Just remember, I warned you."

She spotted a colorful bag on her side of her desk. Peeking inside, she shot him a look.

He raised and lowered his eyebrows in rapid succession. "Yeah, yeah, your favorite," Braddock said. "Chocolate dipped in chocolate. Nothing but the best when it comes to what's good for the waistline."

"Dammit, Loo, you know I can't resist. I'll get us the coffee, then we'll talk."

Ten minutes and two indulgently delicious doughnuts apiece later, she got down to business.

"When the bureau took over this case, Tom, did they get all the evidence we had?"

"As far as I know they did. Why?"

"How about from the hospital the night Kettering was booked? Blood was drawn. What happened to it? Did it come to our evidence room, or go directly to theirs?"

"Ours. In fact, I went over to the hospital as soon as I left the police pound and personally took everything back here. Why?"

"When did the bureau come for it?"

"Can't tell you to the minute, but sometime that day."

"Did they get it all?"

Braddock stopped breathing. His eyes began to bug and his face turned crimson. He stood up and nervously tiptoed over to the door. He peeked up and down the hallway, closed the door, and walked back to his seat. Then he exhaled in one long swoosh.

"How in the hell did you know?" he managed to whisper. "Nobody knew. At least, that's what I thought."

She ignored his question. "What did you hold back, Lieutenant?" Her face was deadly serious.

"Oh, man! Shit, Valerie, I thought I was doing the right thing." He looked at his boss, real fear on his face. "I kept a vial of blood, Val."

In spite of herself she began to grin. "Explain."

"There were three vials drawn. Because they were swamped that night in the emergency room, the lab was backed up and nobody had found the time needed to run the analysis. The vials had been labeled, but not yet numbered. The ER report showed what time the blood had been taken, but like I just said, it didn't give a count. So I took them over here and put 'em in our cooler in the evidence room. I tagged 'em myself so as to keep an unbroken chain of evidence. I entered 'two' on the evidence sheet then signed and dated it. As I said, the vials were identified as coming from the cardinal, so the two I logged in I marked, one of two; two of two."

"And what did you do with the third?"

He waited a full five seconds. "Took it home with me when I went off duty. It's in my refrigerator."

"What in the hell did you do that for?"

"To be honest, Inspector, I don't really know. Some little voice told me to hold it back. I just didn't like the idea of turning everything we had over to the prissy little Ivy League types across town. Guess I was pissed. Anyway, that's what happened."

"I see. And it's still there?"

"Better be," he snorted, "unless I mistook it for a beer."

Her grin gave way to a full-throated chuckle. She raised a fist and punched at the air in delight. "*Yes,*" she stage-whispered. "*Yes*!"

"*Phew*! Man, I thought I was in deep shit there for a moment. Tell me, how did you know?"

She brushed his question aside with a regal wave of her hand. "Not telling. That's why I'm the head knocker around here. I know everything." Inside she was laughing. She had had no idea Braddock had withheld anything when she'd popped the question.

"You want me to bring it back?"

She thought for a second. "No, it's probably safer at your place for the time being. I don't know quite what we're going to do with it, but I thank God for giving me such a smart, yet devious detective-lieutenant. The next round of this diet food is definitely on me."

* * *

It was a shot heard around the world.

On Wednesday morning Justin marched into court and petitioned the judge to throw out the bill of indictment.

"The action of the grand jury is illegal, and therefore invalid."

"Explain, Counselor."

"Your Honor, only the federal court system has jurisdiction over cases involving foreign officials. There's no question that Ambassador Kettering is a foreign official. In order for me to respond to the indictment handed up against my client, it must be brought in the court with the proper venue. With all due respect, Your Honor, yours is not the proper court. I fear that in their haste for publicity my colleagues for the prosecution did not pay attention to the law governing such matters."

Ten minutes later Justin was on the street. The court had given the prosecution ten days to respond.

A very peeved Cardinal Miglianico summoned Justin to the embassy at noon. He was leaving for Rome within the hour but he wanted to talk before leaving.

"Mr. Scott, this morning's proceedings reminded me of the defense attorneys' many trifling actions in the farcical case of your Mr. O. J. Simpson several years back. It looked to me as if you were splitting technical legal hairs, and I fear justice was not served this day. Remember, it's the Church that insisted for the entire world to hear that we resolve this issue in court. We said at the time that we have nothing to hide. But your actions today belie that stance. It looks as if we have everything to hide, namely a guilty cardinal."

"Not so, Cardinal Miglianico," Justin said in a steady voice. "And may I remind you, this is my arena, and I will not be second-guessed. What I presented to the court this morning was critical for two reasons. First, if I have to go to trial, and, God forbid, if I have to go to an appeal, then I want to make sure that we're on solid legal ground every step of the way. Second, this morning's action throws the prosecution into a tizzy. They were sloppy, and I embarrassed them publicly. To speak in the vernacular, I rattled their cage. But in the process I bought myself time; as much as twenty extra days. And those are days I desperately need to use to our advantage to try and find the real killer. So, no, I have not split legal hairs. But I have alerted the opposition that they'd better do their homework. They're now furious at their stupidity, and they're going to be pointing fingers at each other for the next few days as to who should shoulder the blame for such an elemental blunder. And the press is going to belittle them for it. Cardinal Miglianico, this isn't a game. It's for keeps, and your colleague is the one who must pay the price if I lose."

Miglianico had been pacing liked a caged bear as Justin spoke. He stopped, and looked toward Kettering, who had remained seated and silent throughout. Both prelates then shrugged their shoulders in unison.

Miglianico raised his hands, palms upward. "I'm sorry. I didn't know. You said a few days ago that you could not be second-guessed, and I confess, that's exactly what I was doing." Miglianico let loose with a smile. "Lesson learned. It won't happen again. I leave for Rome confident in your abilities. God bless you. I'm truly thankful you're with us."

* * *

The opposition quickly let loose a round of their own, timing the shot to be the lead story on the evening news. It was reported that the FBI had released the results of the blood samples taken from Kettering on the night of the murder, and his blood alcohol level had registered .10 percent alcohol by volume. The man had been legally drunk when apprehended.

By the next morning, the press had expanded on the story, and the suggestion now fully out in the open was that the cardinal had been engaged in a long-standing affair that had gone sour, and that the woman had threatened to go public. There was innuendo of blackmail. No quantum leap of imagination was required to rationalize a motive for murder.

* * *

During the next three days of almost non-stop meetings with Kettering, Justin HH came to see him as arrogant yet complex; a man both angry and mortified at finding himself in such a predicament. For the first time in his adult life he was not in control, and his frustration showed.

Justin had insisted they record and transcribe everything, and at the end of each day he made sure all documents were locked in a special safe he had had brought into the ambassador's office. For the sake of security, all material would stay in the embassy. Any documents that did leave would go only as far as his office, carried by either O'Bryan or himself, and deposited in his safe until he could transport them back to the embassy.

This was Saturday, and his fifth meeting with Kettering. O'Bryan had accompanied him every time.

Kettering had turned alarmingly morose on supposedly hearing the identity of the woman for the first time.

"Mr. Scott, all I can say is, yes, I know who she was, and no, I was not having an affair. And I categorically deny that I was drunk. Anyone who knows me will affirm that I never touch alcohol." Kettering was speaking at a session hastily called after the story had been the lead item on the networks' evening news.

Justin shook his head. "Not true."

Kettering reacted angrily. "I'm not a liar, sir."

Justin rose from the conference table and began to pace. He continued to stalk, making his way around the table until he was standing next to Kettering's chair. He bent down until his lips were up against the cardinal's ear. "I have it on good authority you imbibe every day. What do you say about that?"

"Are you here to defend or to destroy?"

"You celebrate mass daily, Your Eminence," Justin replied, straightening up, his mind racing back to his undergraduate days at The University of Notre Dame and the required courses in theology. "The miracle of the Eucharist involves wine, water, and unleavened bread."

Kettering was exasperated. "Everyone knows that."

"No, everyone *doesn't* know that," said Justin returning to his chair. "But those who do can make a pretty convincing case for priests becoming alcoholics because of a daily intake of wine that doesn't stop at the ritual of the mass. Unfortunately, your ecclesiastical ranks are littered with the afflicted, and if push comes to shove it's something I can maybe use to your advantage." He wheeled toward O'Bryan. "You see where I'm going?"

O'Bryan nodded that he did.

"Transubstantiation," Kettering shouted, before O'Bryan could reply.

"Yes," Justin said, turning on a dime to come face to face with Kettering. "The miracle of the mass. The essence of Catholicism. The transforming of the bread and wine of the Eucharist into the body and blood of Christ."

"Mr. Scott, you're treading on dangerously thin ice," replied Kettering, "and I don't like it." He was worried that this layman was leading them all into a theological minefield.

Justin sat back and shook his head. "Cardinal, I'm heading nowhere, at least not for the moment. But think about this. Blood drawn from you that night shows you were drunk. That, sir, is a fact. So I'd better be ready with a damn good explanation. Something a jury will buy. He leaned forward. "All right, let's move on to other matters." He was not about to get sidetracked. He flipped his legal pad to a clean sheet and said, "Now I want you to tell me everything you know about Maritha von Snellenberger, and I do mean *everything.*"

* * *

Later that evening Justin called Valerie. He hadn't seen her since the meeting in her office.

"Hi, Justin. The newspapers say you've been hired to handle the

Kettering case. And not just as an investigator but as a full-fledged lawyer. I'm impressed, Justin, I really am. Congratulations."

"Val, I'm calling to let you know that I'm really still just the detective. The lawyering part you see in the papers is only a smoke screen. But if you repeat any of this I'll simply deny it. Look, if and when it comes down to a trial I've already been told that a real lawyer named Sean MacMillan will be brought in. He's some kind of a big cheese at Harvard but for some reason Kettering hates his guts, and no one will tell me why." He sighed. "In many ways this Vatican crowd is a real weird bunch."

"So why the call?"

"Val, I want you to know that I don't expect you to pass along any more information you uncover about the official investigation. Because in my newfound role of attorney, and even though it's strictly for show, my relationship with you and the authorities has obviously changed and I can no longer reciprocate. So I'm just calling to say thanks for the offer you made the other day."

"That's really sweet of you, Justin." She was silent for a few moments, then seemed to come to a decision to speak further. She lowered her voice. "I'm not telling tales out of school when I say it doesn't look good for Kettering. Without going into details, the evidence I've seen adds up to a very formidable circumstantial case against your client. You'll be seeing it in discovery," she added with a rush, "but I just wanted to give you a heads-up for old times' sake."

"I appreciate that, Val, but I didn't phone to pump you about Kettering, so say no more. No compromises. No *quid pro quos,* okay?"

She laughed, fully relaxed for the first time since she'd picked up the phone. "Okay, Justin. Got to run. Bye."

CHAPTER 7

Two weeks had passed since the murder, and this Sunday morning found Justin in his Watergate Plaza office along with O'Bryan, and Paula Bateman, his secretary. Paula had willingly followed him from the bureau. They were a team.

Unable to afford such a posh address by himself, he shared the expense of the upscale suite with two successful personal injury lawyers. Each maintained responsibility for his own offices and staffs but split the cost for the two conference rooms, the library, and salaries of both receptionists. It was a sensible arrangement for all concerned.

Justin now stood in the smaller of the conference rooms, his back braced against the gleaming black cherry conference table. He was dressed in shirtsleeves, his expensive slacks held fast by colorful suspenders. His weakness for clothes went as far back as he could remember, and he often joked that in this one regard he was worse than most women he knew.

He plopped a file down in front of O'Bryan, then its twin in front of Paula. "Before we get into those," he began, "let me tell you what I gleaned from a source late last night from inside the bureau. He told me how the feds really got their tip on the identity of the victim." He sauntered back to his seat but remained standing, thumbs hooked inside suspenders. "Seems a handwritten fax came into the headquarters from somewhere in Italy. It read: *Attention FBI: The woman is Maritha von Snellenberger, Gagny, Switzerland.* That's it. No accompanying message, no sender's identification block. Only that one sentence."

"And from that they were able to trace it back to the source?" O'Bryan asked, more than a little surprised.

"Nope. Had it come in on one of the high-tech, dedicated network fax lines, the bureau could have intercepted that information automatically. Instead, it came in on a regular commercial line into the coffee shop. Can you believe it? The coffee shop! Seems they use a fax because people all over the building send them their breakfast, lunch, and dinner orders rather than phoning. Saves time, and it gets the orders right. Anyway, the message sat there for the better part of the day until the manager just happened to show it to an agent. She acted on a hunch, and the rest, as they say, is history."

"So how do you know Italy was the country of origin?"

"Because those bureau boys are good, *Padre*."

"Thank God for small favors. Cut to the chase, Justin," O'Bryan mumbled with a feigned exasperation. He found Justin's dry sense of humor contagious.

Justin ignored the good-natured dig. "Seems a real faint image bled through from the reverse side of the paper the sender used. Not much, mind you. A hint of a logo and two fuzzy letters. But enough for the lab to work with. They reproduced the logo for the Venus de Milo Hotel, and two letters: M, and A. The last two letters of the word, *ROMA*. Neat, huh?"

"How in the blazes did someone in Rome pinpoint the identity of an unknown homicide victim in America? Doesn't make sense."

"Does too if we have a conspiracy, Jack."

"You mean like Kettering had an accomplice?"

"Ah, so you *do* believe the cardinal's guilty, is that what you're saying?"

O'Bryan turned red. Paula placed a well-manicured hand in front of her mouth to hide a spreading grin. "Uh, uh, no," he stammered, "What I meant was, uh …."

"Forget it. We know what you meant," Justin said, winking at Paula. "Look, it's entirely possible the sender deliberately used that hotel's stationery just to throw the bureau off, then faxed it from somewhere else in Europe. But the bureau doesn't think so. Anyway, I'll be checking out that wrinkle further. Now, let's open our folders."

"Before we do, let me suggest another possibility," Paula said.

"And that is?"

"It could be a *Deep Throat*, you know, someone intentionally wanting to steer the authorities in the right direction."

Justin arched an eyebrow and lowered the corners of his mouth. He mulled over what she had said, then slowly nodded.

"Good point. I took a pass on that idea earlier, but it still could hold water. Thanks for reminding me. Now, let's take a peek inside our folders."

They opened their files, which contained several photographs and several typed pages.

"Notice how each picture has a number on the back," Justin began, "a number that corresponds to an accompanying bio, also in your folders. The first two shots are of an Inspector Tobias and Lieutenant Braddock of the Metropolitan Police. These two are handling the case for the local authorities, but word has it they're not on speaking terms with the bureau boys because the *federales* are running the show and are slow passing information back to the locals. That just might be something we can take advantage of.

"Both cops have solid credentials," he continued, "and are well regarded by their peers. I've known Tobias for a dozen or so years," he added, choosing not to expand further on the innocuous statement. "She's the highest ranking female officer in Metro, but she didn't get to where she is today because of affirmative action. The woman's good. Remember that. I've met Braddock on several occasions over the years, the last time at a fund-raiser barbecue back in April. There's a picture in your folders of a group of us hamming it up for the camera."

The photo showed Justin, Tobias, Braddock, and two unknowns toasting the photographer with cans of beer. All seemed in rare form. Braddock was closest to the camera; beer held high in his left hand, his right pointing proudly to his sweatshirt. *NOTRE DAME* was emblazoned across his chest in white letters bordered in gold and resting on a black background.

"Braddock's an alumnus of the *Fighting Irish*," Justin explained. "Played ball all four years but was considered too small to make it in the pros. The guy will bore you to tears with stories of his glory days once he's had a snootful. He glommed onto me because I also happened to have graduated from Notre Dame before going on to Fordham Law a thousand years ago. You can read it in their biographies, but not now."

He moved them deeper into their folders. "The next set of pictures are of the commanders of the task force the feds have put together. My source tells me fifty agents have been assigned to this case, and not a rookie in the group. Four of them went packing off to Europe yesterday morning looking for everything they can find that will link Kettering to the victim. Judge MacAllister, it seems, has a hard-on for the cardinal." As soon as the words were out of his mouth, he glanced up. "Sorry about that, didn't mean to offend anyone."

"The director's not alone," replied O'Bryan. "Kettering has quite a few enemies. Rarely does someone reach his position without honking-off more than just a few folks along the way. Politics in Rome are no different than politics in Washington."

Justin continued. "I stayed up until almost two o'clock last night going over what Kettering had told us about his relationship with the victim. On the surface his story sounds good, and I'm hoping he's telling the truth. But, I suspect, not the whole truth, and not by a long shot. Because his story's too pat. He's leaving big chunks out of the dialogue, and that puzzles me. So I need to start digging on my own."

He turned to Paula. "Hate to have to cancel at the last minute, kiddo, but I'm going to have to take a pass on the fishing trip with you and Ben, and I'm going to ask you to stay behind, too. I'm really sorry. I'll be taking off for Switzerland in the morning," he explained, "because I need to get ahold of the same information the bureau boys will be getting, plus some of the stuff they'll miss. I'll need you to stay here and help Jack."

Paula bowed her head and scribbled feverishly. "Point us in the right direction and give us our marching orders, but first I need to pop into my office to call Ben and tell him of the change of plans. I'll be back in a jiff."

"Thanks, Paula."

She returned as quickly as promised and nodded at Justin to continue.

"Okay, here goes. I want a list of all the cardinal's credit cards: American Express, Master Card, Visa, phone cards, everything. Going back as far as we can. I want the same for all his bank accounts, and I want to know where his money goes. Is there a pattern to his spending? Is there a pattern to deposits outside of what the Church provides?" He looked at Paula. "That'll be your assignment."

"Sounds like we've become the prosecutors," O'Bryan remarked.

Justin shook his head. "Uh-uh, Jack. I just don't want whatever other lawyers are eventually brought in to help with the trial finding themselves blindsided because I didn't do my homework. If there's dirt out there, I want to discover it myself. That way I can prepare a solid explanation for rebuttal. That's called damage control, and it's what I do best."

He made a tick mark on the legal pad beside his open folder then hurried on. "Jack, I need you to work up a biography of the cardinal. Not the rah-rah stuff the Vatican puts out, but stuff with real meat on the bones. I need a complete history of the man, including information on all his postings as he shot up the ecclesiastical ladder of success. And be prepared to air express it to me in Europe if I call for it."

O'Bryan let out a low whistle as he pondered the task ahead. "I'll do what I can, Justin."

"Not good enough. 'I promise results,' is what you meant to say," Justin corrected, as he flipped his pad back to its front page. "Okay, let's go over what the cardinal has told us about his relationship with Mrs. von Snellenberger. As I said, there seems to be a ton of stuff missing from his story. Everybody ready?"

Paula peeked at her watch and wiggled restlessly in her chair. "Boss, Ben's still heading for Northern Maine at three o'clock, and I have to drive him to the airport. We've flat run out of time."

Paula and Ben were both pilots, and they loved to fly their twin-engine Beech at every opportunity. Ben was a helicopter pilot employed by Potomac Power and Light. His job was to fly the hundreds of miles of transmission lines looking for trouble, and also to transport executives around the vast system as needed.

They had invited Justin, along with Ben's two brothers, to join them for three days of fishing at their cabin in Maine. The brothers had already driven up from Boston, and planned to meet the plane upon its arrival at the local airport.

"Just don't pull a fast one and blow town with Ben at the last moment, missy," he pretended to threaten. "You'd probably end up getting the both of you thoroughly lost, and I can't afford the half-hour it would take me to teach your replacement the few simple tasks you sometimes manage to get done around here."

She replied by sticking her tongue out, causing Justin to guffaw at such an unexpected little-girl antic.

Truth was, Paula loved working for Justin, and would willingly sacrifice any holiday to stay and help. In spite of all the lighthearted banter, she knew how important this case was.

* * *

Ben Bateman entered a left-hand traffic pattern at the uncontrolled airfield near Eagle Lake, his altimeter showing him to be bang-on the money: 800 feet above the ground. He looked down and spotted a lone Cessna single tied-down on the grass next to the 4000 foot paved runway, but no sign of a car. That didn't surprise him. He was early, and his brothers weren't due for another twenty minutes. A thick carpet of trees rolled toward the horizon in all directions, a carpet so dense that he knew he could be flying right over them yet miss them completely.

His flight had been uneventful. The plane had handled flawlessly, and the weather en route had been exceptional all the way northward to this corner of heaven on the Canadian border.

Because there was no control tower, he picked up his hand-held radio, triggered the transmit button, and broadcast his position over the field on the Unicom channel, announcing to other planes that might be in the area his intention to land on runway two-seven. A staggered line of seventy-foot-tall maple and birch trees came to a halt less than a quarter of a mile from the approach end of the runway. Instinctively, he set his angle of descent just a tad steeper than normal.

He lowered his gear and made a smooth turn onto final. He lowered his flaps, and nodded a silent approval at the three steady green lights on the dash, indicating his wheels were down and locked. As he eased back on the power and adjusted the trim, he felt the satisfactory rush of adrenaline that came with every perfect approach. The setting sun was now smack in his face, so he lowered his visor.

"Still the world's greatest stick, aren't you, Benny Boy," he crowed aloud.

It was the last sentence he would ever utter.

A Stinger missile launched from the shoulder of a man crouching just inside the line of trees streaked towards the plane's rear at a speed approaching 600 miles an hour. Its infrared, heat-seeking guidance system unerringly made a track toward the greatest source of thermal energy in the sky: the Beech's engines. The resultant explosion whooshed outward; a blinding, expanding orange fireball of aviation fuel which enveloped the plane as it tumbled three hundred feet into the trees. It ignited the forest on impact.

From their car on the roadway less than a mile away, Ben's brothers witnessed the horror.

This can't be happening, they thought as one, knowing full well that it was. Both men screamed.

A lone figure rose from the dirt several hundred yards away in the opposite direction, threw down the spent rocket launcher, punched the air once with a fisted salute, jumped on a Harley Davidson, donned a blue and purple futuristic plastic helmet and sped away, the thunder of his departing machine drowning out the roar of the rapidly spreading man-made inferno.

* * *

Justin sat opposite O'Bryan in a corner booth of Spoto's restaurant in Georgetown. They were dining on Chicago-style pizza. Between bites he gave O'Bryan some last minute instructions. Finally, he wiped his mouth on a tablecloth-sized checkered napkin, then dug into his pocket and pulled out an envelope.

"Before I forget, this is for you. It's ten thousand dollars to cover expenses, as well as the first draw of your salary. It isn't charity. I want you to get yourself into some real clothes, and not from Goodwill," he admonished. "Get a couple of spiffy civilian suits, a sports coat, slacks, shoes, the works. I can't have you running around all the time looking like a priest. It's too distracting. I need us to downplay your Church connection, if that's at all possible. So, Jack, spend some money. Put away the dog collar for a while."

"Thanks. I was going to call Rome and have a buddy ship over some of my things. Any suggestions on what I should avoid? I'm not up on the latest fashions like a certain Beau Brummell I could easily point a finger at."

Justin laughed. "Yeah, stay away from checks and plaids. I don't need you looking like a clown. That would ruin my rep."

O'Bryan flashed a grin, then quickly turned serious. "Straight skinny, Justin. How do you think it's going?"

Justin took a long draw on his soda before responding. "Jack, there have been times in the past two weeks I think I should have heeded my own advice and hoofed it out of here just as fast as my legs could carry me. Kettering's in deep, and it's going to get a lot worse before it gets better. That's *if* it gets better," he added, glumly.

"Well, you sure stuffed the opposition into a blender with that bit about being in the wrong court with the wrong grand jury," said O'Bryan.

"But only for the moment," Justin replied. "When they regroup they're going to come on like gangbusters. The new grand jury convenes shortly, and it'll simply rubber-stamp the bill handed up by the first one. And then the federal attorney for the District of Columbia will formally announce his intentions to prosecute. All I did was buy us some time."

"Then what?"

Justin toyed with the last slice of pizza. "I can't press for discovery until I know who to ask to share the evidence, so I've decided to really muddy up the waters. I'm going to suggest to the media before I leave in the morning that I fully expect the Attorney General of the United States to step in and take charge of the prosecution. This is a town built on giant egos," he continued, "and the very fact that I say this will create a self-fulfilling prophecy. The AG will slap herself silly wondering why she didn't think of it herself, then she and the federal attorney will spend the next couple of weeks snapping at each other as to who should be the top dog." He leaned back and sighed deeply. "All I'm really doing is buying time, Jack. And for what?" he asked dejectedly. He was not the least bit happy with the lack of hard information coming from Kettering.

"Explain to this layman what you mean by discovery."

Justin shrugged. "It's simple, really. Under our system, each side must give the other copies of all the evidence it uncovers. This prevents any surprises in court."

"So, when do they start giving us their discovery?" O'Bryan pressed. "I'm not aware of anything that's been handed over to us yet."

Justin shook his head. "It hasn't. The judge assigned to this case, or any case for that matter, usually instructs the prosecution and defense during what's called the scheduling conference to do so. In theory, it's supposed to be done expeditiously, but, in fact, it seldom is."

"And they're supposed to give us everything they've discovered?"

"Yeah. Supposed to are the operative words. Copies of the autopsy, blood tests, physical evidence taken at the scene. Anything and everything. And we're supposed to do the same."

"Including a copy of a confession, if there was one?"

"Definitely that," Justin said as he stared at his friend. "The smartest thing done to date was the stunt pulled by Monsignor Capelletti at the embassy. He really used his head by getting Kettering back to his legation before anyone in official Washington thought about questioning him at the hospital. Fact is, Capelletti saved Kettering's ass, at least according to those who think he's guilty."

"Amen to that. So if Kettering had confessed to you, would you have to tell the prosecution?"

"You mean confessed to me as his lawyer?"

O'Bryan grinned. "I'm the priest; you're the lawyer. Don't get the two confused."

Justin was too tired to come back with a witty response. "No. That kind of confession is privileged lawyer-client communication.

In reality though, what I would do at that point would be to try to cut a deal with the prosecution. Cop a plea, as they say in the vernacular."

"But if you did that, they'd immediately suspect the guy confessed and would probably say, 'No deal.' Right?"

"Right," Justin replied. "I know I would." He stole a glance at his watch. It was almost eleven. Time to wrap. "How long do you think it'll take you to get the background stuff on Kettering for me?"

O'Bryan answered with a question of his own. "Did you know he didn't enter the seminary until he was twenty-eight? By then he'd already managed a doctorate in philosophy and was teaching at the university in Bonn, and that's when he realized he had a calling to enter religious life. He was ordained at thirty-four, and twenty-two years later was presented with the red hat of a cardinal. Not too shabby, huh?"

"Bloody wonderful," Justin replied with uncharacteristic sarcasm, suddenly weary of all matters pertaining to his stone-walling client. He stood. "I'm beat, Jack, and I've got a long day tomorrow. Let's pay the tab and call it a night."

CHAPTER 8

Monday morning found Valerie and Braddock with their heads nearly touching as they huddled over a copy of *The Washington Post's* Sunday magazine section. The entire cover was devoted to a color photograph of Justin.

CAN THIS MAN SAVE ROME?

Along with the banner caption there was a four-page article inside.

"I think our boy has an impossible task," Braddock said. "Kettering's guilty, period, and we're all going to learn soon enough he'd been diddling that woman for years."

"Sure seems that way," Valerie said, her voice sounding as glum as the look she wore.

Braddock changed the subject. "Val, I want you to know there's no sweat by me if you continue with your classes at Georgetown. I think I can find a way to handle this busy case all by my lonesome for the few hours both evenings you'd be in school. There's sure as hell no need for you to lose out on your education because of a shitty little murder we're not allowed to really work anyway."

"Thanks, Tom. If I were to withdraw I had to do it by the close of business today. I really didn't want to, so I appreciate the backup."

Braddock grinned. "Done deal. You owe me."

The phone rang before she could come back with a witty retort.

"Inspector Tobias." She studied Braddock as she mouthed the words 'It's the chief.' She listened and nodded several times. Finally, she said, "Yes, sir, we'll be there."

She replaced the receiver with exaggerated delicacy then patted it before speaking. "Seems yesterday's article also alluded as to how we're feuding with the bureau, and MacAllister's not happy with all the bad publicity. So to make matters right, we're going to a special briefing in an hour along with the chief, after which we're to be trotted out for a joint press conference just to show the world how we all love each other to itty-bitty pieces. What a crock!"

* * *

"Justin, Ben Bateman's dead. His plane crashed yesterday afternoon."

"What in the hell happened, Jack?" Justin asked in a voice filled with disbelief. He was calling from Vienna.

"Information's still real sketchy, but the state police in Maine are reporting he was hit by a Stinger missile while landing. Apparently his brothers witnessed the whole thing, but Paula didn't hear about it until late this morning."

Justin's thoughts flashed back to the telephone call and the warning the night O'Bryan had arrived from Rome. As if listening to a tape, he again heard the voice politely telling him to take the warning seriously — 'and you can take that to the bank,' the man had promised. *Well, he's fulfilled his pledge*, Justin thought, realizing in the next instant that the assassin had planned his attack to take both Paula and him out as well. He started blaming himself for ignoring the warning.

The killer had to have known my travel plans, Justin quickly reasoned. *He knew I'd be with the Batemans. And the only reason he and Paula were still alive was because of his last minute change of plans. No way anyone would have known that, because he hadn't known himself until deciding to do so yesterday morning. Which meant the son of a bitch had already been in place, waiting for the plane to land.*

Justin suppressed a mounting anger and willed his thoughts to turn to Paula. She had to be devastated. He came to a decision. "Jack, I'll be on the first plane to Washington. As soon as I've firmed up a flight, I'll call you back."

"No, Justin," O'Bryan replied hastily. "Even though Paula's still in shock she specifically asked that you don't return early. There will be a private memorial for the immediate family on Thursday, then one for the public sometime next month. She pleaded with me to tell you she'll cope, and to let you know her son is arriving from Korea tomorrow morning. He's an army captain," O'Bryan finished lamely, his words trailing off.

Justin felt the searing pain of Paula's loss in every cell of his being. "I know," he replied. "I only met him once, and that was right after he graduated West Point. They were so proud." He knew he was rambling, but somehow couldn't stop.

"Ben never had a chance," O'Bryan said. "Paula believes it was really you and her they were after. But no matter what, she wants you to stay over there and she's insisting on coming back to work right after the funeral. Her son can't stay in town and she said she'd go mad if she doesn't keep busy. That's one very special lady, Justin."

Justin knew that Paula was bang-on with her theory, but decided this was not the time to tell O'Bryan of the warning he'd received. Maybe later, he reasoned, after he had time to think things through with a clearer head. He forced himself to change the subject.

"Jack, I want you to go to the embassy tomorrow morning and lean on Kettering. This takes priority, so forget working the biography for the time being. Also, forget the man's a cardinal; see him only as a murder suspect. Crank up the heat for me, Jack. You've got to get him to tell you the truth about Maritha. I'm counting on you."

"Yes, sir."

"Okay, I'll stay in touch. I'm going to ring Paula as soon as we hang up. God knows that's one call I'm dreading to have to make." His voice was beginning to crack under an onslaught of guilt. "Bye," he managed, and broke the connection.

* * *

The following morning O'Bryan arrived at the embassy girded for a free-for-all with Kettering. He owed that much to Justin, to Paula.

Before he could open his briefcase, there was a knock on the door. A look of exasperation crossed his face. "What is it?" he called out.

Monsignor Capelletti entered, eyes falling on O'Bryan. "I'm sorry, Monsignor, but Mrs. Bateman is on the phone and she says it's urgent. I've directed the call here. You can take it at the ambassador's desk."

O'Bryan nodded, and the man was gone.

"Paula, what's up?" he asked, his voice full of concern.

Kettering, seated a few feet away could hear Paula's small, tinny voice speaking rapidly. He noticed O'Bryan's jaw slowly tighten. "I understand. I'll see you back at the office."

He replaced the instrument and stared at Kettering, his jaw still clenched, and his face now flushed with anger. He returned slowly to the table and sat. For a minute neither spoke.

Finally Kettering said, "More bad news, Monsignor?"

"Damn right it's more bad news, Cardinal Kettering," O'Bryan replied, his choice of words a deliberate reflection of his ire. "Let me give you the short version. The attorney general took the bait Justin offered before he left town, and she's announced that she'll be spear-heading the prosecution. So far, so good. That's what Justin wanted to hear. But what he *didn't* want to hear was that she's released a follow-up to the autopsy report, and guess what little nugget of information's just been made public?"

Kettering slowly shook his head. "I don't know."

"Oh, I'll bet you do," O'Bryan countered in a voice heavy with mockery. "It seems that the late Maritha von Snellenberger was almost two months pregnant at the time of her death. The FBI's been sandbagging that information, waiting for just the right moment to drop it on the press. Now there's no doubt in anyone's mind as to motive, is there, Your Eminence?"

Tears welled in Kettering's eyes, and spilled down his cheeks. He remained silent.

O'Bryan wasn't finished. "It doesn't take a rocket scientist to know what the next announcement will be. Care to guess?"

Again Kettering shook his head.

O'Bryan answered his own question in a sarcastic voice. "DNA testing to look for a match between you and the fetus, that's what." He was full of righteous wrath. "They've had two weeks to run the preliminary tests, and I guarantee you, they already have their match. The sophisticated tests take about ten weeks, but what the hell; all that'll do is verify in minute detail what's already known. No wonder the attorney general wants the case for herself. The village idiot could prosecute this one."

O'Bryan glared at the silently weeping Kettering, his face devoid of all pity. "Just when do you plan on telling us the truth?" His anger increased. "You really are beneath contempt," he said as he stood up. "Tell me one last thing. When did you find out the woman was pregnant?"

"I knew for less than a month." The words were spoken in a whisper and O'Bryan had to strain to hear. "But I swear to you, it's not what you think. The child is not mine. I have never broken my sacred vow of chastity."

"Enough of your lies. You're single-handedly doing more to destroy the Church in less than a month than the communists tried to do in seventy years. Congratulations. I'm going outside for some fresh air because something's dead in here!"

O'Bryan realized that any basis for a pretense of a trial was gone. He would call Justin with the terrible news as soon as he got back to The Watergate.

* * *

"Who would have ever thought!" exclaimed Matthew Tuchmann. He was in the FBI director's office along with Valerie and Braddock. They had been invited by MacAllister to join him for lunch following the news conference which had been delayed for one day at the request of the attorney general. Tuchmann was feeling his oats. It looked as if the case had been solved, and nobody in his command had lost his or her head in the process.

He posed a question to MacAllister. "How long before we hear a full-blown confession, would you guess, Judge? Today? Tomorrow?"

MacAllister continued to cut into his chicken breast then sliced the carved piece of meat into quadrants. "Don't hold your breath waiting for a confession, Chief. I suspect the deal's off regarding that cardinal ever seeing the inside of a courtroom. The Vatican will whisk him out of the country under cover of darkness and give the American people some cock-and-bull story that he was insane, and therefore incapable of being brought to justice. I don't envy them the damage control they have coming their way with this one."

"But until then, the attorney general is still going to press for a trial?" Valerie asked. Much as she would like to deny it, she was in awe of her surroundings. The office reeked of power and prestige. And to think she was an invited lunch guest in the very room that J. Edgar Hoover had conferred with presidents and kings.

"That's my understanding, Inspector, and I spoke to the boss less than thirty minutes ago. But I really think it's all a formality at this point."

"Did your agents uncover anything of value in Europe, Director?" Braddock asked. His plate was clean, and for the past several minutes he had been eyeing Valerie's untouched meal.

"We got a ton of evidence, son, and we'll be handing over copies of everything to your department. Basically, the cardinal has known the victim for years, and theirs had been a long-standing affair. Anyway, it's all in the report, and you're free to read it at your leisure. The bottom line is this: we've got the son of a bitch cold." The director sat back in his chair and let out a long, contented sigh.

"It's a shame," he continued. "It really is. Kettering had been seen off and on in the company of this young woman since her teens. Claimed she was a family friend since childhood. Funny, though, no one suspected anything untoward in the relationship. At least that's the story my agents got from those they interviewed. Well, I say bull. We've pieced together a money connection going way back, but, like I said, it's all in the report." He glanced at the grandfather clock in the corner as it sounded the hour.

Matthew Tuchmann took the hint and stood. "One last question, Judge. Has anyone located the husband yet?"

"No. He's been traveling in Russia, and it seems no one has been able to track him down. With the way that country is now, Christ could be well into His Second Coming and the poor Ruskies would be the last to know. Fortunately that's not our worry, but I do feel for the guy."

Well, we've got to get back to the office, Judge," Tuchmann said, holding out his hand to the director. "Thanks for everything. Always a pleasure to work with the bureau."

MacAllister took the proffered hand and shook it vigorously. "Likewise, Chief. If every police department in the country were as professional as yours, well, we here at the bureau would soon be out of work. My thanks to all of you." He shook hands with Valerie and Braddock as he escorted the trio to the door.

* * *

The only sound O'Bryan heard was the faint whir of the air conditioning compressor outside the embassy window. It was now minutes away from midnight, and he was seated in a small anteroom waiting for a call from Rome. He'd already spoken once to Cardinal Miglianico that afternoon; twice to Justin, and was now waiting for another call from Miglianico. Kettering had duped them all with his protestations of innocence.

The disclosures made public by the FBI almost forty-eight hours ago had been the last straw. He had spoken at length with Justin, and the consensus was that Kettering's position was, of course, untenable. The facts told the whole sordid story. Justin had informed O'Bryan that he should get ready to call in the hotshot Sean MacMillan from Harvard to take over because Kettering was still insisting on going to trial. "I absolutely refuse to defend an out-and-out liar, and Kettering is pathological. You'll see. I'll lay it all out for you when I get back."

O'Bryan found he was physically and emotionally spent.

A civilian secretary entered. "The call from the Vatican has come through on the secure line in the Nuncio's office. Cardinal Kettering is already in there."

Thirty seconds later Kettering and O'Bryan were seated in front of a speakerphone, O'Bryan most definitely the man in charge this night.

"We're both here, Cardinal Miglianico," he began in a formal voice.

"Thank you, Jack. Francis, can you hear me?"

"I can, Rafael," Kettering replied.

"Good. I want there to be no misunderstanding of what I am about to say, so bear with me." He paused, and the duo could hear the rustling of papers a continent away. Miglianico found what he was looking for. "I've just spent the last hour with the Holy Father. This is what I told him the facts of the case appear to be. Cardinal Kettering is accused of murder. The murder weapon has been recovered and only his fingerprints have been found on it. Blood samples show that the cardinal was drunk at the time of his automobile accident. The autopsy performed on the victim shows that she was pregnant at the time of her death. DNA testing will undoubtedly confirm that Francis Kettering sired the child. Those are the facts. Do I have it right, Monsignor O'Bryan?"

Jack nodded wearily. "You have it right, Your Eminence."

"This changes everything," Miglianico continued. "The Holy Father is weighing the idea of admitting guilt on your behalf, Francis, then recalling you. To pursue a trial now would be a mockery."

"Rafael, you can't do that. I'm not guilty, Kettering said in a too-loud voice."

"Control yourself, Francis, I'm not finished." The anger in Miglianico's voice was plain to hear. "Until a definitive decision is reached, and that should be forthcoming, the Pope has instructions for you. Hear me well. First, you will remain in the embassy. You will receive no visitors, save for the two men currently helping you, and any legal friends Mr. Scott should see fit to hire in order to expedite closure. You will not use the telephone unless it's to speak to me. And, lastly, as of this moment, you will not celebrate mass under penalty of excommunication. You are still bound by your holy vows, however. Written confirmation, signed and sealed by the Pope will arrive in the diplomatic pouch tomorrow. Any questions?"

The men were speechless. That the Pope would take such a dramatic step left no question as to where the pontiff stood on the matter of Kettering's guilt or innocence. It was a mortal blow.

Kettering sat mute, his face the color of chalk.

Miglianico continued. "Jack, I want you to stay on and help implement whatever instructions come from the Holy Father. There are going to be some terrible days ahead."

"I understand, Your Eminence."

"One last thing."

"Yes, Your Eminence."

"Mister Scott was here this morning. He left an envelope to be delivered in the pouch. It's for a Mrs. Paula Bateman. He said to make sure Mrs. Bateman gets it with all dispatch. Please see that it's sent over to her as soon as it arrives at the embassy."

"I will, Cardinal. Did Mr. Scott say when he would be coming home?"

"Tomorrow, maybe the day after at the latest. For what it's worth, he did not look at all pleased when I spoke to him." Miglianico rifled through some more papers, then announced, "That seems to be it, gentlemen. I know it's late there and I appreciate you waiting up. Good night, and God bless you."

Two seconds later all O'Bryan could hear was a dial tone.

And a totally shattered Cardinal Kettering placed his head on the table and silently wept.

* * *

Two mornings later, Justin, Paula and O'Bryan met in the main conference room. Justin gently gathered Paula in his arms and the two hugged and swayed silently for a long minute, rocking back and forth in unison to a requiem heard only to themselves. O'Bryan's eyes teared as he watched, devoid of any sense of embarrassment at being a witness to this intimate moment of shared grieving. It rent his soul.

"Thank you, Justin," Paula finally said, breaking the spell as she backed away, but still holding fast both his hands in hers. "Find who did this evil thing to my Ben," she whispered, tears glistening on her cheeks. "Just find him, okay?"

"Count on it," Justin replied hoarsely. "That's one son of a bitch who's toast, believe me, Paula."

She managed a thin smile, brushed her eyes, and then announced in a surprisingly firm voice, "Time to get to work, gentlemen."

A visibly tired Justin dimmed the lights and snapped on an overhead projector, displaying the first of the material he had forwarded to Paula in the diplomatic pouch from Rome. She had arranged everything in the order Justin had spelled out on an accompanying tape recording.

"It seems that Maritha von Snellenberger came into the cardinal's life around the time of her fourteenth birthday," Justin began without preamble. "He was a monsignor with a parish in Vienna, and the girl and her mother were members of the congregation. The woman was a widow, and a rather poor one to boot. Anyway, Kettering took the girl under his wing and arranged for her to attend the best Catholic girls' school in the city. From all accounts, she was an outstanding student. She also blossomed into a drop-dead gorgeous young woman." While he spoke, he put up several slides of the girl, some going back to her teen years. He had retrieved them from school files, and newspaper clippings.

"A couple of years passed. The monsignor became a bishop and was posted to Rome. In due course the girl graduated high school, and guess where she decided to go to college?"

"Rome?" said Paula.

"Rome," Justin replied, as he changed transparencies. There were several more pictures of the girl taken at what seemed to be various university functions, and in every photo, all eyes were on Maritha. She was breathtaking, seemingly incapable of presenting a bad likeness.

"She continued to be an outstanding student," Justin said, "and apparently helped with her own support by teaching other students how to use the library for research. Seems she was quite the expert. In fact, there's a whole article about that.

Justin continued. "Anyway, the years went by and Kettering remained a force in the young woman's life. He was known as a friend of the family, and on several occasions Kettering, Maritha and the mother were seen in public together. It seems the mother never suspected a thing, or if she did, she apparently kept her mouth shut. I was able to dig up records showing that Kettering gave gifts of money to them both, and I've made copies of checks from over ten years ago proving that he paid for the girl's college education and living expenses. I also learned that the cardinal has some family money, so I'm not making an accusation that Kettering was possibly skimming from the collection plate."

"If only that had been the case, and the extent of his problems," O'Bryan said.

"Good point," replied Justin. "Unfortunately, it wasn't. Seems our man was a regular Henry Higgins, cultivating a very captivating Eliza Doolittle. God only knows when the relationship turned physical, but it must have been several years back. There's a long paper trail showing that Maritha was in various foreign cities at the same time as Kettering where he supposedly was attending religious conferences and the like. Sometimes she went alone; at other times she went with her mother. Can you believe the nerve of that man?"

Neither replied.

"Well, she finally met Mister Right, Manfred von Snellenberger, a Swiss banker, about three years ago. After a two-year courtship, they got married, July, a year ago. Everybody who was anybody in European society was at the wedding except, guess who?"

"Kettering?" Paula asked.

"Kettering. The good cardinal was traveling in Australia at the time, I guess on a mission to convert the Aboriginal people. Or maybe he was just scouting for the next Eliza. My hunch though, is that he was consumed with jealousy and wanted to be as far away as humanly possible on the bride's big day."

"Summarize." O'Bryan had heard enough.

"It looks like the cardinal had been engaged in a long-term affair with the woman. If indeed there was a rift around the time of her wedding, it was soon patched up, and life continued as before. But here's something to chew on. It seems the newlyweds had visited a fertility clinic in Bern, and on more than just one occasion. My guess is because Manfred had some sort of a deficiency, if you get my drift. The couple just couldn't produce the bambino everyone says they so desperately wanted. There was even talk among their friends that they might adopt. But, boom, suddenly all that changed." Justin shut off the projector. "Maritha von Snellenberger was pregnant the day she died. That's a fact. And my hunch is that she came to Washington to tell Kettering that he was the father. Maybe she wanted blackmail money, maybe something else. But whatever it was, Kettering wasted no time in deciding to kill her rather than be exposed as the most sanctimonious, hypocrite of a priest in all of Christendom. What a truly despicable character he's turned out to be."

Justin stood. "I'm sorry it had to end this way. We were hoodwinked, and I know it hurts. Because in spite of the evidence from the very beginning, we still allowed Kettering the benefit of every doubt. Turns out he didn't deserve our support. It's my guess the Pope will make a public announcement very shortly, and we can then wrap things up on this front as quickly and as quietly as possible." He looked at O'Bryan. "If that creature still insists on his day in court, Jack, then get the Harvard jock to defend him. Once you've done that, get as far away from this mess as you can, and stay away. And this time I really mean it."

He was about to say something more when the duty receptionist slipped into the room and handed Paula a note. Paula read the message, then read it again. She looked toward Justin, eyes full of wonder, and shook her head.

"What is it, Paula?"

She rose, walked over and handed him the paper. Justin stared at the message for almost half a minute, his face frowning, his mind racing. He finally turned to O'Bryan. "This just came in on the fax line from Europe. It seems that Paula's *Deep Throat* has a message especially for us.

"*All is not as it appears. Kettering is telling the truth. Trust me. Keep looking.*"

CHAPTER 9

Because of its proximity to the home of the vice-president at the U.S. Naval Observatory, the pickets outside the Vatican's Embassy were limited to six. There were two uniformed metro officers assigned to ensure peaceful protest. The marchers were relieved every ninety minutes, and in the two weeks they had been parading at the corner of 34th Street and Massachusetts Avenue, all had proven to be law-abiding citizens.

Justin moved his car at a crawl around a sawhorse barricade and into the compound. He and O'Bryan caught a glimpse of a couple of the professionally printed posters.

MURDER IS A CARDINAL SIN.
THE CATHOLIC ANSWER TO ABORTION IS TO
MURDER THE MOTHER.

"This meeting will be for all the marbles," Justin said as they waited for someone to open the front door. "Let me be the bad cop, okay? If my plan backfires, then I'll take the heat, but we'd never forgive ourselves if the message was right and we ignored it."

A very skeptical O'Bryan begrudgingly assented. "Do what you must, but I think we're wasting our time."

At a few minutes past ten, they were ushered into Kettering's office. Justin suddenly realized this could well be the last time he'd ever meet with the man.

Kettering rose from behind his desk. He had been writing letters in longhand, and he now fussily arranged the vellum sheets into a tooled leather folder and placed them in the center drawer. His face was drawn.

"Good morning, Your Eminence." Justin neither smiled nor offered his hand. He passed over a copy of the fax. "Have you any idea who might have sent this message from Europe?"

Kettering studied the document. He looked up at Justin and shook his head. "No, Mr. Scott, but I reiterate, the contents speak to the truth. I am not guilty, no matter how bleak things appear; no matter the evidence against me."

Right, and there are no guilty men on death row, thought Justin.

The cardinal sat stiffly, his face a study in torment. Then he seemed to come to some sort of a decision because his features visibly softened, and he began to speak in a subdued voice. "I've struggled for weeks with certain information," Kettering began, "and I confess, I still don't know where to turn, or who to trust. You see, there's a terrible cancer growing within the Church, a cancer which has spread its poison and corruption to the highest levels."

Justin motioned with a flutter of his right hand for O'Bryan to sit, thinking that this could well be confession time. "Please continue."

Kettering sighed. "I only ask that you listen with an open mind."

"Fair enough."

"History is replete with tales of intrigue and chicanery inside the Vatican. Most, thankfully, are patently false, but some are terribly true. We all admit that at times in the past the Church has engaged in conduct none of us are proud of, but through it all the papacy survived. That was Christ's promise to Peter. The Church and its truth would survive."

Justin waited patiently for Kettering to continue.

The cardinal turned to O'Bryan. "You work for the Holy See, and you know firsthand the obscene power plays which take place behind closed doors. You have lived among the rumor-mongers. I'm sure you remember the stories that surfaced after the untimely demise of the first John-Paul. Vicious rumors of murder found their way into the press, but those of us in the know scoffed at such talk. The man died of a heart attack, God rest his soul. He was a good man, and he would have made a fine Pope. But God works in mysterious ways, for his successor was truly an inspired choice, proving that sometimes the College of Cardinals is capable of making the right decision. Well, this was one of those times. Our present Holy Father is a gift from the Creator, but I fear his days are numbered. Not from another attempt on his life, mind you, such as we witnessed in the very close call many years ago. No, I think the time is fast approaching for God to call him home. He is a sick, tired, worn-out soul, but because of his absolute goodness, he is oblivious of the misdeeds taking place around him. There is a conspiracy underfoot, and it's being orchestrated from very close to the Throne of Peter."

"I see. And how did you come to be aware of such goings on?" It was all Justin could do to keep a growing skepticism from creeping into his voice.

"I learned of it from Maritha von Snellenberger," Kettering replied, in a voice barely heard.

That was not the answer he had expected. Justin arched a questioning brow. "I see. And once you learned of this conspiracy, as you call it, why didn't you go to, let's say, Cardinal Miglianico, and share such an important discovery with him?"

Kettering's eyes bore into Justin's, then flickered for an instant to search out O'Bryan's. He did not answer.

It took Justin but a moment to realize the significance of Kettering's action and sudden silence. He pursed his lips, then nodded sagely. "Let me see if I've got this right," he began slowly, as if searching for just the right words. "You didn't tell Cardinal Miglianico because you feared he might be in on this conspiracy. And because Monsignor O'Bryan works for Cardinal Miglianico, well, there's a good chance he's in on it, too. That about the size of it?"

"You don't believe me."

Justin leapt from the sofa. "Damn right I don't believe you. In fact, I think you're willing to go to any extreme to save your skin. Well, I've got a news flash for you. Your little problem isn't going to miraculously disappear simply because you've decided to unload a conspiracy theory on us at this late hour. Do I honestly look that stupid?" He made a half-turn and pointed at O'Bryan. "Does he?" Justin appeared to be at the end of his rope. "Unless, of course, you're laying the groundwork to show us you're mentally unbalanced, hoping to cop an insanity plea." He paused long enough for his disgust to register. "You never stop, do you? It really tests my threshold for anger to think that you would stoop so low as to infer that Monsignor O'Bryan could in any way be a part of this phantom plot when the man has worked day and night to save your hide."

Kettering still said nothing.

O'Bryan spoke up. "You say that Mrs. von Snellenberger told you something evil was unfolding inside the Vatican?"

"Yes." It was barely a whisper.

"And just how did she come to have such knowledge?" O'Bryan pressed.

Kettering shook his head sadly. "Quite by accident, and she paid with her life."

"Didn't she just!" Justin was steaming. "As my southern friends like to say: This dog won't hunt. And the facts of the case scream for justice. You murdered the woman solely because she was carrying your bastard. Well, I sure do hope you go to trial," he mocked, in a suddenly lowered voice, "because even if you get a jury as brain-dead as O.J Simpson's, they'll still find you guilty and make sure you're put away for life." He turned to O'Bryan. "Jack, we're out of here."

"Wait, Mister Scott," Kettering pleaded. "That's not true. I would never have hurt Maritha. I couldn't have. She was my everything. She was my life!"

Justin stopped mid-stride, turned, and faced the cardinal. "Is that your roundabout way of finally acknowledging she was your mistress, that she was carrying your child?"

The tears began to flow. Kettering cried out from the depths of his pain, his face a grotesque study of anguish. "No, no, no!" he wailed. "Maritha von Snellenberger was not my mistress. She was my daughter! The child she was carrying was my grandchild!"

Justin was speechless. With mouth agape he turned and stared myopically at an equally shocked O'Bryan. Then finally his eyes focused on Kettering. Thus transfixed, he retreated and slowly sank onto the leather sofa. "Oh, my God," he whispered, then repeated the phrase as if in prayer. "Oh, my God."

Five minutes later a somewhat composed Cardinal Kettering was able to continue. "Let me explain, as best I can, the reason for my protracted silence. There is still a lot I either cannot remember or even make sense of in my own mind, but once you hear what I have to say, hopefully, you will understand why I trust no one, including Cardinal Miglianico." He took a moment to make himself more comfortable, then began to tell what he knew.

"It all started when a very distraught Maritha informed me she suspected her husband of infidelity ...."

The three remained sequestered until darkness overtook the city.

* * *

"*Confiteor Deo omnipotenti* ... I confess to almighty God. Would that I could hear those words from Francis," exclaimed the Holy Father as he walked stiffly beside Cardinal Miglianico. They were in the private gardens of the Vatican, and the pontiff leaned heavily on a cane for support. The man had aged alarmingly in the past eighteen months, and a behind the scenes jockeying for power by potential successors to the Throne of Peter had already begun. The Pope was fully aware that the jackals were circling, waiting.

Cardinal Miglianico paced his friend. "A couple of weeks ago I had such high hopes that Francis would confidently face the world and rightfully proclaim his innocence. But now I only seem to dread the news each passing day brings."

"It can't get worse, I'm afraid," replied the Pope. He paused, looked worriedly at Miglianico then added, "Or can it?"

The cardinal shrugged. "Only if more bodies are uncovered, I suppose."

"Don't even think such a thing, Rafael!" The Pontiff eased himself onto a wrought iron bench beside a bed of late summer flowers. Miglianico followed, and the prelates sat in momentary silence enjoying the waning afternoon sun. They were alone save for a gardener trimming a hedge in the corner furthermost from the building, and a multitude of noisy sparrows at home in the several shade trees near the walled perimeter. This garden was serene, and the septuagenarians drank in the beauty of their surroundings. Both were keenly aware that they were well into the autumn of their years, and daily gave thanks to God for whatever time remained.

"What does Monsignor O'Bryan suggest our next step should be? How is he handling the situation?" The Pontiff grimaced and let out an involuntary gasp as he moved his left leg to a more comfortable position. His suffering was evident to all who encountered him. He refused all offer of prescription painkillers from his doctors, reasoning that since he was an old man, he could ill afford to become a befuddled one as well. Because he was so frail, he realized he could soon grow dependent on such medications. His constant suffering was willingly offered up as a never-ending prayer to the greater glory of God.

Miglianico extracted a Ziploc bag from somewhere deep inside his cassock then busied himself broadcasting seeds close to their feet. A lone sparrow boldly approached the bench and was rewarded for his brazen behavior. Spotted by his neighbors, he was quickly joined by a multitude of excited, chattering friends. Both men smiled.

Miglianico brushed his hands together before answering. "Jack O'Bryan has been magnificent, Holy Father. Indeed, I can say the same of all of the people in America working on our behalf. But it looks like they're at the end of the road, I'm afraid. The monsignor's now just waiting for instructions from you, even he can't perform the miracle we need. It's a tragedy of the first order."

"Whatever possessed Francis to take such a terrible step? How could he have possibly thought he could get away with it?" The Pope shook his head in despair.

"God only knows what's been going on inside Francis' mind," Miglianico replied. "I suppose all people who adopt such desperate measures somehow feel that they can commit the perfect crime, or else they would never take that first fateful step toward the abyss. Maybe Francis Kettering would have gotten away with it were it not for the car accident. Who knows?" His eyes wandered into the distance; his mind followed. Soon he was lost in deep thought.

Neither man spoke for several minutes.

The birds, silent but expectant, sat patiently eyeing the provisioner on the bench.

Miglianico returned from his reverie, reached into his trove and scattered another handful of seeds, making a soft chirping sound with his lips to validate the pleasure he felt in the company of these creatures.

"What am I going to do with Francis, Rafael?" the Pope finally asked. "Once he's back here, then what? The Vatican has no jail. Do I send him away to the foreign missions and simply ignore his misdeeds?"

Miglianico shook his head. "I must prepare for that eventuality also. I intend to speak to the American secretary of state within a day or two to lay the groundwork for Cardinal Kettering to be declared *persona non grata* by the President. It's now clearly in the best interest of both governments to conclude the matter quietly.

But I fear the press will crucify us in light of our stance of only a few short weeks ago. I suppose I can't blame them," he added glumly. "I for one had such high hopes. Now there's just no good spin we can put on the whole turn of events."

The Pope rose slowly, then stood facing his friend of many years. "Come, we have work to do."

Cardinal Miglianico walked slowly beside the Pope. "Where's Monsignor Caffarone?" he asked. "I just realized that I haven't seen him for the past couple of days. He's not ill, is he, Holy Father?"

The Pontiff shook his head. "No, Ignacio's fine. It's his sister who's ailing. He's gone to Genoa for a few days to be with her."

Miglianico glanced sideways at the Holy Father, an inadvertent frown furrowing his brow. "I see."

But he didn't see. Cardinal Miglianico knew that Ignacio Caffarone was the youngest of three brothers. There was no sister. At least not now. Years ago when he was still Archbishop Rafael Miglianico, of Genoa, Italy, he had celebrated a Requiem Mass for one Beatrice Caffarone, a spinster, who had died on her fortieth birthday of uterine cancer. Father Ignacio Caffarone, the youngest brother, was a junior member of his staff in those days, and Miglianico had gotten to know the up-and-coming priest rather well. Why in the world would Ignacio now be lying to the Pope?

He could not come up with an answer.

* * *

The following morning Monsignor Ignacio Caffarone returned to Vatican City, and after a hectic several hours, finally found the time to slip into a small, private office adjacent to the Pope's, where he dialed the embassy in Washington. He had been given his instructions the day before; instructions he would follow to the letter; not from the pope, but instructions from men who know not the meaning of the word failure.

He had been assured that Kettering would take his call, but within moments he realized something was wrong. Caffarone was not a good improviser, and he instinctively realized, too late, that he was squared against the American lawyer, Justin Scott, even though he was speaking to the boorish Jesuit, Monsignor O'Bryan. His intuition told him that Justin Scott was lurking in the background along with Kettering. He broke out in a sweat.

"What do you mean, Cardinal Kettering refuses to obey?" Caffarone now asked, his voice filled with incredulity. He had just informed O'Bryan that the nuncio was to return to Rome with all due dispatch. Justin and Kettering heard it all on extensions.

Caffarone's tone of disbelief turned to one of anger. "Understand, Monsignor O'Bryan, I'm relaying the wishes of the Holy See, and Cardinal Kettering must abide." He spoke in precise, grammatical English, wanting to make absolutely sure he was not being misunderstood. He was unused to hearing people say no.

Kettering leaned forward as if to speak, but Justin put his index finger to his lips to indicate that he was to say nothing. For added emphasis, he shook his head and mouthed the word no.

"We are not discussing matters of faith and morals, Monsignor Caffarone," O'Bryan replied calmly. "This is a secular issue, and as such it must be resolved in a civil arena, both for the good of the accused, and for the good of the Church," he said emphatically. "It is Mr. Scott's decision that his client will remain in Washington."

"So much for your Jesuit's vow of obedience to the Pope!" Caffarone hissed, deliberately belittling those of the society's members who were known as professed fathers; a cadre who enjoyed a unique status among priests in that upon ordination each swore a special fealty to the papacy. And because Caffarone knew O'Bryan to be a professed father, he was now throwing the insult in his face. "You've always been an outlaw, and I've repeatedly warned the Pope and Cardinal Miglianico of your true nature. You're nothing more than a renegade, a disgrace to everything the Church stands for!"

"Thank you for your kind words of support, Monsignor Caffarone," O'Bryan said in a voice laced with sarcasm. "I promise to remember you in my prayers." He abruptly severed the connection, not in the least concerned with the gravity of the conversation just concluded.

"I cannot disobey the Holy Father," Kettering spoke up, visibly distressed by the turn of events.

O'Bryan shook his head. "You're not," he replied, confidently. "Caffarone wasn't speaking for the Pope, I guarantee you. The slimy little sycophant was posturing, nothing more."

"How can you be so sure, Jack?" Justin interrupted, thinking that maybe Kettering had good reason to be worried. This was ecclesiastical law the priests were discussing; something he knew next to nothing about.

O'Bryan replied with a knowing smile, and a voice oozing confidence. "Because he cited his authority as coming from the Holy See, the central governing body of the church, that's why. He's a sharp rascal, I'll grant him that. The Holy See addresses *concerns* of the papacy," he went on to explain, "but it is an amorphous body, and a pronouncement issued under its auspices does not begin to carry the weight of a Papal Bull, signed, sealed and delivered in the name of the reigning Pope. And under these circumstances, such a document would be delivered from Cardinal Miglianico's office on behalf of the Curia to the American secretary of state. It would outline Cardinal Kettering's crimes, and at the same time inform the American secretary of his official recall. The Pope wouldn't wait for his ambassador to be declared *persona non grata.* No, he'd issue a Bull, and its contents would be made public." O'Bryan's voice reflected his disgust. "But to invoke the name of the Holy See is merely a clever ploy, one often used to intimidate those in disfavor with the Curia. Caffarone was usurping the power of the papacy to further some unknown agenda. Now why would he do that? But more importantly, who put him up to it?"

"Are you sure you're not just splitting legal hairs, probing into the fine nuances of semantics, Monsignor?" Kettering asked, sounding a lot like the devil's advocate, yet obviously impressed at just how sharp O'Bryan's mind was when dealing with such matters. "Surely a Papal Bull would not be used to address this issue," he concluded by way of observation.

O'Bryan was ready. "To recall a sitting ambassador accused of murder?" he challenged, but not unkindly. "I beg to differ, Cardinal Kettering. Under the circumstances, the Pope would want the whole world to know that you no longer enjoyed his support. It would be Rome's public admission of your guilt. And it would become an historical document, one which would be studied for years in musty law libraries everywhere."

O'Bryan stood, and switched gears. "No, I'm not splitting legal hairs. At least I don't think so," he allowed, begrudgingly. "But I also don't think Monsignor Caffarone is about to call my bluff."

He began to pace, his mind racing. "The Pope would never use Caffarone as a conduit in so delicate a matter," he reasoned aloud. "Any such instructions would have come through Cardinal Miglianico, and he hasn't said a word. The papal secretary is up to no good, I'm afraid, but I can't fathom why." He continued back and forth, lost in thought. After a minute, he asked: "Just how did

Caffarone come by his appointment? Was he a particular friend of the Pope's?"

Justin sat silently transfixed as he followed the conversation.

Kettering shook his head, eyes following the moving figure. "No, at least not to my knowledge. You must think back some years. When the then-cardinal from Poland was elevated to the papacy he was as much surprised to be chosen as were so many others in the College of Cardinals. He was something of an outsider, and had no coterie of close friends to call upon for advice. It was Cardinal Miglianico who stepped forward and recommended Ignacio for the position, and the new Pope simply acted on the suggestion." As soon as the words were out of his mouth, Kettering realized the importance of what he had just said. His face paled.

O'Bryan stopped and held up his hand. "Not so fast, Your Eminence. Let's not jump to conclusions," he cautioned. "In all probability Miglianico was truly acting in the best interests of his Polish acquaintance. The new pontiff must have been in a state of utter bewilderment at the time, and I seem to recall that Monsignor Caffarone had worked for Cardinal Miglianico in a similar capacity. Let's face it, why wouldn't Miglianico want a confidant so highly placed? By virtue of his office, Caffarone's a gatekeeper directing the flow of all matters coming before the Holy Father. Quite a powerful position, wouldn't you agree? But think about it. Chances are it was nothing more than smart politics on Cardinal Miglianico's part. Remember, he'd been offered the top job at state only hours after the eligible cardinals had selected the new Pope, yet he unselfishly offered the pontiff his own trusted secretary. And, yes, this appointment assured him of a ready access to the ear of the Pope. But so what? There simply doesn't have to be a more nefarious reason than that." He looked squarely at Kettering, shrugged, and smiled thinly. "I sure hope I'm right about this, but only time will tell."

"Suppose the Pope does recall me. What then?" Kettering was still unsettled, but he had addressed this last question to Justin.

"Then you'll have to make a choice," Justin replied. He had given that possibility a lot of thought over many days, drawing little comfort from his conclusion. "You can obey, and be publicly disgraced for all time with no hope of ever clearing your name," he explained, "or you can choose to stay and fight. If you decide the latter, then you'd have to relinquish all your rights afforded under the umbrella of ambassadorial protection, and face the real possibility of life imprisonment should a jury find you guilty." Justin could see the cardinal was listening intently to his every word, but the man's face spoke volumes. He was not happy with either choice.

"*But*," Justin concluded with a deliberately upbeat observation, "we're going to prove your innocence long before such a decision has to be made. And I still have complete faith in Cardinal Miglianico, and his promise not to interfere with our strategy. So, chin-up, Cardinal Kettering, we're going to win this one, and win in a grand way. There'll be a whole gaggle of folks who'll be very uncomfortable and embarrassed knowing that they didn't support you in your darkest hour."

"Thank you for your vote of confidence, Mr. Scott." He stood and thrust out his hand. It was the first time he had done so.

Justin did not hesitate. Responding in kind, he stretched, and warmly shook the cardinal's hand.

Simultaneously, both men realized that a bridge had been built, that something much more than an uneasy truce had been forged with that handshake.

Kettering turned and offered his hand to O'Bryan.

The three parted company; not yet friends, but definitely no longer enemies.

CHAPTER 10

It was midmorning, Monday, and Inspector Tobias and Lieutenant Braddock had just left the Fourth District Station. In a little less than a week three street dopers and small-time pushers had been shot; all in broad daylight. The shooter had been seen by at least a number of people, and still the police couldn't nab him. Valerie was not happy with her detectives. Neither was the district commander.

"He's just eleven years old, for God's sake. The little darling's been positively identified by four witnesses, and we know he lives with his grandmother in this district. So get off your butts, folks! I want that one-man war machine off the streets and in juvenile hall before sundown. We're all just lucky no one has been killed—yet."

"Could be smoke on the ID, ya know," someone had grumbled from the back of the room. "Our perp could be a midget."

"Spare me." She turned to the shift lieutenant. "You've got your marching orders, Tilly. Make it happen!"

Now they were heading back to headquarters, Valerie driving the unmarked Dodge.

Braddock let out a chuckle. "Could be a midget," he mimicked.

Valerie laughed. "Go back—oh, I guess it was about eight or so years ago—to when we had the schoolgirl bandit. Three bank heists in a month. She'd waltz in, pretty as a picture, all decked out in her school clothes and a satchel full of dynamite instead of books?"

"Yeah, but, if I remember it right, third time sure as hell wasn't charm."

"No, it wasn't. She started shooting during the getaway, and the people on the street damn near rioted when she went down. But it quickly turned out the 'she' was really a 'he-midget' but instead a mean little bugger to boot."

"Well, our pint-sized punk in this case ain't no midget. Where's this shit all going to end?" Braddock asked angrily, turning to face Valerie. "Little kids offing people without any sense of remorse." He took a deep breath, gazed out the window, and changed the subject. "You born in this town, Val?"

"No. Khartoum."

"*Cartoon*? Where in the hell is *Cartoon*? Some place in Iowa?"

"*Khartoum*, Tom, as in the capital of Sudan."

"No shit, Val. Man, I'd never have known. You even speak English like a native. Who would have guessed?"

"*My parents are Americans*!" she shouted. "*They were with the embassy. They worked for the State Department, you moron*."

Braddock began laughing like a deranged kid. Tears clouded his vision as he beat a two-fingered tattoo on the patch of exposed seat between his knees. "Oh, Val, you should see your face. You're ready to pop. Oh, wow. I haven't had such a good laugh in months." He blew his nose and wiped his eyes "Thanks for being my straight man, you were great!"

"Up yours, Braddock." She, too, began to laugh. "For a moment there, I really thought you just might be that stupid. Mondays you're usually kind of dense."

"Had me a good weekend, Inspector. Watched a little football; made a couple of bucks on some bets that went my way; and sucked down some brewskies. Guarantee you, I had more grins and yuks than our cardinal friend."

"Speaking of who? ... whom? ... ah, hell, whatever. Anyway, I looked at the evidence the bureau finally turned over to us last Friday. I stayed late, unlike some people I know, Thomas Braddock."

"Yeah, and what did you come up with?"

She came back with a question of her own. "When you saw the victim in the trunk that morning, did you get a good look at the murder weapon?"

"If you mean, did I study it in detail, the answer's no. It was a candlestick. Kind of big. Also, looked damn heavy. You go down after being whacked on the head with that baby, you ain't getting back up. Why do you ask?"

"Seems the bureau went to great lengths studying that candlestick. Turns out it was one of a pair owned by Kettering, and the story line is that they were made by Michelangelo Buonarroti as a coronation gift for some pope. Apparently they have his mark, or brand, or whatever they call it, stamped on the base. However, historians argue that they were probably cast by one of the maestro's students. But in any event, they're priceless."

"*B'wandarotti,* or whatever it was you just said. That the painter's last name?"

"It was."

"I'm impressed you'd know that, Val. I always thought the guy had just the one name, like Cher, or Elvis, you know?

Anyway, how did Kettering get ahold of them?"

Valerie smiled and waved at an unmarked unit coming out of the Daly Building parking area as she started up the ramp. "Hi, Maria," she mouthed to Detective Delgado, and Maria waved back. She pulled into her reserved space, shut off the motor, and sat quietly listening to the engine tick as it cooled. Finally: "You want irony, Tom?"

"Hit me."

"Maritha von Snellenberger gave them to Kettering last year for his sixtieth birthday. You see, she'd just married a guy with more money than God. Anyway, the report goes on to say that the cardinal claims to have spotted the same candlesticks in some painting in the Vatican by Michelangelo a couple of months later, and that's why the big to-do about their value. The story got a lot of play in the European press at the time. The file the FBI sent us has copies of the clippings. Makes for some interesting reading."

"And Kettering used a priceless candlestick to bash in the lady's head? Doesn't make sense," Braddock said.

"No, it doesn't, Tom. But, pray tell, what does in this whole affair?"

"You've got me there. He sure didn't need to kill the lady." Braddock opened his door. "I've got the time, Val. Let's go study together what the crewcut crowd has finally dumped on us."

Three hours later, at one-thirty, they called a truce and ordered in pizza. The FBI files were scattered over the length and breadth of Valerie's office, and the two detectives had been enthralled at what they had read.

Valerie sat back, sated. She took a long pull on her soda. "You've got to give credit where credit's due, Tom. These guys have sure done their homework."

"Granted. The autopsy will stop anyone cold; the blood work is first rate; and the forensics and history lesson on the murder weapon is outstanding. No question about it: When the bureau's got your number, you can run, but you can't hide."

She thought about his comments for a moment, then replied. "You know, the cardinal must have realized there had to be a better solution to his problems. Remember, the woman was married; they could have palmed the kid off as being legit." She held up a hand anticipating the response. "I know, I know. The happy honeymooners were having a hard time conceiving. Still, I'll bet she could have convinced her husband that the baby was his." She reached for the last slice of pizza as the phone rang. She snatched up the receiver.

"Tobias."

"Tilly here, Inspector."

She punched a button on the high tech console, activating the speakerphone. Braddock leaned forward.

"So talk to me, Tilly."

"Inspector, we have your one-man gang. We caught up with him less than ten minutes ago."

"Now, that wasn't so hard was it, Loo?"

Tilly paused for two beats before answering. "Nah, not for us, it wasn't, Inspector. But it also wasn't all candles and cake for junior."

"What do you mean?"

"We found him in a dumpster on Eastern Avenue near the railroad tracks," Tillman replied. "The kid's been there for at least a day, all wrapped up like a birthday present in plastic garbage bags, and with a hole in his head the size of Brooklyn. Probably a forty-five, but that's just a guess according to the uniforms who made the find."

She didn't know what to say. She buried her face in her hands, and shook her head in dismay.

"This is Braddock, Tilly. Good work. Look, the inspector will get back to you shortly." He severed the connection, sighed deeply and pushed himself all the way back in his chair. "It's like I said this morning, Valerie. Where is this all going to end? Sure isn't the same world you and I grew up in. Eleven years old, for God's sake. A giant waste, Inspector. A big fat zero!"

* * *

"It's on again," Justin announced, his excitement spilling over to O'Bryan and Paula. "As of right now, we're back in the picture, and we're going to prove our case in court if need be. I really do believe Kettering's innocent. His story's too preposterous not to be true, so now it's going to be our job to prove it." Justin was a general laying out the order of battle to his army of two.

He turned to O'Bryan. "Jack, I want you to go to up to Harvard tomorrow to lay the groundwork for your Professor MacMillan to come on board. I'm a humble enough lawyer to call for help when I think I might need it, and both you and Cardinal Miglianico seem to think this guy's your man. Plan on flying to Boston tonight. I'll drive you to the airport."

"Justin, before we say anything more I've got to ask you something. Do you know for a fact these offices aren't wired?" O'Bryan said, his voice dropping off, embarrassed to be even questioning the expert.

The question took Justin by surprise. "I didn't realize you were so paranoid, Jack. But to put your mind at rest, the place is clean. The phones, too. I have the entire suite electronically swept twice a month."

"Why? paranoia?"

Justin rubbed his face and chuckled. "*Touché.* Nah, habit. Before I came on board neither of the other two lawyers gave it a thought, but security's a big deal now. The computers are also bug-free, and I constantly check to make sure no one can tap into my database. I do the same for the partners. So, relax, we can talk freely."

O'Bryan's relief was audible. "Thanks. In light of what we now know I wanted to make sure our conversations went no further than the three of us."

Justin plopped down on the small sofa by the window. "You're starting to sound like you've got the makings of a top-notch investigator," he added approvingly.

O'Bryan actually blushed. "I'm working on it, but still I need to lean on the master for answers." He knew he was laying it on a bit thick. He hurried on. "So, my question is simple; Where do we go from here?"

Justin popped his tongue rapidly against the inside of his cheek, repositioned himself, then spoke. "I gave that quite a bit of thought after we left Kettering last night, and I came to the conclusion that it's back to Europe for answers. Who would have thought it?" He shook his head in wonder. "Like the old song says: 'What a difference a day makes.'" He paused long enough to stand, then continued in a more serious vein. "In light of what Kettering's told us, there's no doubt in my mind this is going to get a lot more dangerous from here on out. We'll be up against folks with a lot to lose, and killing one or all of us means zip to them. I have to tell you, I suspect that's what happened to Ben," he added, all the while looking at Paula. "This is the big leagues where all the participants play for keeps."

"Comforting thought," Paula observed.

"I'm deadly serious, Paula," Justin said, "and I must place a heavy emphasis on the word deadly. Once the word is out that we're sniffing where we shouldn't be sniffing, then we can expect the opposition to do all in their power to shut us down. Believe me, fear is a big stick these people have learned to wield to great advantage. They have the wherewithal to make even the toughest, meanest cops look the other way, or simply, go away. And I mean far, fast, and forever."

"But you intend to stay the course?" O'Bryan wanted to know. "You're not going to go all wobbly on us, are you, like Margaret Thatcher asked George Bush Senior before the start of the Gulf War?" It was obvious he was razzing his friend. It helped relieve the tension.

"I ain't going to go all wobbly on you, kid," Justin replied in a hard-boiled, bang-on imitation of Humphry Bogart. "I still need a good challenge, so I'm stuck with you for the duration. Like I said, it's back to Europe, only this time I want you coming with me. I might need your ties to the Vatican to loosen some tongues; open some doors. That'll be the official line should anyone ask, but the real reason is I need a lackey who can speak French, German, and Italian," he added with a grin.

Paula interrupted the light banter. "Justin, have you thought of the possibility that someone might try to move against Kettering?" Her face reflected genuine concern. "I'm thinking he needs a much closer watch than he has right now, even though he's restricted to the embassy."

Justin nodded. "You're right, Paula. I'll remind Capelletti to stay on his toes." Justin stretched, groaned, then turned to O'Bryan. "Monsignor," he announced in a formal voice, "I plan on us being on our way to Europe as soon as you get back from Boston, so pack your woollies because it might get cold where we're going. The weather in Europe's been known to get squirrelly in September."

"Pray tell, where do you think I've been living the past decade: Arizona?"

"Oops, I forgot." Justin laughed. He pretended to punch O'Bryan on the shoulder as he sidled past him on his way out of the office. "*Adios, amigos* and *amigoettes*, duty calls. See you both later."

* * *

Justin led O'Bryan into the welcome relief of the air-conditioned American Airlines in Terminal 2 at Ronald Reagan National Airport. For the past hour he had sensed a reluctance in O'Bryan at having to go to Boston, but it was also obvious his friend had no intention of giving voice to whatever concerns he was harboring. Though puzzled, Justin elected not to press for an explanation.

They paused at the ticket counter long enough for O'Bryan to claim his boarding pass and answer a slew of questions. They then made their way to the departure concourse. The TSA agent had let him go through after he showed his FBI credentials. The place was all but deserted.

"Good luck, Jack. I really hope you don't have a problem convincing your hotshot Harvard pal to come on board. If he's like every other attorney I know, excluding yours truly, of course," he added, with a cheeky grin, "then he'll turn cartwheels at the opportunity for fame and fortune. The man's guaranteed to become a media event, then a full-blown star."

O'Bryan shook his head, having none of it. "Not this guy," he replied, in a serious tone. "Sean's very much his own man, so, I'll tell you up-front, this is going to be one tough sell." He fell silent, a signal to Justin that he would volunteer nothing more on the subject of Sean MacMillan.

"Well, whatever. I'll see you back here tomorrow, then it's off to Europe for us. I feel good about where we're finally heading with this thing."

They shook hands, and Justin turned heel as O'Bryan stepped up to the end of the small line at the last security checkpoint.

Justin retraced his steps to the parking garage, his brain wilting in the heat. His body was simply responding to autonomic reflexes as he headed for his car.

He stepped out of the stifling elevator on the fourth level and started up the gloomy incline, digging his parking ticket out of his shirt pocket as he went. He paused in the middle of the ramp to squint at his ticket when his inner voice told him that the noise he was hearing required his immediate attention. He looked up.

A motorcycle roared into view at the top of the dimly lit ramp. The rider braked only long enough to align his metal steed then gunned the engine in a blatant display of machismo. With no further warning, the huge Harley reared, and as the bike lunged forward, its front wheel came crashing down with a force that fully compressed the heavy-duty springs. As if alive, the monster grabbed ahold of the pavement and headed right for him, the deafening noise from the engine vying for dominance over the screaming protest of peeling rubber. The cacophony of sounds echoed off the concrete canyon walls.

This son of a bitch has every intention of running me down, Justin suddenly realized as he threw himself headfirst across the trunk of a Lincoln parked a step away. His shoulder struck hard on the rear deck as he swung his legs up and out of the path of the madman. He felt a rush of air thick with exhaust as the Harley thundered by, the rider's face completely hidden behind a blue and purple futuristic plastic helmet.

His cellphone tumbled to the ground from his jacket pocket which had been ripped apart on the car's partially retracted radio antenna. It was followed by a procession of coins scattering in all directions.

Two seconds later the bike reached the bottom of the ramp and fishtailed as its driver slowed and glanced back over his shoulder to look directly at Justin. He quickly regained control, gunned the motor once, then tore around the corner and disappeared. The noise trailing in his wake was deafening.

Justin seethed as he brushed himself off. He saw the incident for what it obviously was, some smart-ass punk who had simply seized the moment to scare the shit out of the doddering geezer standing in the way—namely him. *It's all about getting-off at someone else's expense, nothing more,* he told himself.

He tested his phone by punching the power button and waiting for the screen to light up. Miraculously, it was fine. Next, he patted his shoulder holster, confirming that his .357 Colt was still secure; then he stooped and picked up two quarters lying at his feet. The rest of his change would become fodder for the road sweeper.

Still furious, he squinted once more at his parking ticket and saw that he had gotten off on the wrong level. His Jaguar was parked two ramps higher. Muttering epithets, he returned to the elevator and rode the oppressive aluminum box up to level six accompanied by an ancient Japanese couple who crowded fearfully into the right rear corner convinced he was a modern-day Jack the Ripper.

Justin exited the elevator and looked down the ramp, only to spy his car playing host to two teens in the act of stealing its hubcaps.

"*Hey, dammit,*" he roared, starting toward them, suddenly filled with rage at this latest, last-straw insult.

Two skinny kids rose in unison and began laughing derisively at the old fart heading their way. Devoid of fear, the tallest of the duo flicked a middle finger and stopped laughing long enough to yell, "This yo' wheels, bro?" Then not bothering to allow time for an answer, his accomplice added in a high-pitched voice, "Watch this, you mother," as he jumped onto the car's trunk.

A nanosecond later the Jaguar was lifted off the floor by a horrendous explosion. Both left side doors were torn off by the force of the blast, and cartwheeled through the air in slow motion toward him. He had just enough time to see the two boys disappear inside the fireball before he threw himself to the ground and covered his head with both arms.

The shock wave rolled over him, dragging in its wake a curtain of incredible heat. Ragged bits of metal and glass clanged and dinged in an obscene shower all around him, some pieces actually landing on his clothing, burning their way through to his skin. He smelled the awful stench of scorched flesh and hair, wondering wildly if it was his or that of the two shredded teens.

He glanced up and took stock of his surroundings. His Jaguar was a fiery hulk, as were two other cars parked beside it. In spite of the hellacious ringing in his ears, he managed to hear an alarm sounding in the distance. It was soon joined by several sirens, their electronic wails and yelps seemingly coming from every direction.

Crawling painfully to the side of the ramp, he began swatting wildly at his clothes and hair, hoping to extinguish those hot spots he couldn't see. He glanced again at what was left of his car, understanding in that briefest of moments that only a bomb could have caused such carnage; and also realizing that the expected war he had warned O'Bryan about three hours earlier had started.

He pulled out his cellphone and speed-dialed Valerie. When she answered, he briefed her on what had just happened, insisted he was okay, and suggested she dispatch a homicide team. "Tell them to expect to find two juveniles torn into a thousand charred pieces. And, Val, warn them it won't be pretty."

"I copy, Justin. Tobias out," Valerie replied in her most professional voice.

CHAPTER 11

Settled into his hotel room, a very antsy O'Bryan set to the task of telephoning Sean MacMillan. He had deliberately not called ahead simply because he did not want to tip his hand. He had already noted that a Sean MacMillan was listed in the Cambridge directory, the number a match to the number he had in his wallet. Ten minutes to ten, he observed as he listened to the phone ringing somewhere out in the city. He found he was nervous.

"Sean MacMillan," announced the familiar voice.

No turning back now. "Hi, Sean, it's a voice from across the sea. How have you been?"

Silence. Then finally, "Who is this?"

"Jack O'Bryan."

"*Jack!* It's been a while. You in town?"

"Briefly. That's why I'm calling. To see if maybe we could get together tomorrow. I only have the one day."

"I see." More silence. Then: "Tell me, could it have something to do with our mutual acquaintance currently in residence on Embassy Row in Washington?"

"It could."

A shallow laugh. Not derisive, not mocking. A laugh revealing nothing. "Tell you what, Jack, meet me at the Savoy Grill at noon. It's in the Savoy Hotel on Boylston, facing the Common. I've got a faculty meeting in the morning," he explained. "Law school starts next week, but I'll be through by eleven-thirty, twelve at the latest."

"Noon it is. See you tomorrow. Thanks, Sean. Goodnight."

"Good night."

O'Bryan was already seated and into his second coffee when Professor Sean MacMillan arrived, dressed like the lawyer he was. A charcoal gray pinstriped suit, white shirt, rep tie, and gleaming, black, tasseled shoes. He stood a shade over six-foot-two, hair more silver than black, tanned and relaxed, a man without a care in the world. At forty-six he was where every lawyer aspired to be.

"How are you, Jack? Still working for the MiG?"

"You know it. Good to see you, Sean." He pumped the other man's hand enthusiastically, giving him the once-over as he did. "Looks like the academic life agrees with you."

"It's a living." The lawyer pulled back his chair and sat. He grinned. "Jack O'Bryan. I still find it amusing how the name neatly rhymes with Jack Ryan, the CIA sleuth made famous by that super storyteller, Tom Clancy. Guess that qualifies you to be the Vatican's very own honorary spy. What a world!"

O'Bryan laughed. His name had been the source of good-natured ribbing from many of his friends for the past twenty years. Jack O'Bryan had become a marked man. He took it in stride, shrugged it off, but secretly enjoyed the comparison.

"Just remember, I had first dibs on the name Jack O'Bryan, ergo, good old Tom Clancy had no choice but to settle for second best."

Both men laughed.

"Okay, Jack, okay. Now, on to important matters. Let me suggest the scrod. There's not a restaurant in the city knows how to do it better. You won't be disappointed."

"Done."

Forty-five minutes later, both passed on the temptations of the cake trolley and settled for coffee. The easy banter enjoyed throughout the meal turned serious.

"To answer the unasked question, Jack," MacMillan began, directing the conversation to the yet unspoken purpose of the meeting, "I've been following the story of our friend Kettering ever since it broke. Who hasn't? It's been headlines in every edition of *The Globe*, as well as all the other newspaper in the country. And, let's not forget TV stations, radio talk shows, and corner pubs. It's no exaggeration to say that this is as big—or bigger, than the O.J. Simpson mess. Speculation as to Kettering's guilt runs rampant, as those establishment seekers of the truth are wont to editorialize. And I'd be less than human if I didn't admit to a fair amount of media voyeurism myself. God forgive me."

"So, you think he's guilty?"

MacMillan motioned to the passing waiter for refills. "I admit there's not a soul alive who could be accused of harboring greater pleasure than me at the very real possibility of Kettering's complicity. I think about it constantly. But you know, Jack, I just can't see that paragon of virtue doing such a thing. It sounds oh so self-righteous, even to my ears, but I mean it." He shook his head as he poured cream into his cup. "Frankly, I have a hard time believing any of it. Anyway, I expect the Vatican to recall him momentarily, regardless of his posturing statements, and a demand for a trial to clear his good name. It very well may come to a showdown, since the second grand jury will reach the same conclusion of probable cause as the first. So for the sake of the Church, I hope you guys are really not considering going along with his foolishness."

It was O'Bryan's turn to shake his head. "There are still other avenues being considered," he said, "including the one where the Holy See would actually allow Francis Kettering to be bound over for trial, if that's the right terminology. They would suspend his diplomatic immunity but not revoke it."

"Which horse's ass came up with that bright idea?" MacMillan slammed his cup down, sloshing the contents onto the pristine tablecloth.

O'Bryan said nothing.

"Please tell me *you* aren't the horse's ass, Jack."

O'Bryan started to fidget, a look of misery crossing his face. He remembered most vividly the seamless logic of his argument in favor of just such a move only a couple of weeks ago in Cardinal Miglianico's office. Now he was being chastised, and it stung, all the more so because he wasn't free to respond. He had not been empowered to divulge the gist of Kettering's startling exposé. That information had to remain secret.

"So, it seems that you're not only a secret agent, Jack, but a lawyer as well. My, my, what talents you hide. You must indeed be a good one to have inspired Miglianico to not only to listen, but to actually heed such inspirational counsel. Congratulations." A derisive sound followed. "That's the absolute worst advice I've ever had the displeasure of hearing. It's so bloody moronic it shouldn't be dignified with a rebuttal. The only thing is Jack, and it's such a trifling technicality really, but should you lose, then that course of action could very well lead to a thorough disgracing of the Church. And, Jack, I don't use those words lightly."

"Then what do *you* suggest?" O'Bryan was miffed at being brought up short by the older man. He felt like an errant child. He had used the same argument with Miglianico who had accepted it as right. And the secretary of state was definitely nobody's fool.

MacMillan snorted, the sound loud enough to cause nearby patrons to glance their way.

He let out a deep breath as he leaned in toward his friend. "Jack, here's my advice. Distance yourself right now from this mess. I mean as far away, and as fast as you can. I'm already picturing the power play unfolding in the Vatican, and I'm seeing bigtime winners and bigtime losers. And the losers will forfeit their heads."

He sounds just like Justin, O'Bryan thought, as he managed a one-word response. "Why?"

"Just cut and run. You're way, way out of your league on this one. Frankly, I think everybody who has anything to do with defending Kettering is."

O'Bryan mimicked his companion and likewise leaned forward, his elbows searching rudely for the middle ground of the table. "I can't, Sean. I'm committed, whether I like it or not. In fact, I came here for the expressed purpose of feeling you out to see if you'd consider helping Justin Scott mount a defense for Kettering in the event a trial becomes necessary."

MacMillan's jaw dropped. He sat transfixed, a statue with living eyes staring across the narrowed divide, looking to O'Bryan much like a man whose mind refused to understand what it had just heard.

"That's right," O'Bryan pressed. "Justin wants you on the defense team. So does Miglianico. So do I. Who better?" he asked, his eyes riveted to MacMillan's. "Answer me that. Who knows more about what's at stake here than you?"

MacMillan kept his silence until he'd recovered his composure. He took his time to formulate a response. Finally he spoke. "Monsignor O'Bryan, you can't be that naive. You probably know more about what has transpired than the police. The Vatican always knows. Maybe Kettering's already confessed."

"He hasn't," interrupted O'Bryan.

MacMillan waved his hand; a signal for silence. "Maybe, maybe not. But what *is* true is that Kettering would rather go to jail for the rest of his life than be defended by me."

"Not if the Holy See directs him to accept you as counsel. He still must embrace his solemn vow of obedience, and the Pope could well enter the fray with a command he accept you for the good of the Church."

"That would be just dandy," MacMillan replied sarcastically. "An unwilling client with an unwanted lawyer defending him on a charge of capital murder. And the two just happen to be mortal enemies. But, hey, the accused must accept the lawyer because of a solemn vow he's sworn to uphold. It even sounds like a bad movie plot. This wouldn't play in Peoria, and it sure won't play with Kettering!"

"Let me be the judge of that, okay? I just want you to consider the possibility. Think about it. All I ask is that you think about it."

The waiter brought the check and MacMillan paid with his American Express card. After signing the receipt he turned to O'Bryan. "I've got other commitments," he said coldly. "I'm a law professor, remember? Class starts next week and I have a full load. I'm not your man. End of discussion."

"It's not too late to have someone else fill in for you. Let's face it, as soon as the school hears why you need the time off, the governing board will instantly see it as a major coup. It'll bring them a gazillion dollars' worth of free publicity. They will think they've died and gone to a monetary heaven. One of their own has been asked to join the defense team to represent the accused in what is already shaping up to be one of the highest profile murder cases seen in years. You'd be just like Alan Dershowitz jumping on the successful Simpson Dream Team bandwagon. Another feather in Harvard's academic cap."

"You're dreaming, Jack. Things don't work that way in the real world. And anyway, Alan went on to make an absolute ass of himself over the Bush, Gore, Florida hanging chad election thing."

Both men rose, and started toward the door.

"I'm going back to Washington this afternoon, but I want you to think about it. I'll call you."

They stood on the sidewalk, hugging the façade of the building, trying to stay out of the heavy flow of pedestrian traffic. MacMillan was visibly agitated.

"Jack, why do you persist? It's not going to happen. Tell you what, though. Just to prove my heart's in the right place, let me recommend a few good law firms. Some here, some in New York, and some in Washington. Don't worry, I'll recommend men I'd want for my defense if I were similarly situated. Speak to them all, because I'm sure any or all would love to join your Mr. Scott. But remember this: no matter who you finally choose, it's going to cost a ton."

O'Bryan ignored the offer. "I'll call, okay?"

Thoroughly exasperated, MacMillan finally vented his anger. "Why do you persist?" he repeated. "Why can't you acknowledge the real reason I want nothing to do with the man? Is it something you've conveniently forgotten, Jack? Well, let me be as blunt as I can: I don't want the job! Remember, it's because of Kettering I am where I am today. Unlike you, I'm a defrocked Jesuit priest, and Kettering was the one who enjoyed pulling the plug on me. Have you suddenly acquired a case of selective amnesia and forgotten that insignificant little fact? Francis Kettering can hang for all I care."

Without another word, Sean MacMillan plunged into the noontime crowd and disappeared.

O'Bryan felt crushed under the heavy weight of defeat. He had gambled and lost. Justin was now on his own.

* * *

Paula was a study in efficiency. She had accepted delivery of the first batch of evidence files from the attorney general, delivered by pre-arrangement at a few minutes past seven. The first thing she did was to digitally scan and copy each page into the computer. Then the originals were filed by subject matter in specially prepared folders. Each was assigned a color. The autopsy file was red, chock-full of information on the victim and fetus. Next, all physical evidence was assigned a blue folder, which contained everything relating to the victim, the auto, and the accident scene. Evidence solely relating to Kettering was housed in a green folder; and lastly, all information from Europe was secured in a yellow one. Every page was color tabbed, and sequentially numbered. In all: 343 pages. The process took six hours. She suspected that this represented only the first of many such batches to come her way in the ensuing weeks.

Now Justin could really go to work.

* * *

Justin sat dressed in red sweats and running shoes, clothed for comfort and the long day ahead. He had planned to get the task started while Jack was in Boston.

He and Paula began with the autopsy file. Not because it was the thickest folder, but because it contained the essence of the case.

Both were saddened to learn the details of the young woman's death. It was tragic beyond words.

They viewed the FBI-created video of Maritha von Snellenberger, seeing the lady for the first time in the fullness of her life.

Justin was awestruck. "She's more beautiful than the stills we've seen of her, Paula. She must have caused a sensation every time she appeared on the street."

Paula smiled sadly. "Maritha was in a class by herself." She peered at the video, and continued with her observation. "You know, in spite of all her beauty she seems to have had that certain something, that mysterious, intangible something which was inexplicably non-threatening to other women, and from what I've read, she seems to have been blessed with a personality to match her beauty. The likes of a Maritha come along but once in a generation. She reminds me a lot of the late Princess Diana."

"Let's get started, shall we?" Justin said, not willing to dwell any longer on the loss of Cardinal Kettering's child.

He plucked out the file detailing the extensive blood workup done in the FBI labs across town, while Paula settled in to read from the pathology report. They worked silently for the next hour, the muted clicks of the keypads on their laptop computers confirming that serious work was in progress. Then it was time to exchange information.

"Here's what the blood shows," Justin began. "She was in her first trimester, evidenced by the increased levels of estrogen and progesterone. Her white cell count was also slightly elevated, and possibly climbing. And an elevated ferritin reading suggests she was on iron supplements." He glanced at Paula. "The bureau knew from the get-go she was pregnant."

He scrolled to the next screen, and continued. "No evidence was found of illegal drugs or nicotine, although there is a side-bar notation that subsequent hair and lung analysis during autopsy showed she had smoked in the past. But not for at least six or seven months. She was doing everything possible to present herself as a perfect host for fertilization to take place. Then there's a lot of chemistry results listed to validate these findings, stuff that only a chemist or hematologist would understand." He tapped up the next screen.

"Here's an interesting finding. At the moment of death there was no indication of elevated levels of adrenaline in the blood, suggesting the victim was neither fearful nor frightened. She had not been struggling, which meant Maritha was comfortable in the presence of her attacker, and with her surroundings. When the blow came, it came out of the blue, and she never knew what hit her. Thank God for that!"

"Amen."

"The only thing missing, of course, is any indication of DNA testing." Justin sat back, finished.

Paula frowned. "Not unexpected. What would they have been looking for in her blood? Maternity was a given. The fetus was still inside her. They weren't searching for a match. Ergo, no need for DNA testing of the victim."

"But we know differently."

"How so?"

"DNA testing and typing will establish the genetic link claimed by Kettering to Maritha. It will let us know for sure whether Kettering is telling the truth or whether he's the world's most accomplished liar."

"You still have your doubts, Justin?" she asked in a subdued voice.

He shook his head. "Nah, I believe we'll see he's telling the truth. But I do want to get a sample of her blood from the bureau so we can run our own tests, but at the same time I don't want to tip our hand as to what we're up to. They haven't thought of the possibility that a genetic relationship could exist between Maritha and the cardinal, which explains why the fetus would carry Kettering's markers. The FBI lab types found what they expected to find. A match with the cardinal. But a match for all the wrong reasons. They just didn't look for other explanations. After all, the man was a priest." He looked solemn. "That's something we keep to ourselves for the time being, Paula. Our ace up the sleeve. Or at least one of them." He then cleared his screen, sat back, and asked: "What have you got?"

Paula began without fanfare. "Well, other than the cause of death, the obvious finding during the postmortem was a confirmation of pregnancy. The victim was into her eighth week, established by a study of the fetus, and supported by the physiological changes seen in all of Maritha von Snellenberger's organ systems. There was no evidence of anything other than normal conception. She probably would have delivered a healthy child at term."

Paula clicked over to her next screen. "Now, let's look at the cause of death, shall we?" She studied the display for a second, frowned, then continued. "The blow was struck towards the center of the left side of the occipital bone, shattering the external occipital protuberance, thus driving skull fragments into the brain. The impact came from left to right, not from above or below. It's as if the candlestick was swung like a baseball bat."

Justin interrupted. "Does the coroner speculate that the assailant was left-handed?"

Paula shook her head. "No. He does state for the record that the evidence could point in that direction, but, he cautions: not conclusively. The position of the head at time of impact could account for that seeming to be the case, so he advises against ruling out that the assailant was right-handed."

She went on. "We know death was instantaneous, because of the lack of exsanguination. The heart stopped immediately; so no blood was pumped." She entered the next screen. "Time of death has been put at between midnight and 2:00 a.m., and it's noted that the body was moved from the scene of the murder to the trunk of the cardinal's car. But there is also evidence indicating she was placed inside another car's trunk, transported to an unknown location, then transferred into Kettering's vehicle. They know this because there were microscopic fibers found sticking to the wound and to her clothes, fibers which match the matting material used only in late-edition Chrysler products. But Cardinal Kettering was driving a Ford Crown Victoria."

Justin wandered over to a sideboard and helped himself to a cup of coffee and a doughnut. He returned to his seat facing Paula, softly chewing and sipping as he listened to her summary.

"The body bore no other marks of violence, nor were there any signs of past injuries or surgeries. There was a small purplish discoloration on her right middle finger, but it turned out to be an ink stain, probably from a leaky fountain pen. A highly unusual color of ink though," she observed, then went on.

"Maritha only had two small fillings, both on the lower left side of her jaw. The posterior premolar, and the molar directly behind it. The work was done with cosmetics in mind in that the material used was a white compound, not an amalgam as is still commonly used by dentists in Europe." She passed several 8x10 color glossies to Justin. "These are the close-ups of the head wound."

Justin spent a couple of minutes studying the pictures, his face a mask. Paula used the interval to prepare some hot tea. By the time she was again settled in her chair, he had finished with the last photograph. He stacked them neatly and pushed the pile over to Paula's side of the table.

Without a word she handed him three more. They were even tighter shots of the head, but, surprisingly, not of the wound. In each, the thick, blond tresses had been parted to reveal scalp. Paula sipped her tea; eyes riveted on her boss.

Perplexed, Justin looked up and scrutinized her face. "What am I supposed to see? Why close-ups of normal hair and scalp?"

"Look at the hair, Justin."

He was still puzzled. "Okay, I'm looking, but I don't see anything. Help me, woman."

"Okay, try this," she said, pushing over a small, powerful magnifying glass. "Look closely at the roots."

He followed her instructions. Finally, he shook his head, impatience and exasperation on his face. "Just tell me, okay?"

"Justin, Maritha's not a blond. Her natural hair color is white. Not the white of an albino, but the white found in hair that has gone from blond, to gray, to white. If you look very carefully at the roots you'll see it's the color of snow. And that same color is found on the pubis. But both have been dyed; the head done professionally at least once every ten days, the other done by Maritha herself. I'll bet not too many people were aware of her little secret, including her husband." She paused, then added almost as an afterthought, "I wonder if the cardinal knew?"

"I'll grant you it's highly unusual, but what's the significance? I mean, so what?"

"I'll tell you, what. The cardinal has a headful of beautiful snow-white hair. I'm sure you've noticed. Find out at what age his hair began to turn. That's a hereditary trait, Counselor. It would simply be more proof that Kettering's telling the truth."

Justin grinned. "Good work, girl."

"Thank you, though I suspect the praise is premature." Still, she blushed with pleasure. "However, I'm glad to add in some small measure to the body of evidence that will hopefully prove our case. Now, let me finish before I get too swellheaded, okay?" Paula spoke for another ten minutes.

"One final observation," she said by way of summary. "Only the toenails on her left foot were painted, which tells me that something interrupted her, something important enough for her to stop what she was doing, and move onto something else. And that something else had to have been pretty important, trust me."

"Well, let me leave you with a something to chew on, too, Paula. Somewhere out there in the city is a woman's handbag. I don't pretend to know much about women, but I do know they never go anywhere without a purse, or a bag of some kind. Maritha's purse wasn't listed among her personal effects. The reason I know is because I glanced at the evidence folder before we started, and for some reason that missing purse jumped right out at me, and bloody well screamed for attention."

"Good point." Paula rose. "But it's break time. In fact, I'm calling an hour's recess so we can go search for the perfect Rueben sandwich. I'm starved."

In an unspoken agreement, neither had broached the subject of the explosion and carnage of the night before. They both knew the score.

CHAPTER 12

"Got a minute, Inspector?"

Valerie looked up and smiled. "Sure, come on in, Maria. What's on your mind?"

Maria Delgado strode into the office and plopped down in the chair in front of her boss. "It's a circus out there this morning, and not yet nine o'clock. I'm so pissed I could scream."

"Well, if it'll help, scream to your heart's content."

Detective Sergeant Maria Delgado vigorously scratched her head with her right hand while waving a sheaf of papers in her left. "How do you stay sane, Valerie? I mean; what's the secret?" She dumped the bundle onto the desk.

"Coffee, and lots of it. I've got a new machine. Care for a cup?"

"If it'll help, pour away."

"No, you pour, I'll listen."

Maria jumped out of her seat and began to prepare them each a mug. She spoke while she worked. "Braddock's called in sick; the humidity's turned my hair to frizzy shit; and I've got a sexual harassment charge dumped on me by one of my detectives." She placed a mug before Valerie. "Can I just go home?" she pleaded, deliberately sounding like a whiney child.

"No, you cannot. Sit."

Maria sat.

"Now, sip." Valerie followed her own advice, and stared at the younger woman over the rim. After a few moments she started to grin. "Okay, give it to me slowly, and give it to me from the top. First, you say Braddock's sick?"

"Sick of this place, if you ask me, but yeah, he called in just before roll call saying his dauber's down. Mumbled something about the flu, but I think it's the cure that's doing him in." She placed her steaming mug on the desk, then mimicked someone holding a bottle and chugalugging the contents. "My guess is he just got knicker-ripping drunk last night. The loo does that about once every couple of months, you know."

"Okay, so Braddock's a no-show. I'll come back to that in a moment. Your frizzy hair I can't do a thing about, which leaves the last item, namely a sexual harassment charge. What gives?"

"One of my junior detectives is being propositioned by a very unwanted suitor who's looking for a new main squeeze. Pamela Reardon."

"Son of a bitch, I'll have his nuts. Who's the idiot?"

Maria Delgado drew a noisy swallow of coffee before answering. "It's not what you think, boss. This is one crazy world we're living in. Turns out our Lothario ain't a real Lothario. Our he is a she. Linda Pulling, a secretary in the steno pool."

"*The Mouse? The Mouse is hitting on one of my detectives?* The same Linda Pulling who breaks down crying if you so much as say boo to her?"

"The very same. Seems she's been writing love letters in her spare time, and mailing them to Reardon at home. Also, she's sending flowers, candy, the works. Internal Affairs traced the letters back to the Mouse's computer. She's confessed."

Valerie Tobias sat back, mouth agape.

"Boss, Pamela has asked that the woman not be fired. She doesn't want to cause her any grief. She just wants her to knock it off. Anyway, it's your call."

"What do you think, Maria?"

Maria ran both hands through her frizzy hair. "The Mouse is scared shitless. She's promised to never, ever, look at or speak to Detective Reardon again unless spoken to first. And only then in the line of duty. She's been with the department ten years and she's a good worker. I say give her another chance after you read her the Riot Act, Inspector. When all's said and done, you've kind of got to feel sorry for her, you know."

"All right, I'll speak to her today."

"Thanks, boss."

"Now, about Braddock. I'm aware that he ties one on every once in a while, but it's unusual for him to do it on a weeknight."

"Scuttlebutt has it that he's taken some heavy hits in the gambling department lately, mostly on college football games," explained Delgado. "Even some of the troops he's palled around with on those rare occasions in the past have sensed a change. The loo's always been a loner, so no one really has a handle on what's going on."

Valerie nodded. "It's no secret the guy likes to bet, and I've got no problem with that. Lots of folks do. Even straight-arrow cops will bet in an office pool during the World Series, or the Super Bowl. And a lot of people drink too much, Tom Braddock included. But once it starts to affect his on-the-job performance, then it becomes my problem." She studied Maria. "Tom needs about two more years to get his twenty in," she said quietly. "He's a damn good detective, but long ago his personal life nixed any chances for his going higher. It's already cost him his wife and kid. Anyway, keep it quiet if you can. I'll have a word with him." She smiled. "That it?"

Maria Delgado stood. "That's it. You sure have a way of making problems disappear. No suggestions for my hair?"

"None. You're on your own in that department. One last thing, Maria. Word came down yesterday you've been selected to attend the winter term *Advanced Investigations Course* at the FBI Academy at Quantico. Class starts on January 15, and goes for four weeks. You were the only one picked from Metro, so that's quite an honor. You'll be with the best of the best from select departments from around the country. Congratulations, Detective. Do us proud, okay?"

"Are you serious?" she whispered.

"I am."

"I don't know what to say. I know you must've gone to bat for me, Val, 'cause the competition for that course is out of sight. Promise I won't let you down. I don't know what else to say except thanks, and that I'd better get out of here before I start to bawl. Bye, boss."

Valerie felt good as she began to attack the mountain of paperwork before her. But not for long. Her thoughts kept returning to Braddock, and she shook her head. *He really is his own worst enemy!*

CHAPTER 13

On the drive back from Ronald Reagan National Airport, O'Bryan told Justin of Sean MacMillan's refusal to have anything to do with the case. He explained how three years ago Kettering had chaired a tribunal in Rome which had found MacMillan guilty of an interpretation of Catholic dogma it deemed heretical. A prolific writer on Liberation theology ideas, MacMillan had finally been ordered to cease and desist. He refused, and Kettering convinced the Pope to approve the draconian measures recommended by the three cardinals sitting in judgement: Defrock the renegade Sean MacMillan, and expel him from the ranks of the Jesuits.

Justin shook his head, thinking O'Bryan and Miglianico patently naive to have even hoped that the outcome could have been any different. He found himself giving thanks that O'Bryan had said nothing of Kettering's confession to the disgraced priest. It was time to move on.

* * *

Justin and O'Bryan had arrived in Bern, Switzerland, the previous evening.

Now, after a solid night's sleep, they were in a rented Fiat heading southeast toward the town of Fribourg with O'Bryan driving. Traffic was heavy, and although their journey was a scant twenty miles, in the past forty minutes they had covered only half the distance. The bright, 9:00 a.m. sun was thankfully to their rear, but posed an obvious hazard to those motorists entering Bern from the west. That patience was a virtue to be practiced this morning had definitely crossed Justin's mind. He decided to ask O'Bryan a question that had nagged him for the last couple of hours.

"Tell me honestly, Jack, could Miglianico be a party to this obscenity? Is it possible that's the real reason Sean MacMillan doesn't want anything to do with you guys? Could it be he suspects your boss is a ringleader in some wild attempt to dethrone the Pope? and that citing his personal problem with Kettering is nothing more than a smokescreen?"

O'Bryan thought carefully before answering. "Justin, had you asked me all those 'could it be' questions last week, I'd have lit into you with righteous indignation." He scratched his jaw. "I've worked for Miglianico for almost eighteen months now, but have known him for several years, and I've always seen him as a rock; both morally and spiritually." He shook his head sadly. "But after what Kettering's told us, I don't know what to believe, or who to trust anymore."

"Let's just drop it for the time being, okay?"

"Fine by me." O'Bryan quickly grabbed the opportunity to change the subject. "So, when are you going to tell me why we're going to Fribourg?"

"Looking for clues."

"Better tell me what I'm looking for if you want my help."

Justin scrunched up his face and made a pretense of deep thought before replying. "Okay, wise guy, here's the plan. When you need information on a subject, any subject, where do you go?"

"The library?"

"Very good, Jack. The library."

"Excuse me," O'Bryan interrupted with feigned sarcasm, "but I'll bet there are at least four libraries where we've just come from. You know, that little backwater village called Bern which also just happens to be the capital of Switzerland."

"Hear me out, hotshot."

O'Bryan pretended to pout. He enjoyed the relaxed atmosphere which somehow seemed to naturally envelope Justin. It was contagious. The man had a gift to make others like him. He was unaware of this ability, which only added to his charm. Yet one also instinctively knew that Justin Scott would be the man you would want to have in your corner if push ever came to shove.

"I'm aware that the libraries in Bern carry more than coloring books," Justin began, "but I'm playing a hunch. If you remember, Maritha had been fascinated with libraries ever since she had learned to read. She saw the library as a haven, and oftentimes while traveling she would spend hours in a city's library. She knew how to do research, and according to the article I uncovered during my last trip, she collected library cards like other folks collect stamps. So, knowing all that, I'm betting our Maritha von Snellenberger was looking for certain information, but she didn't know who she could trust to turn to for help. Kind of like us right now. My guess is it was something profoundly personal, and that possibly she felt she could be too easily spotted and recognized at any of the libraries in Bern. But she desperately needed the information, so my hunch is that her overwhelming need drove her to the safety and anonymity of the neighboring cantons.

"But our answer may not be found in Fribourg," Justin continued. "We might have to go to Neuchatel, or head out in the direction of Solothurn. Maybe even Lucerne. Or to every other library in Switzerland. And maybe my hunch won't pan out at all. That's the nature of this business. Hours upon hours; days stacked on days; weeks followed by more weeks; sometimes even untold months of boring, tedious, tiring legwork. *'Seek, and ye shall find.'* That's what drives us ever forward."

"All right, so far so good, Justin. But once we get to the library, what exactly will we be looking for?"

Justin explained. "We know from Kettering that Maritha turned to a private investigative firm to help her with her problem. She suspected infidelity. Trouble is, we have no easy way of finding out which firm. Sure, we could spend the next twenty years calling every private eye in the country, but, Jack, this Mountain Paradise was founded on secrecy. It's the magnet which attracts people from all over the world to its banks. The Swiss have a thousand-year history of keeping their mouths shut. And especially if the client is rich and powerful, such as you-know-who. So I'm thinking she went to a library in a neighboring town, but one far enough from home in case anyone should stumble across her while she was doing her research.

"Can't you just picture it?" he said. "Up comes Mrs. Busybody who lives next door, plunks her ample behind down next to Maritha and starts to read over her shoulder. 'Oh, Maritha, looking for private detectives? Trouble at home, dearie? Do you suspect your husband of infidelity? Oh, Maritha, I promise not to tell a soul.' That kind of gossip would spread like wildfire. It would become a self-fulfilling prophecy in that it would damn well destroy her marriage no matter whatever the outcome of any investigation."

O'Bryan agreed. "We know that's what Kettering said she was worried about, and supposedly what drove her to seek help. But, you tell me this, Justin. Was that the real reason, or was it just a red herring she used with Kettering?"

Justin sighed. "I don't know. But whatever it was, it's a fact she finally did turn to private investigators for help. And in the process she uncovered something far worse than just a cheating husband." Justin had extracted a small photo of Maritha from his jacket pocket as he spoke, and studied the likeness. "I can't imagine any man two-timing this lovely lady," he added quietly.

"Speaking of the erstwhile cad, it's been weeks since the murder, and still no sign of the husband, although it's said he's traveling in Russia on business. What does that really mean, Justin?"

"It means don't rush to judgment. We only know from Kettering that infidelity is what she says she suspected. We have no proof that's what she discovered. Learn a lesson from Kettering's case. The whole world knows the guy's guilty, right? An airtight case? Just like the O.J. affair. But we know better. Things aren't always as they appear. That's the first lesson learned by any investigator worth his salt, and it's also the easiest to forget."

"Let's go back to the husband for a moment, Justin. Why haven't we heard from him? News from the outside world eventually finds its way into Russia."

"My gut feeling's not a good one, Jack. The man's disappeared. You're right. The whole world knows of Maritha's murder, but still no sign of Manfred. After this many weeks, even he's got to have heard. Something's fishy."

"Russia's still in a state of total collapse," O'Bryan replied, as he studied the road signs leading into Fribourg. Traffic was bumper-to-bumper, and the little Fiat became part of a living metal snake inching its way forward on a ribbon of concrete. "Law and order there is a thing of the past. Anarchy reigns. It's every man for himself. Even the KGB's been stripped of its power, and the military has all but disintegrated." He shook his head slowly as he tried to visualize Russia. And he knew it was probably ten times worse than any images he could conjure up. He verbalized his feelings. "That's what the husband's disappeared into. Maybe he's in trouble somewhere."

"There's been no hint of that," replied Justin. "Believe me, the bureau and Interpol have some deep feelers out on that one. And while we're on the subject of missing persons, I'll tell you something else that's really sticking in my craw. Where's Maritha's mother? Why hasn't she come forward? Kettering says she's still alive. So why isn't she squealing like a stuck pig?" Justin looked glum. "There's a lot that stinks about this whole affair, Jack, and in all probability Francis Cardinal Kettering doesn't know the half of it. But enough of that for now. Let's go find the library."

Ten minutes later as they entered the library, Justin paused at the edge of the lobby.

"You're on," he whispered loudly to O'Bryan.

"What?"

"I can't read German. I can barely *Sprechen* enough *Deutsch* to ask people if they speak English. Most can. But this?" He swept the room with his right arm. "I haven't a clue where to go, where to start, and I sure don't want to have to ask."

"What exactly are we looking for?"

"The reference section. I want to look at the directories which list the private investigators; stuff like that. When people use those books they invariably leave some clue. A flag, a marker, something indicating that they've been there. Hell, I've found whole pages of notes left in such books. Sometimes people will circle what interests them. The point is they usually leave a trail. I'm hoping Maritha held true to form."

"Then this is your lucky day, old man," whispered O'Bryan. "I'm glad you're finally recognizing my talents."

"And all this time you thought it was your boyish charm. Hokum. I dragged you along only because you can natter in a couple of languages. I trust you can read them, too." He playfully slapped the cleric on the shoulder. "You're my lifesaver, boy. Lead on."

They did not find what they were looking for in Fribourg. There was nothing to indicate anyone had ever used any of the reference books. They left, and headed for Neuchatel, the next town on their list. An hour and a half later they drew a second blank.

But in Solothurn they hit pay dirt.

"That's it!" exclaimed Justin, as they peered at the fine print in the directory before them. "See that pen mark in the left-hand margin beside the firm's name? Unusual ink color," he remarked, as both studied the purple dots, "but it's identical to an ink stain discovered on one of Maritha's fingers during the autopsy. "See the other mark on the right-hand side by the phone number? The asterisk?" Justin continued, pointing to the spot in question. "Those marks made it easier for her to come back to her place on the page as her eyes went back and forth while she wrote down the information she wanted."

"You're really sure these were her little marks, Justin? Somehow it seems like one tremendous leap." O'Bryan sounded dubious.

"After twenty-nine years in the business, you develop a sense," Justin replied. "You listen to your instincts, and follow your hunches.

Nine times out of ten, your first plan of action proves to be your best, chiefly because it's usually the simplest. It's even got a name. *Ockham's razor,* attributed to a Middle Age monk, and is also known as the "*principle of parsimony*". He looked O'Bryan in the eye and chuckled. "Bet you're super impressed, Padre, that I would even know of such stuff, huh? Well, kiddo, while I'm in an expansive mood I'll let you in on another little secret. When I was here in Europe last week, I learned some things I haven't had time to tell you, or Paula, for that matter. Weren't important. Or so I thought. Things such as learning that Maritha's real maiden name was *Ibel,* not *Furstenburg,* which appears on all legal documents. The same as in *Ibel & Laufenburg.* You dig? I'm thinking she chose that firm as much for the name as for anything else. Maybe she saw it as an omen. But whatever the reason, I'll bet the farm those are her purple ink marks. By the way, what year was this thing published?" he asked, a frown crossing his face.

O'Bryan flipped to the cover. "It's two years old."

"Do me a favor, Jack. Hunt down the telephone directory for Lausanne."

Lausanne was the town listed as the home of *Ibel & Laufenburg, Investigative Services.* The firm was described as having expertise in several facets of investigations, including domestic surveillance. Their ad stressed that confidentiality had been the corporate watchword for more than thirty years. That, Justin knew, would certainly have held sway with Maritha von Snellenberger.

O'Bryan found the directory and returned within two minutes. He rifled through the tissue-thin pages, his finger finally coming to rest on the correct line. And there it was! Purple pen marks in the margin. The phone numbers matched, a surefire confirmation to a searching Maritha that the information she had retrieved on the firm was indeed current.

"*Bingo*!" Justin was delighted. He winked at O'Bryan. "Thank your lucky stars this isn't the United States. Back home, folks would simply tear out the whole damn page and stuff it in their pocket. Over here, they're still civilized. Maritha left us a trail. We're off and running."

"What now?" O'Bryan asked, glancing at his watch. It was going on four o'clock.

"Back to the hotel to figure out our plan of attack for tomorrow." Justin looked around. "Jack, I need a phone. Correction, you need a phone. My cellphone is useless here. It ain't yet rigged for Europe, but I need a secure land line."

"Oh?"

"Yeah, I want you to call *Ibel & Laufenburg* and set an appointment for tomorrow morning. And, Jack, don't take no for an answer."

O'Bryan picked up the directory and set out in search of a phone.

Several minutes later he returned. "You're on for ten o'clock sharp. Anything else, my *liege*?" he asked in a pretend-groveling tone of voice.

Justin laughed as he heaved himself up from the hard wooden chair. "Nothing pressing, vassal, but I am feeling my oats. So, as a sign of my pleasure, I'm going to allow you to buy me a beer as soon as we get to the hotel. *And* I'll let you drive back. How's that for being an all-round wonderful master, and Mister Nice Guy?"

O'Bryan laughed. "Can't deny the obvious, Justin. You're a true prince."

Justin pretended to shove the priest toward the door. "Yeah, yeah, that's what they all say."

CHAPTER 14

They had headed out for Lausanne at dawn, and standing now on the curb in front of the four-story granite building, were thoroughly confused. The address was clearly marked on a simple brass plate bolted onto the granite façade to the left of the imposing double door entry; but nowhere was the name *Ibel & Laufenburg* shown. Indeed, to all appearances this was simply another private residence on a street of equally imposing structures.

"Well, here goes nothing," Justin announced as he climbed the steps and pressed the buzzer. They waited in silence, shuffling from one foot to another, feigning interest in a study of the formidable exterior.

Justin had decreed they wear their 'Sunday best' for the occasion. He was in a conservative blue pinstripe; O'Bryan in his black suit and Roman collar. "We want them to think this is official business," Justin had explained.

The door was opened by a woman in her early twenties. She smiled and beckoned them to enter. "Please follow me, Mr. Furlan is expecting you." She led them up a flight of stairs to the second level, then down a well-lit, carpeted corridor lined with magnificent museum quality paintings. At the far end she led them through French doors and into a spacious sitting room. "Please make yourselves comfortable. May I offer some coffee, or tea, perhaps?"

Both declined. Before she could turn to leave, a man entered the room from a side door. "Thank you for greeting our guests, Mrs. Heydrich." Striding forward he held out his hand and introduced himself. "I'm Klaus Furlan, the managing director of *Ibel & Laufenburg*. How do you do, gentlemen?" As he spoke, he motioned with his left hand , inviting them to sit.

Furlan appeared to be in his early sixties, every man's image of a prosperous banker, or maybe a lawyer, but certainly not a private investigator. "So, how may I be of service?"

Justin answered without preamble. "Mr. Furlan, we were hoping your firm could shed some light on an investigation we're conducting on behalf of the Vatican. I'm referring to the matter of Cardinal Kettering, and the murder of Mrs. von Snellenberger."

"A terrible thing," Furlan replied, the right amount of sadness leaking out in his voice, "but I'm not quite sure what it is you are asking. Is it that you want to contract with my firm to undertake an investigation regarding the matter?" He replaced the echo of sadness with just the right degree of feigned puzzlement.

Justin shook his head. "No, sir, we would like you to tell us what you can about the arrangement your firm had with Maritha von Snellenberger. We know she hired *Ibel & Laufenburg* to investigate her husband. Somehow, that investigation led to her death. We're merely asking you to help us understand why."

Furlan absently toyed with his watch chain, then replied. "Mr. Scott, when Monsignor O'Bryan called requesting this meeting, I made some inquiries of my own. For example, I know you are a retired FBI agent, and that the Monsignor is employed by the Vatican. And, of course, I know that you have been hired to defend Cardinal Kettering. But I do not understand why you would think that Mrs. von Snellenberger had any business dealings with us. I fear that somehow you've been misled. I'm sorry if that is the case, but I assure you, I cannot help you in this matter." He paused to study the Americans, then added solemnly, "But even if it was possible, you must realize that any such information could not be forthcoming. You see, our clients expect confidentiality. That's why they hire us, and that's what they receive." He began to rise. "I'm truly sorry, gentlemen. I know your time is precious."

"Mr. Furlan, we know for a fact you were hired by Mrs. von Snellenberger. The woman is dead, and you possibly have information which could lead to the apprehension of her murderer. Even Switzerland has laws covering the obstruction of justice, and your reticence could certainly be construed as being just that. However, it's our hope that you can confirm certain facts; corroborate, if you will, information we have gained from other sources. That's all we ask. We have no intention of making public what you tell us. In fact, no one need ever know of this meeting."

Furlan stood and allowed a hint of anger to creep into his voice. The light from a crystal chandelier flashed off his rimless glasses as he moved his head to face first one, then the other. "That sounds very much like a threat, Mr. Scott. May I remind you, this is not America. We Swiss do not conduct our affairs in such a crude manner. Now, permit me to show you out. Good day, gentlemen."

Justin appeared relaxed as he stood. "Very well, Mr. Furlan, we'll leave. But let me tell you what I intend to do." He smiled a most insincere smile. "Within the hour I'm going to call Washington with a recommendation that the FBI take over. And it will. I will then see to it that word immediately leaks to the press of this new development, and I'll do so with the expressed purpose of making sure that your firm becomes a household name before the week is out. I will infer that you are deliberately harboring knowledge of criminal behavior. And that's just for starters. At the same time, Monsignor O'Bryan will guarantee that the Vatican puts its considerable clout behind a squeeze on *Ibel & Laufenburg*. The Holy See will launch an official complaint of misconduct with your foreign office. Then, with all the precision of a fine Swiss watch, the U.S. government will be persuaded to do likewise. Mr. Furlan, you and yours are going to be famous. That's not a threat, but a promise. I'm sure your clients will approve. Have a nice day, *Herr* Director."

Furlan turned to O'Bryan, a hint of uncertainty and fear creeping into his voice. "Monsignor, does this man speak for you?"

Though O'Bryan seldom ever stretched the truth, he felt it necessary this time to achieve the desired end. "He does, and I concur with everything Mr. Scott has said. Rest assured my government views this matter most seriously. The Holy See has vowed to show no quarter in its search to uncover Mrs. von Snellenberger's murderer." As he spoke, he ambled to the edge of the Chinese silk carpet and straightened a knotted tassel with the toe of his shoe. A mesmerized Furlan gave the cleric his undivided attention.

"You know," O'Bryan continued, seemingly admiring the results of his labor, "the Swiss and the Vatican have enjoyed a special relationship dating back to the Middle Ages. Why, the men responsible for the protection of the popes down through the centuries are your own Swiss Guards. No other country can claim such an honor. So I daresay neither the Swiss people, nor their government, has any desire to see a strain put on such a long-lasting friendship.

But it could come to pass, and all because of you. Not an enviable position for you to be clinging to. Untenable, really," he concluded.

Just then a phone rang on a secretary's desk nestled in an alcove at the back of the room. Furlan held up a hand signaling them to wait. He picked up the receiver and identified himself. He nodded repeatedly as he listened, all the while staring intently at the two Americans. Something being said on the other end apparently did not sit well with him. He became agitated, and spoke rapidly, making no attempt to shield the conversation from the visitors. Back and forth the words flew for almost two minutes. Furlan hung up.

He seemed to have reached a decision, or one had been made for him. And it was obviously not one to his liking. His changed demeanor told all.

"May I request you call me later, say about four o'clock? I might further ask you to be prepared to return shortly thereafter. Can you fit that into your plans for today?"

"We can," replied Justin. "Thank you for your time, Mr. Furlan." He did not offer to shake hands, and the director wordlessly escorted them to the front door.

Ten minutes later they were in their Fiat, heading toward the center of the city. O'Bryan was driving, and Justin began fumbling with something he had pulled up from below his shirt collar. The priest stole a quick peek just in time to see Justin screw a small plug into his left ear. "Okay, Jack, let's see what we got."

"You recorded the meeting?"

Justin held aloft his left hand requesting silence while he listened. A moment or two passed, then he began to grin.

"Why, you rascal, Mr. Furlan!" he exclaimed. "You either knew, or at least suspected I was wired, so you zapped me. Probably with a magnetic field hidden in the doorjamb so that when we left, any recording would be erased."

"So we lost it?"

"*Au contraire, mon frere.* My toys are a lot better than his toys! The cassette is shielded in lead, but I just got a signal telling me what he'd tried to do. Nope, I got it all, Jack. Now, let me fast-forward to the phone conversation. I should have been able to pick up both ends. Then you can jump in and translate."

"You're kidding? You recorded both ends?"

"I told you my toys are good. Look, if we can read a license plate on a car from thousands of miles out in space, this, my good fellow, is a piece of cake." He then turned serious. "What language was Furlan speaking when he got on the phone?"

O'Bryan shook his head. "Not sure. Hebrew, maybe Yiddish."

"Damn! No wonder he didn't try to conceal anything. He knew he'd erase any tape recording before we left, and he was cocksure we wouldn't understand a word, anyway. Chalk one up for Klaus Furlan."

O'Bryan didn't miss a beat as he drove into increasingly heavier traffic. "No sweat, Justin. Let's stop at the Vatican's consular office so I can call Rome and play it to one of my pals in the archives. Those eggheads speak every language known to man. Good chance we can have a translation before we have to call *Herr* Director back at four."

"Good man. I knew I was one smart fellow for dragging you along. Go find the consulate, Jack; time's a wasting."

But O'Bryan was slightly troubled. "Let's hope we do get the answer before four, Justin, because something mighty important took place with that phone call for him to change his mind so fast."

* * *

O'Bryan came up a winner on the first roll of the dice.

They had marched into the Vatican's consular office where O'Bryan displayed his credentials and requested a secure line to Rome. Within minutes he was talking to a friend in the library.

"So play it already." Simon Chertoff was a man of few words. He was scholar on loan from The University of Tel Aviv, his specialty being Hebrew manuscripts dating back to antiquity. The Vatican Library was the world's foremost repository of such documents, and Simon Chertoff was happily spending his days rooting among its treasure-laden shelves.

"You might have difficulty because of the quality of the recording, Simon," O'Bryan apologized.

"Jack, just play it, please," replied Chertoff, doing his best to sound exasperated. "I can enhance it if I have to."

After a couple of minutes, Chertoff asked, "Is that it?"

"Yes."

"You were right. It's Yiddish, but a dialect that hasn't been in vogue for over a hundred years. It's still spoken by a few in Western Russia, some in Austria, and by a smattering of souls in the Balkans. Very interesting."

After Chertoff had relayed both sides of the taped telephone conversation he remarked, "Sounds mysterious, Jack. I've got to admit, some of what they said seemed like they were speaking in riddles, so I might not be right-on the money with my translation. You in some kind of trouble?"

No, but I'd appreciate it if you'd keep this under wraps. It's important, and I can't tell you how grateful I am. You're a genius."

"Flattery will get you everywhere, Monsignor. And my lips are sealed. But let me pass along a little something for what it's worth. Rumor here has it that Cardinal Miglianico has been trying to get in touch with you, but that you've disappeared. Might be time for you to call home."

"Thanks for the tip, Simon. I'll be in touch. *Ciao, addio.*"

* * *

They ate lunch at an outdoor, lakeside restaurant that was protected from a stiffening breeze by a ten-foot wall of tempered glass. The balmy, sunny weather of the past two days had fled, dragging in its wake low-scudding clouds, and wind-driven whitecaps to Lake Geneva. A dozen sailboats were about, and two hearty souls dressed in formfitting black neoprene suits were beating their way through the waves on windsurfer boards.

They dined in silence, taking in the scenery on the last day of summer. Chertoff's translation of the tape had given them much to think about.

Justin ended their reverie moments after they ordered coffee.

"You know," he said, "this is one of those times when a good Cuban cigar sure would be welcome, Jack. To just sit back and puff away while the old brain searches for answers." He looked across to O'Bryan who was still seemingly a million miles away. "You with me, lad?"

"I'm here." O'Bryan stared at Justin. "So, do we tell Mr. Furlan up-front that we know he's having us followed?" That nugget had come from Chertoff, along with more telling information. But it was the least of their newfound problems.

"Yeah, we'll lay down the law when we see him later, but we now know from your pal that he's worried about where this thing's heading. Apparently it didn't take them long to realize that they'd stumbled into a hornets' nest after they'd hired on with Maritha. But once they did, all they wanted was to get the hell away from her as fast as possible. And when the lady was taken out, they probably thought they were home free. Then we showed up. They've got to be scared witless."

"I'd love to get a look-see at those photos," mused O'Bryan. "Whoever was on the other end of the line more than suggested they should have burned them along with the rest of the file."

Justin smiled thinly. "Maybe you don't want to see them, *Padre.* Maybe they really are bad news, and maybe *Ibel & Laufenburg* knows that if certain people should learn of their existence, they could all end up like Maritha. Now that would get my attention if I were in their shoes. No, Jack, they see us as a couple of loose cannons, too stupid to know what we're getting into, and, by default, dragging them over the edge of the cliffs with us."

"At least they seem to know something about Maritha's mother, and that'll be a big help if we can manage to get to her. The guy hinted that her continued well-being was crucial to their survival, which sounds to me like there's some sort of heavy-duty blackmail involved."

Justin shook his head. "Remember my advice earlier about jumping to conclusions, Jack? It could be something entirely different. We'll just have to wait to see how it plays out." He tossed a wad of crumpled notes in the direction of his plate and pushed back his chair. "Let's take a stroll and work off this grub. It'll be good for the guys following us to get some exercise."

* * *

CHAPTER 15

They arrived at *Ibel & Laufenburg* at four-thirty. Justin had decided to say nothing about being followed, reasoning that he didn't want to tip his hand and acknowledge that he had successfully recorded the previous meeting.

Furlan opened the door while they were still climbing the steps, and immediately led them to the room on the second floor.

"The bank closed at three today, so we will not be disturbed."

Both Americans were puzzled by the comment.

"There's a bank in the building?" Justin asked.

"There's been a bank here for the past eighty years. It was founded by Messrs. Ibel and Laufenburg to protect the assets of a dozen wealthy Russian families just before the outbreak of The Great War. Both had emigrated from Russia some five years earlier. They had sensed the future; and the future proved them right. Ours is a private bank called *Credit Lausanne*. Over the years we've maintained a constant twelve clients. If and when any should leave or die, another on a long waiting list is discreetly invited to take his place. That is why they have come to be known amongst the staff as the twelve apostles."

"And is it still just Russians who avail themselves of your services?" Justin asked, enthralled with this new knowledge. It was so typically Swiss.

Furlan shook his head. "Not exclusively. We now represent a couple of other nationalities, mostly because of marriages, but the number of clients remains at twelve, and the majority are still Russians."

"Did you ever uncover a Judas Iscariot?" Justin asked, humorously, as they walked into the sitting room.

"What a prescient question, Mr. Scott." The reply came not from Furlan, but from a man seated at the desk in the alcove. He rose as the trio entered, and came forward to meet them. He appeared to be about forty, with a rugged complexion, powerful build. He was dressed as though headed for the mountains. "I'm Count Rudolph Laufenburg," he said with an unmistakable emphasis on the title. He shook hands with a grip that could have bent iron. "Yes, we did uncover a Judas Iscariot, Mr. Scott, but that was long before my time. His name was Iosif Vissarionvich Dzhugashvili. However, that would mean nothing to either of you." His eyes betrayed a slight smugness; his face a veil not quite hiding his contempt.

As he sized up the count, Justin realized he was the man Furlan had spoken to on the phone earlier.

"Like most, we're more familiar with his other name: Joseph Stalin," O'Bryan said, holding out his hand.

Dolph bowed slightly. "*Touché*, Monsignor. How stupid of me to forget you hold a doctorate in international affairs. Of course you would know of such things."

"Was Mrs. von Snellenberger ever one of the apostles?" Justin asked.

"No, Mr. Scott. She was the wife of a banker, so she did not have need of our services. However, I'm not telling tales out of school when I say that her husband's bank had been experiencing some difficulties in the not so distant past." The count took a seat and, seemingly as an afterthought, beckoned with an imperious wave for the others to follow suit. He glanced quickly at Furlan, gave a slight shrug, and continued. "However, as you suspected, she did indeed come to *Ibel & Laufenburg*. The investigators, not the bankers. So, in the interest of clearing up any misunderstanding from this morning, we have decided to tell you what we can of our brief relationship with the lady. And believe me, it's not much."

Justin knew that the condescending tone was meant to convey the feeling that the count had more productive endeavors to follow than to waste his precious time with two boorish Americans. He refused to be baited. "Please go on."

The count made a deliberate show of studying the face of his expensive Patek. "I must be brief as I have to leave shortly. I'm supposed to go hiking with some fellow enthusiasts."

He turned to Furlan. "Would you be so kind and get the folder while I begin?"

Furlan gave a slight bow as he embarked on the mission for the man who was obviously his master.

Laufenburg began to explain. "Mrs. von Snellenberger suspected her husband of infidelity. That is why she came to us. They had been married for a little over a year when quite suddenly, and for no apparent reason, her husband's amorous attentions suddenly ceased. He had become short-tempered, and was spending more and more time away from home on business. And he'd started drinking heavily. Maritha was devastated. She had waited until she was in her late twenties to marry, you understand, and she very much wanted to start a family. Now it looked as though her marriage was falling apart. She was aware that the bank had been going through difficult times of late, but she had been told repeatedly that it was but a passing downturn. Things would soon return to normal, he told her. But she was not so easily convinced."

"Why not believe him?" asked Justin. "A business reversal is a very real reason for anyone to become agitated and withdrawn, and from everything I've been told of Mrs. von Snellenberger, she seemed to be the type of wife who would rally behind her husband in difficult times."

Laufenburg nodded his agreement of that assessment. "For richer, or for poorer, and so forth? So true. Anyway, she went on to mention several small things, things I need not recite chapter and verse in order to set the stage. Suffice to say events were such that in her mind she had reason to suspect there might be another woman in her husband's life. That is why she came to *Ibel & Laufenburg*. And, I must stress, she was mortified in feeling the need to be driven to do so."

Furlan came back carrying an accordion file which he handed to Laufenburg. The count placed it by his feet and continued. "I'm the one who took her case, assuring her that I would get her an answer, good-or-bad, quickly, and quietly. If worse came to worst, I assured her there would be no scandal. If a divorce was inevitable, then I told her our lawyers would handle it if she so chose. But I tried to be upbeat, telling her that in all probability Mr. von Snellenberger was not engaged in any dalliance, but that simple business pressures were the cause of his preoccupation. I suspected at the time she thought I was just being kind, but that was truly not the case. I fervently hoped I was right. I couldn't bear to see such a woman hurt." He stared defiantly at them both. "Would that I had met Maritha von Snellenberger ten years earlier. How different both our lives might have been."

He scooped the folder up from the floor, placed it on his lap, and extracted a sizeable manila envelope. "Three weeks later I was able to report back with my findings. They were what she had prayed for. Her husband was indeed telling the truth. You see, I followed him on three trips, and each was indeed strictly business. There were no trysts, nothing untoward whatsoever. On all three occasions he met only with businessmen, and on all three occasions I was able to take photos. The pictures were snapped in three different cities, and all with telephoto lenses. I assured the lady that no one was aware that I had done so. I showed her the pictures, explained in detail the settings and circumstances for each, and pointed out that at no time were any women present. I also told her that I had monitored his hotels, and could truthfully report that he always retired alone." Laufenburg sighed as he recounted the last. He'd obviously been smitten by the exquisite Maritha.

He continued. "Well, she was elated. She began crying, apologizing for wasting my time, thoroughly embarrassed that she had thought the worst of her spouse. I told her I was pleased to be the bearer of such good tidings, and reiterated that no one would ever hear of her doubts. Then I showed her these photos." He divided a dozen or so 3x5 color glossies into two piles, then handed one to Justin, the other to O'Bryan.

The Americans studied the photos intently, Justin taking a little longer with each print. The photos revealed groups engaged in intense conversations in disparate settings. There were a total of eight men pictured, but never all together in any one frame. Some of the shots were taken in restaurants; a couple in quiet corners of hotel lobbies; several at outdoor cafés. They were as the count described. Although it was a different grouping at each session, in all the pictures the same four men were conspicuously present; the husband, and three others.

"Any chance we could get a copy of these?" O'Bryan asked.

The count shook his head. "I would rather not. I offered them to Mrs. von Snellenberger, but she wisely declined. She reasoned that she had no need for the pictures because her questions had been answered. She did not want the possibility of her husband coming across them and knowing she had spied on him. As I mentioned a moment ago, she was embarrassed. These are the only copies. Even the negatives have been destroyed. To be honest, I should have done away with these at the same time. I don't know why I didn't. But that's what I intend to do as soon as we're finished here. The case is closed, gentlemen, and that's the extent of my firm's relationship with the late Mrs. von Snellenberger."

Laufenburg dug into the folder and extracted a single sheet of paper which he offered to Justin. It was printed in German, but Justin could see it was some sort of a final bill. And in the lower right hand corner was Maritha's copperplate signature written in that unusual purple ink. He handed it back.

"When I learned of her death, it saddened me beyond words," the count said. He glanced at his watch as if willing the passage of time to exorcise the fond memories of Maritha von Snellenberger he still carried.

"Did she inquire about any of the men in these photos?" Justin asked as he handed his set back to Laufenburg. "Did she seem to recognize anyone?"

The count stiffened, but only for a moment. He shifted uncomfortably in his seat and looked quickly at Furlan before answering. "She never said, but, yes, I could tell from her expression as she studied the pictures that she did. None of the faces were familiar to me, and, of course, I had not been hired to uncover their identities." He indicated that the meeting had ended by placing the folder on the floor. He stood. "Now you know all that we know, gentlemen. As I said, it really was much ado about nothing."

"One last question," Justin said. "Do you know how or where we might find Catherine Ibel?"

Count Laufenburg was brought up short by the mention of the name. *"Catherine Ibel*?" he blurted, genuine puzzlement in his voice. "*Aunt Catherine*?" He shook his head, truly bewildered by the question. "But my aunt's been dead for thirty years. Uncle Martin's the last of the Ibel family still with the firm. He and Catherine had only the one child, a daughter, and she died hours after her birth. My aunt followed her to the grave soon thereafter, dead from despair, her doctors said, and my Uncle Martin never remarried. Why in God's name would you ask about Catherine, Mr. Scott?" Suddenly Count Rudolph Laufenburg realized that to have taken this American for some sort of lightweight had definitely been a mistake. Just what was it he was looking for?

Justin shook his head slowly. "I'm asking about Maritha's mother. That Catherine Ibel."

"Maritha von Snellenberger's maiden name was Ibel, not Furstenburg?"

Justin nodded. This was not the reaction he had expected, but allowed his face to betray nothing.

Rudolph Laufenburg sat heavily, the breath escaping from his lungs in one loud burst. "You're telling me this Catherine Ibel is missing?" He stared helplessly at Furlan, his now-paled face reflecting utter disbelief. He was but a shadow of his pompous, assured self of only a few minutes ago.

Furlan had likewise paled, fast becoming a clone of the confused count. Both had become like fish out of water; mouths spastically opening and closing, each seemingly trying to outperform the other in a desperate but failed attempt to draw a stabilizing breath.

Justin broke the spell. "Look, I have no reason to think those Ibels are in any way related to your family. It's just a coincidence that the name's the same, that's all. The mother's dropped out of sight, and I was wondering if you could point us in the right direction to help find her."

Rudolph turned to his companion and began speaking in a whisper. And in Yiddish. Furlan just stood and listened. When the count finished, he seemed to suddenly remember his visitors. He struggled to his feet, valiant in his attempt to recover his still badly shaken composure.

"You most certainly took us by surprise with that information. We had no idea. However, if we should hear anything as to that Mrs. Ibel's whereabouts, we will get word to you. Now, I really must go. I hope we have been of some help." He held out his hand, willing it with every fiber in his being to remain steady. "As you can see, we had nothing to hide." But his ashen face and wintry smile belied the words. Laufenburg was not a happy man.

"Thank you," Justin replied for them both. "Enjoy the weekend hike, Count Laufenburg."

As earlier, Furlan escorted them to the main door. The meeting had lasted a half-hour.

During the time they had been inside the weather had turned considerably colder, the biting north wind forcing them to scurry for the protective cover of their car. Although barely five o'clock, it was now almost dark.

With O'Bryan again driving, Justin wasted no time testing his recorder. He nodded his satisfaction, then fast-forwarded the tape, searching out the Yiddish words. He gave O'Bryan a thumbs-up, then asked, "What do you say, Jack? We did pretty damn good, huh? You're probably thinking: it's too bad we didn't get to keep the pictures."

Unable to contain himself any longer, Justin let loose an earsplitting whistle, releasing the pent-up energy of the past half-hour. "But we did get 'em, Jack. Click, click, click. I got 'em all with my trusty little three thousand dollar camera hidden in here." He held up his watch for O'Bryan to see. "They're all in there, and they're in digitalized color."

But O'Bryan was not to be persuaded to join in the celebration. "I'm not so sure I want those pictures," he remarked in a low voice full of worry. "At the very least they should have been sealed in Pandora's box. But they weren't, and now we're on a collision course with bigtime trouble."

"Oh, come on, Jack. Relax. Back off the doom and gloom predictions, lad. Have some fun. Let's enjoy our triumph. We've earned it."

O'Bryan pulled the car over to the curb, and shut off the motor. He turned toward Justin and spoke in a flat monotone, his face fully revealing the unease he felt. "I recognized three of the men in those photos. It was the three who were in all the shots along with Maritha's husband."

"Yeah? Well, that's great, Jack. Saves us a whole bunch of time and trouble ferreting out their identities. So, tell me, who are they?"

"The youngest, the pudgy one wearing the double-breasted number and the goofy, plastered-down hairdo? That was Monsignor Ignacio Caffarone, personal secretary to the Holy Father. And the old man that looked like a starving stork? Archbishop Dominico Torrelli, the *numero uno* at the Vatican Bank. And the last one is a guy named Pasquale Sabatini. Rumor has it he's way, way up in the Mafia. We've got big problems, Justin."

Suddenly Justin was no longer the carefree spirit of moments ago. O'Bryan had rudely snatched him from the clouds, and none too gently hurled him back to earth.

"How about the count?" he finally asked. "Despite his denial, do you think he really recognized anyone? No, scratch that. My question should be: Does he suspect that *you* recognized anyone?" He reflected for a moment before asking, "And how about Maritha. Do you think she was able to make those guys?"

"Justin, she lived in Rome for years. Of course she did. She had to have met the two clerics through Kettering, probably dozens of times, and everyone in Italy over the age of two knows who Sabatini really is. He's their John Gotti. Only difference: Sabatini's still alive." O'Bryan looked morose as he posed his own question. "Why would Caffarone and Torrelli be meeting on the sly with these guys, in out of the way places, and dressed in mufti, to boot?" He immediately answered his own question. "Because they didn't want to be recognized. This really sucks." Staring ahead, his face alternating between shadow and light in the headlights of each passing car, he summed up his feelings. "Oh, our Maritha received great news about her husband, all right, but those photographs were somehow her undoing because whatever it was she uncovered, she paid for it with her life." O'Bryan studied his friend. "When you went through the pictures, did you happen to take a good look at the husband's face?" He didn't give Justin a chance to reply. "That was the face of a very worried, very scared man."

Justin sat still and listened while his brain struggled to digest this torrent of information.

O'Bryan allowed him a full minute, then added more grist for the mill. "Both Dolph and Klaus were blindsided by your asking about Maritha's mother. They weren't acting, that's for sure. They really might not have known that her maiden name was Ibel, but I'll bet they could tell us a lot more than they let on. They know something about the mother, and I'll also bet it isn't good. Otherwise, why the sudden need to start jabbering in Yiddish?"

"She could be dead," remarked Justin, still staring out the window, realizing as he spoke that he was disobeying his own counsel to O'Bryan about jumping to conclusions. "Maybe Simon Chertoff misinterpreted what they said on the phone," he suggested, but without conviction. "He did note that they seemed to be talking in riddles, and he emphasized more than once it was an obscure dialect they were using. And he warned us that he could be a little off with his translation. Well, maybe he was a *lot* off!" Justin sighed, then straightened in his seat. "I just don't know. Anyway, it's time I prepared a package to send to Paula. When we get back to the hotel, I'll download the film, write a short report, microdot the whole kit and caboodle, and deliver it to the Vatican Embassy in Bern. She should get it in the pouch within forty-eight hours. Meanwhile, we don't speak to Miglianico, or anyone else in the Church for that matter, except maybe your pal Simon. It's going to be a long night, so I suggest we find a place to grab a quick dinner then head for the capital."

O'Bryan started the motor, put the car in gear, and eased into a thin line of traffic. It had begun to drizzle, and the gray dampness matched their mood.

"One last thing," O'Bryan said moments later. "Why in God's name did Laufenburg decide to keep a set of the pictures, and not just destroy everything at the same time?"

Justin sighed and shook his head. "Got no answer for that one, Jack. You're right. It doesn't make sense."

Neither man was aware of the voice-activated microphone hidden deep in the back seat, sending information to a recorder wedged behind the spare tire in the trunk.

Later that night its small spool was removed from the Fiat, and quickly whisked away to be heard by anxiously awaiting ears.

* * *

Nestled among the foothills of Rome, in a building strikingly similar to the manor house of *Ibel & Laufenburg,* lights shone from every window on the ground floor. It was five o'clock, Saturday morning.

A young man in his late twenties, already dressed for the day in a conservative double-breasted suit, patted down his slicked-back hair for the umpteenth time, then smartly rapped on the door to a corner office. "Uncle, it's Marcello." Without waiting for a reply, he turned the ornate handle and slipped into the room. "I have a translation of the tape recording," he explained, waving a folder as he approached the seated figure. "There was some trouble with the high-speed transmission from Bern, but we got it all. I've highlighted the important parts."

The old man smiled briefly as he lay a journal in his lap and held out his hand. "No, you tell me what they had to say. I must save these old, tired eyes. Sit, Marcello."

The young man brushed his lips against the back of the proffered hand, then sat. Without a wasted word he summarized the conversations, and ended by pointing out the problem now facing them—namely that Justin had made copies of Laufenburg's photographs. "We know from the recording that the Americans are unaware of the identity of some of the men in the pictures, but they certainly have the resources to find out. However, I must tell you, you were definitely spotted, Uncle."

Marcello stood and patted his head in several places. "But that's not all that's bothering me. It's Laufenburg. I think he too will soon learn the identity of our partners, and when he does, his Russian masters will pull out all the stops to destroy them and us. There's too much at stake to do otherwise."

Again, Marcello's hands shot back up to his head. "Who would ever have thought this would be the result of the von Snellenberger woman stumbling into the arms of *Ibel & Laufenburg*. And all because she suspected her husband of infidelity. Just look at the grief it's caused us."

The old man had been sipping from a cup of hot water as he listened, drawing in little swallows like a sparrow, his black eyes never leaving his nephew's face. He licked his lips, then slowly placed the cup on a side table. He removed the journal and a light-weight cashmere blanket covering his lap, then rose unsteadily to his feet.

"You're right of course. Laufenburg must not be allowed to interfere." The old man let loose a small sigh, then continued. "Truth be told, I rue the day we agreed to do business with the Russians. But we must make the best of a deteriorating situation by staying focused on the grand prize after Russia falls into our hands. The Throne of Peter. So, here's what we'll do. I'll contact our people in St. Petersburg and inform them that they must get rid of Laufenburg. He's their problem; let them handle it. However, the Americans are ours, so I want you to do the honors. But you must act fast before they leave Switzerland. Get the word to our colleague in America to be ready to get rid of the Bateman woman if I deem it necessary. And, lastly, I needn't remind you that all copies of those photographs must be destroyed. Now, help your old uncle across the hall to the chapel. That's a good boy."

The clock on the mantle chimed six. Daylight was still an hour away.

Ten minutes later, dressed in vestments the color of the liturgical season, the old man stood before the altar, closed his eyes and blessed himself. He then whispered in Latin the opening prayer to a two thousand-year-old ritual.

"*Introibo ad altare Dei*…I will go to the altar of God."

With those words, Archbishop Dominico Torrelli began to celebrate the never-ending mystery of the Eucharist.

CHAPTER 16

Justin called Paula. She confirmed that she had received his package and had scanned everything into the computer, including the photos. She asked if he had an idea when they'd be coming home.

"Soon. We've just about wrapped things up here. There's one more stop I'd like to make."

Paula made a suggestion. "Justin, how about seeing if you can locate the clinic where Maritha and her husband had been treated for infertility? It'll only delay your return by one day; two at most, but it could pay handsome dividends."

"Why? What do we gain?" Justin wanted to know.

"Samples of blood, semen, maybe even a fertilized egg. We can run our own DNA tests to prove that Maritha's husband was the father. As long as he remains missing, I don't see any other way to get the material we need."

Justin relayed her suggestion to O'Bryan who was standing beside him, and asked the priest for his guidance. They were tiptoeing into uncharted territory here, and Justin was well aware of the Church's position regarding *in vitro* fertilization. To avail oneself of this method of conception was anathema to a Catholic. Indeed, Kettering had told Justin and O'Bryan how he had expressed his displeasure with Maritha when she informed him of what she had done.

O'Bryan answered slowly. "If all you collect is a blood sample, then I can agree. But if the only material available is either semen or fertilized eggs stored in liquid nitrogen, then my answer is an emphatic no. We would be destroying a human being, and I cannot allow that to happen. And even if I did, know Kettering would rightfully turn his back on the lot of us. Those are my conditions. Can you agree to that?"

Justin nodded. "I'd be less than truthful if I said we don't need a fertilized egg," he said. "Genetic markers from that source would go a long way in establishing a match to the fetus directly from Maritha, but, yes, even if all we recover is blood, we can live comfortably with that." He pursed his lips, then added, "But I don't know that I'll be able to locate the clinic; it's a long-shot at best. Got to run. We'll see you soon. Bye."

Paula hung up, gathered the photos Justin had taken, and put them in an envelope. Because of the conditions under which they had been shot, several frames were off center; two were out of focus; at least half held a partial image of Justin's right hand.

She made a note to remind him to take them over to Kettering when he got back to see if the cardinal could identify any of the men.

* * *

As Justin lay in bed later that night, his mind kept going over Paula's suggestion. He was doubtful of success, suspecting that the Swiss guarded such secrets with the same efficiency as they did numbered bank accounts. He rolled over and punched his pillow. He had promised Paula to think about it, and he would.

* * *

It took several moments for Valerie to realize that the ringing was coming not from inside her head, but from the phone on the nightstand. With a bobbing, open hand she reached out blindly, made contact, and picked it up. She was still in a twilight state: too groggy for anger; too dulled to resent her husband's blissful snoring.

"Tobias, here, and it better be good," she warned the caller in a loud whisper.

"Inspector Tobias?" The voice had a tentative quality, as though the speaker was not happy to be calling.

"Speaking." She shook her head slightly to focus her brain, perplexed at not recognizing the voice. "Who's this?"

"Sergeant Avery, Atlantic City P.D., Inspector. I've got a problem I'd like to shut down before it goes any further. I'm putting my head on the block as it is."

She was wide-awake now. The bedside clock told her in bold red numbers it was 4:15 a.m., smaller letters announced the day was Saturday. She squinted. Wrong. It said Sunday. She was off for the weekend. *Couldn't someone else handle this?*

"What have you got, Sergeant Avery?" She deliberately used his name to reinforce her memory.

"A guy here who should be booked on a D and D, Inspector. The only reason I don't have him on ice already is that he claims to be one of yours. And unless they're stolen, his badge and credentials confirm it."

She quickly sat up, and with her left hand wrestled impatiently with the covers, freed her legs, got up, and stood by the side of the bed. Drunk and Disorderly. Dammit!

"He's a Lieutenant Tom Braddock, and he's one nasty son of a bitch. We pulled him in for beating the snot out of a bar patron, and for tossing around a couple of my guys before they could subdue him. It wasn't until he was being booked that we ID'd him. He dared us to call you for a confirmation, so that's what I'm doing. He's a first-class prick with an attitude, Inspector."

"Please describe your man, Sergeant."

"I'll do better than that. Hold on. You can talk to him yourself."

A second later Braddock came on the line.

"It's a bullshit, setup charge, Val. I was ...."

"Shut up, Tom. Just put Avery back on."

"I take it he's one of yours, Inspector?" Avery said.

"I should just tell you to throw the book at him, Sergeant," she replied, her voice dripping with disgust.

Avery waited a second or two before replying. "That what you want me to do?"

She sighed. "No. Not that he doesn't deserve it, but if a newspaper reporter covering your night beat picks up his name from your booking sheet, or from the arraignment proceedings later this morning, then all hell will break loose here in metro. For starters, the chief will have my ass, and God only knows what he'll do to Braddock. Probably fire him, at the very least." She paused for a few seconds while pacing in the dark, then said, "Get the idiot out of earshot, okay? I'd like us to talk freely, one-on-one."

She heard Avery give a command for someone to take Braddock to an office and hold him pending further instructions. She clearly heard him tell the officer not to start the paperwork for the booking process. He came back on the line.

"Okay, Inspector, spell out what you want done."

"Was he carrying his piece?"

"Nah, just his badge and credentials. Probably stashed his service revolver in his car. Smart move for such a dumb ass. He got caught in any of our casinos carrying a piece, wouldn't mean jack that he's a lieutenant in D.C."

"Is he still shit-faced?"

"Not *too* bad, Inspector, but I wouldn't recommend him driving for a while."

She thought the situation over. "Can you put him in a hotel with orders not to checkout until noon? Tell him I want him to get a time-dated receipt when he leaves. Then have him shag his butt back here with instructions to be in my office at nine Monday morning."

She continued. "I'll dock him a week's pay, but in such a way so as not to leave an official paper trail. I'll send you his personal check made out to your favorite charity. I'll write up a report, but I'll hold it from his file for six months. If he stays out of trouble for that length of time, then I'll destroy it. If not, I throw the book at him. That's my promise to you, Sergeant Avery." She lowered her voice. "He's only two years away from getting in his twenty," she explained, hoping that Avery would understand. "I fully expect you to make a report, but I ask that you hold it from going any further. I'll call you six months from now, and if Braddock's kept his nose clean, maybe you could agree to destroy yours. I know I'm asking a lot, so it's your call, Sergeant Avery."

"Well, my guys weren't roughed-up too bad. You know, more a case of wounded pride than wounded heads. I guess we can keep a lid on it here. As to the charity thing, yeah, have him make out a check to the American Cancer Society. I understand if you officially dock his pay then there's got to be a potful of explanations. So, if he's not totally brain-dead, he should get down on both knees and thank God he's got you for a boss. It should work, Inspector."

"Thanks, Sergeant. I owe you."

"Not you, ma'am. Him. One last thing, though. When you see him, tell the turkey to stay the hell out of my town from now on, okay? Goodnight, Inspector."

She sat on the side of the bed, fingers drumming rhythmically on the top of the phone now resting in her lap, staring at the nothingness of a barely visible wall.

Damn Tom Braddock to hell. He was spinning out of control. Wouldn't see twenty at this rate. Just what in the hell had gotten into him lately? She was wide-awake now and fully working herself into a foul mood.

It was only a few days ago that Maria Delgado had alerted her to his most recent bout of heavy drinking. Well, thirty hours from now she fully intended to come down on him with both feet. This shit had to stop. She put the phone back on the stand and climbed back into bed. Avery was right. Braddock could be an obnoxious prick at times.

CHAPTER 17

The day dawned cold but brilliantly clear. Gone were the rain and wind of the last twenty-four hours. This was the picture postcard Switzerland.

O'Bryan had celebrated Sunday mass in his room an hour ago, and now both men were on the streets of Gagny, a small town at the foothills of the Alps. Justin had decided to relocate there the previous evening, and they had settled into a quaint bed-and-breakfast dominating the northeast corner of the main square. Gagny—the place the von Snellenbergers called home—was minutes from Bern.

"It'll be a scouting expedition," Justin had explained. "We'll just be following our noses."

They walked the spotless streets of the residential district, and twice passed the von Snellenberger mansion. There was nothing to indicate that anyone was there. No smoke drifting upward from chimneys, no cars on the pristine gravel driveway behind the tall iron gates. But the absence of activity did not necessarily mean that no one was in residence. They kept walking, and after twenty minutes headed back to the commercial district.

At eleven o'clock they were treated to a joyous outburst from the carillons of the town's churches, all telling of Sunday worship taking place inside Gothic walls.

They were marking time until the restaurants and sidewalk cafés opened. The day was getting noticeably warmer.

During their stroll, Justin said that he didn't think the task Paula had suggested was doable.

"And all this time I thought you were Superman."

"Not in Switzerland, I ain't, and definitely not on Sundays. If I were home and still with the bureau, it'd be a piece of cake. But not here. No neat little telephone directory tricks to fall back on this time. The process would take weeks. I'm just going to have to tell Paula: No can do."

"Are you implying that you did your share of breaking and entering when you were with the government?" O'Bryan pretended to be flabbergasted. "The legendary Mr. Hoover condoned such goings-on?"

"You don't want to know the half of it," Justin said.

"Did you ever meet Mr. Hoover?"

"Several times, but like every other agent, I went out of my way to stay the hell out of his. He was tough, and everybody in and out of the bureau was scared to death of him." Justin smiled at the thought. "When I joined, you had to be either a lawyer or an accountant, and it was a definite plus if you were also Catholic and Irish. The boss died when I was still a pup." Justin was on a leisurely stroll down memory lane.

"There were no women agents in those days, so when we needed female decoys we simply shanghaied them from the steno pool. We were true-blue all the way, tough as nails, as honest as all get-out, and respected by everybody. Mr. Hoover would have it no other way. Everybody was afraid of the guy, including presidents. He had the goods on all of 'em, and they knew it!" Justin shook his head in wonderment of the memories.

"After the old man died, things changed," he said, a hint of genuine sadness in his voice. "Women came on board, standards were lowered, and more than one agent turned traitor. That rotten bastard Bob Hanssen is only the latest, sad to say. Then suddenly-brave people began badmouthing the director. Stories floated that he had been a closet gay, that he had enjoyed wearing frilly silk party dresses on special occasions. Some damn nasty things were written about him, too, including stuff that he helped railroad innocent men. But none were proven. There'll never be another Mr. Hoover, Jack. Never!"

"Justin, I don't even know if you're married. Was it allowed?"

"It was damn near a job requirement. Hoover was always promoting the image of the family man even though he never got hitched himself. Yeah, I got married the week I graduated law school. Sally and I never had kids, and about three years ago we drifted apart. We're not divorced, and we've remained friends. She even gave me this sweatshirt for Christmas," he announced proudly, opening his windbreaker and displaying a Notre Dame University jersey.

"I'm sorry it didn't work out," said O'Bryan.

Justin shrugged. "That's life."

There were now knots of people descending on the square, and Justin suggested they find a table before all were taken. The temperature was rising, so the thought of eating outdoors was pleasant and welcome. They agreed on the small café right outside their inn, ordered coffee, and studied the menu.

It was forty minutes later, after they had doffed their jackets and had been talking about everything and nothing, that O'Bryan leaned toward Justin and remarked that the two women facing them from the table in the corner seemed to be showing undue interest in him. "They don't know you're still a married man, you old reprobate," he kidded. "Look up slowly. See for yourself. They can't take their eyes off of you, especially the one with the dark hair." O'Bryan chuckled, enjoying teasing his friend. "God only knows what they see in you."

"Good taste always shows, sonny," replied Justin, drawing himself up just a tad. He turned casually in the direction of the women. They realized that he had seen them, and unabashedly burst out laughing. Justin's face turned a deep red and he busied himself pretending to drink from his long-emptied cup.

O'Bryan began to laugh, then cut it short. "Oh, oh, buddy, they're heading this way. What are you going to do now?"

They approached Justin, one on each side of his chair, both grinning broadly. The one with the dark hair spoke.

"Forgive us for staring and laughing so rudely. We apologize for our behavior, but, please, let me explain. You are both Americans, no?"

"Guilty," replied Justin.

"It's your shirt," the older woman explained in perfect English but with a pronounced German accent. She pointed a manicured finger in the direction of Justin's chest. "You see, I first saw one of those shirts last June, worn by a man right over there," she explained, now pointing toward a café on the opposite side of the small square.

"I asked him if he had purchased the shirt at the cathedral, you know, *Notre Dame,* in Paris. I had never seen one before, and I was infatuated with the thought that they were now selling such things." She laughed. "Well, he explained that it was from a university in America. I felt so stupid. But he was a very nice man, and he told me all about his Notre Dame. He said he had been a footballer there, a long time ago, but that he now was just an old man who still loved his alma mater."

Both women smiled, pleased at the innocence of their confession. "So, when I saw your shirt from Notre Dame, I just had to reminisce with my daughter."

The Americans stood and Justin motioned for the women to please sit. Without being asked, the waiter suddenly appeared with four coffees. His fawning suggested that the women were well-known, and well-liked patrons.

Justin introduced O'Bryan and himself as businessmen in town for the day, and in return the older woman made their introduction. Diana and Leslie Steiner, mother and daughter. All four shook hands.

Justin studied the women casually as they prepared their drinks. And he had thought they were sisters. He could now see that one was indeed quite a bit older than the other, but admitted to himself that he would never have suspected mother and child. This is how Maritha might have looked fifteen or sixteen years from now, he thought, sadly.

"Our *Notre Dame* is probably the most famous university in America, with the possible exception of Harvard," O'Bryan explained. "But, I've got to admit, your idea of selling sweat shirts in all of the world's great cathedrals is intriguing, to say the least."

The mother laughed a deep, sultry, Marlene Dietrich laugh. "Of course, the best one in any collection would have to come from St. Peter's in Rome!"

Leslie spoke up. "The man last summer offered to give mama his shirt, but she said no. She told me later that she really wanted it, though." The daughter was enjoying tattling on her mother, but the woman just laughed at the disclosure.

"Ah, he was nice," Diana said. "He said he was a friend of Mr. von Snellenberger, whose wife was killed in America a short while ago. Maritha was a dear friend, and I'll miss her until the day I die." The laughter had faded. "However, the von Snellenbergers were not at home at the time, so the man from America missed visiting with his friend. He was sad."

Something clicked inside Justin's brain. Something the woman had just said moved him into overdrive. What was it?

"This American, was he a banker?" he probed casually as he stirred a large measure of cream into his coffee.

She shook her head, her face taking on an expression suggesting she was trying hard to remember the conversation. "No, he was not a banker, but worked in your capital, I think."

"Would you excuse me for a moment? I'll be right back. Jack, entertain these lovely ladies." Justin smiled, rose, and hurried toward the front door of the inn.

He was back within five minutes. He handed a photograph to the mother. "Is this the man you met?"

She recognized him instantly. "That's him! The one in the front row pointing to his Notre Dame shirt." She turned to Justin, her face aglow. "He's a friend of yours. Ah, look! I see you in this picture also. What a truly small world."

O'Bryan leaned over and looked at the photograph. His heart skipped a beat. The man in the picture was the police lieutenant from Washington who was working the murder case. Lieutenant Tom Braddock. It was the photo of the group of Washington police officers taken at the April barbecue get-together. He looked up at Justin who immediately shook his head ever so slightly, and pursed his lips at the same time indicating that he didn't want O'Bryan to say a word.

Justin handed the woman a second photo; a head and shoulders close-up of Braddock dressed in a business suit. She nodded again. "Oh, yes, that's the same man. What was his name?" she asked, her smooth forehead now suddenly lined with furrows.

"Tom?"

"That's it! Tom Braddock from Washington, the capital of America. How could I have forgotten?" Her face radiated pleasure at the sudden remembrance of the man's full name.

"Are you sure he wasn't here in August?" Justin asked, nonchalantly retrieving the pictures and placing them inside his coat's pocket still draped over his chair.

She shook her head. "Positive. Late June; early July at the latest. I remember, because we were going to our home in the south of France for two months and I had some last minute shopping to do. That's how I ran across your friend. I was not here for most of July, and not at all in August, so it had to have been the end of June."

Leslie asked, "Do you know the von Snellenbergers?"

Justin replied without missing a beat. "No. When our friend Tom Braddock heard we were coming to Bern on business, he asked if we would stop in Gagny and offer his condolences to Mr. von Snellenberger. We've never met either of them," he added, truthfully.

"Such a terrible thing," said Diana, eyes welling as she spoke. "Maritha had so much to live for. She was positively ecstatic when she realized she was pregnant. She had confided in me that she had gone to a fertility clinic for help, so she truly saw her pregnancy as a miracle."

"You were a close friend?" O'Bryan asked.

"Our family lives directly across the street. My husband and Freddy—we never called him Manfred—have been chums since they were little boys. I met Maritha for the first time shortly before the wedding, and we just clicked. Is that how you say it? Ah, they were so happy. Now Maritha's dead, and Freddy's vanished. It's like a Greek tragedy. But, unfortunately, at the end of this play the actors don't get to take bows in front of the audience, smile, then go home."

"So Mrs. von Snellenberger said that the treatment she received at the clinic here in Bern had worked?"

The woman appeared puzzled by Justin's question. She shook her head emphatically. "No, no. The Antonni clinic in Bern specializes in rejuvenation therapy. You know, injecting fetal tissue into old people, that sort of thing. Rumor has it that Pope Pius XII was a frequent patient in the 1950s. Of course, in those days they used monkey glands, sheep glands, that kind of stuff. Ugh!" She involuntarily wrinkled her nose at the very thought. "Maritha certainly didn't need that. She went to the other Antonni clinic; the one specializing in fertility problems. The one in *Milano.* And, yes, they definitely performed a miracle."

"Do you think Cardinal Kettering killed her?" Leslie blurted out. "The papers all say they were lovers!"

Out of the mouths of babes ... thought Justin, as he answered her. "I sure hope not, Leslie. It would make a terrible tragedy that much worse to have a cardinal involved." He picked up the bill and handed it to O'Bryan. "I still don't understand the money here, so you do the honors." He turned to the women. "We certainly enjoyed meeting you, ladies, but we must be getting back to Bern. I'll let Tom Braddock know that we met you. He'll sure get a kick out of that. Especially when we remind him about the *Notre Dame* shirt story."

Again, all four shook hands. The Steiners left arm in arm. As soon as they were out of earshot, O'Bryan bombarded Justin with questions. "What in the name of all that's holy does it mean? Why would Lieutenant Braddock be here posing as a friend of the von Snellenbergers just weeks before Maritha was murdered?"

"Don't know, Jack. Oftentimes it's plain old serendipity that changes the course of history. Those innocent, seemingly inconsequential happenings, which suddenly open a firmly locked door leading in turn to something entirely new. In our case, a new focus for a murder investigation. Meeting those women just now was a textbook example of serendipity."

"What comes next?"

"We pack, and head to Bern. I want to get a message to Paula telling her we're on our way home. It's time for a major powwow. We might have to come back to Switzerland in a couple of days, but this could be the big break we've been praying for. It's only a hunch, but my gut's telling me things won't be the same from here on out. And all because of a spur-of-the-moment decision to wear my *Notre Dame* sweatshirt. Serendipity, Jack."

* * *

They realized something was wrong the moment they entered the embassy. A civilian secretary escorted them to a small, sterile office and instructed them to wait for the duty officer. O'Bryan had shown his diplomatic credentials, said they were on official business, and had asked to use the secure line to Washington.

They were informed rather coldly that they would have to wait for someone in authority. No apologies for any inconvenience, just a command to wait.

It was not the duty officer who finally arrived but rather the chief-of-staff, Monsignor Allenby. They had met Allenby a few days before, and all had shared a good laugh at how a man with such a very proper British name was really a Swiss native with roots going back untold generations. On that occasion Allenby had even persuaded them to stay for tea, and had charmed his visitors with stories of life working for the Pope's representative in Bern.

But not now. There were no smiles as he entered the room. He acknowledged their presence with a nod as he silently handed a slip of paper to O'Bryan. The priest read it quickly, then passed it to Justin.

The message was short and to the point. It had been transmitted a few hours earlier from Rome, and was in the form of a general information bulletin sent to all the Vatican's embassies and consulates throughout Europe. Simply stated, Monsignor Jack O'Bryan was not to be permitted access to the communications facilities at any legation on the continent. His credentials had been revoked by Cardinal Miglianico, and the only accommodation allowed would be for a staff officer to place a call on his behalf to the secretary of state. If the monsignor would not cooperate, then he was to be escorted from the premises.

Allenby relaxed a trifle. "Monsignor, I don't know what it is you've done or not done, but if you want to speak to Cardinal Miglianico, I will place the call right now. If not, then I have no choice but to follow instructions. However, nothing was mentioned about relieving you of your diplomatic credentials, so I won't ask you to turn them over." Allenby was uncomfortable at having to be the bearer of such tidings. "Shall I place the call, Monsignor?"

O'Bryan looked at Justin, and the older man shook his head. "That won't be necessary," O'Bryan replied. "Just inform the cardinal's office that we're returning to America, and that His Eminence can contact me there if it so pleases him."

Both turned on their heels and walked out of the legation.

* * *

They had called the airport before meeting Allenby, and had booked the last Swissair flight to Washington. They would be airborne all night, touching down at Dulles Airport at 9:34 a.m.

As they made their way to the Fiat, Justin asked for the keys. "I'll drive, *Padre.* What's the best way to the airport?"

"Straight out this road to the autobahn, then follow the signs. It's an easy run, and we've got a ton of time."

After a few minutes of driving in silence, Justin shot a sideways glance over to O'Bryan. "You upset at Allenby? The man was only following orders; nothing personal."

"No, I've got no beef with Allenby," O'Bryan replied. "It's Miglianico. I'm beginning to wonder if maybe he's been involved with the bad guys all along. Maybe he's using me, and I've been either too proud or too stupid to have figured it out."

"Could be," Justin said as he floored the accelerator to propel the car up the entrance ramp. He wanted to be moving at the same clip as the highway traffic when it came time to merge.

He did not notice the Volvo several hundred feet back also ease up onto the ramp, it's driver taking pains not to close the distance between them.

"Let's not worry about Miglianico for now," Justin said. "We've had a helluva successful trip, and Kettering and Paula are going to be dancing in the aisles when we tell them what we've got. So cheer up, buckaroo, and that's an order."

O'Bryan found himself forced to smile. "Yeah, you're right, Justin. Screw Miglianico."

Justin laughed. "Atta boy. Now you're back in the groove. Screw Miglianico." As he spoke, he craned his neck to better read an overhead sign as it flashed by. He swung the car into the right lane and headed for the off-ramp.

and a car cruising in the middle lane abruptly swung right, slowed, and followed him, its driver mindful to maintain his distance.

It took O'Bryan a second or two to figure out what Justin was up to. He let out a laugh. "Wrong exit, old man," he said, with feigned exasperation. "The sign didn't say 'exit here' *dummkopf*, it said, '*next exit to airport.*'" As he spoke, a loud clap of thunder shook the car and the skies opened up. The sudden sound startled him. "Where'd that come from?"

Within seconds Justin was blinded by the torrent. He tapped the brakes until the car had slowed to a crawl. The wipers were pathetically ineffectual as they struggled from side to side. Already the windows were starting to cloud up. He fiddled with the defogger, but other than hearing a lot of noise, realized he couldn't see any better than before. He used his right hand to clear a spot on the windshield, then cracked his window in the hope that fresh air would help. He inched his way toward the on-ramp only to come face to face with two huge concrete barricades blocking his path. Despite the deluge, it was impossible not to see the same message written on both.

O'Bryan spoke up in a cheeky voice. "It says, '*detour, follow the arrows.*'"

Justin managed a grin in the glow of the panel lights. "Sure glad I brought you along." He followed several more signs which led him further away from the highway, and after three turns, realized that there were no more signs and that his sense of direction had vanished. He was hopelessly lost.

He was about to comment on their predicament when a wooden arm lowered eerily out of the darkness a few yards ahead. Red lights began to flash on both the descending barricade and the now suddenly-visible pillars at the side of the road. Bells started to clang. A car pulled up behind them and stopped. Its driver courteously dimmed his lights.

"If I were back in the good old U.S. of A, I'd bet that sound meant a train's soon coming round the mountain, Jack." Justin's words were lost in a blast from the locomotive's horn. "What do ya know, it *is* a train. Well, I'll be!"

They saw the high-powered lamp cut a pathway through the rain, shaking them in their seats as it let loose another long blast. It appeared to be flying down the tracks.

A flash of movement in the rear-view mirror caught Justin's eye. He braced himself. The lone car behind them suddenly bolted forward, smashing hard into their rear. In a heartbeat Justin knew what it meant. O'Bryan's head snapped backward, then immediately forward, but his seatbelt pulled him up short, the webbing grabbing him violently across his chest, knocking the air out of him. He was stunned into silence by the impact.

Justin slammed on the brakes. The small Fiat's front-end nose-dived, forcing its rear to fly skyward. But momentum still carried it through the barricade, tearing the lighted wooded arm from its mounting like a discarded matchstick which then sailed upward, and disappeared over the roof. The Fiat's rear bumper dropped hard onto the bumper of the car behind. Both cars were now solidly locked, with the Fiat sitting squarely astride the tracks.

"*Holy sweet Jesus, hang on, Jack!*" Justin managed to shout.

The train's horn sounded again, the noise filling every pore of every living thing in its path. It was the sound of the devil's own trumpet welcoming them into eternity.

O'Bryan sat paralyzed and mute, eyes wide and transfixed on the blinding light barreling toward him.

Justin slammed the car into reverse and mashed down on the accelerator. The two cars remained frozen in place, one pushing, the other resisting, both engines screaming as wheels spun on the rain-slicked, oily surface; smoke pouring from smoldering, shredding tires. Justin caught a whiff of the horrible, acrid smell. He thought he heard the horn of the car behind him, but somehow realized it must be his imagination.

His brain bellowed out a command, telling him to go forward. Heeding instinct, he threw the car into low gear and floored it. Freed of backward resistance, the two vehicles bolted forward still locked in an obscene embrace; one pushing, the other pulling, but both now suddenly in concert and both at full throttle.

Light filled the cabin of the Fiat with the intensity of a thousand suns, blinding both men. A protrusion on the locomotive snagged the Fiat by its roof and spun it around with the ease of a toy in the hands of a deranged giant child. Kinetic energy tore the Fiat free of the car behind, catapulting it into the lowered barricade blocking the oncoming lane. It, too, snapped as easily as its twin, and the Fiat came to rest miraculously still upright, its engine screaming, but now facing the track from the opposite direction. Less than five seconds had elapsed from the moment Justin had been rear-ended. He never saw the other car being swallowed into the black maw of the speeding train's undercarriage.

A line of freight cars thundered past, mere inches from their startled faces. Justin felt a rush of wind. He glanced over his shoulder. The entire rear-end of the Fiat was gone. The roof had been shorn off at a point over the back seat, taking with it the rear window, the trunk, back bumper, and both rear quarter-panels. The gas tank had somehow remained intact, still attached to the exposed Fiat's chassis, its fueling pipe sticking up like a forlorn periscope.

Justin heard the train's brakes being applied, and marveled in silence at the shower of multicolored sparks as they cascaded outward in all directions. The fireworks show continued long after the god-awful, ear-splitting screeching of metal-on-metal had begun.

And the rain pummeled down all the harder.

After two failed attempts Justin found reverse gear, and backed away from the tracks. He turned the steering wheel sharply left, spinning the car in a semi-circle, and came to rest with his back to the still-passing train. A car approached head-on, followed by two more, but all three stopped short as Justin's shredded Fiat was caught in the glow of their headlights. He shifted into low gear and crawled away; a half-car disappearing into the night. It was a scene worthy of Dante's Inferno.

And still not a sound from O'Bryan.

Five minutes later, the rain stopped as abruptly as it had started. Justin cruised down an unlit street, slowed, then swung into a weed-choked alley. He had started to giggle and shake uncontrollably, and through a fog fully understood what it meant. He was headed for the edge; going into shock. He had the presence of mind to shut off the engine, then sat in the dark, staring at nothing, hearing nothing.

After an eternity, O'Bryan finally managed to speak, seemingly to himself. He uttered two words. "*Dies Irae.*"

The vaguely familiar Latin phrase brought Justin up short. He frowned. "I've heard that before, Jack. What does it mean?" he asked in a voice barely above a whisper.

"The Day of Wrath. Judgement Day. *Dies Irae* was a poem written by a Franciscan monk in the thirteenth century, and in hair-raising detail it chronicles that which will come to pass after Christ opens those Seven Seals described by St. John the Apostle in the Apocalypse, the last book of the New Testament. Without fail, those two words have always sent a shiver up my spine. They just popped into my head. Somehow they seemed appropriate after what we've just been through."

Justin had no comeback. "*Dies Irae*," he repeated, and as he did, he involuntarily shuddered. O'Bryan's fear of the Day of Wrath was contagious.

* * *

Two hours later they arrived at the airport still riding an adrenaline high. Justin had realized there was no way he was going to return what was left of the Fiat to the rental agency, so he made the decision to abandon it, and had O'Bryan telephone from the airport to report it stolen. He had rented it by showing both a false passport and international driver's license for identification. Even the MasterCard he had used was untraceable.

* * *

The only luggage left in the wreck had been Justin's small carry-on which he had wedged between the front and back seats. Everything else was gone; scattered helter-skelter along the tracks. They had flagged a taxi after walking for thirty minutes, O'Bryan telling the leery driver in German that their car had broken down on the way to the airport. If the man was ever questioned about his peculiar fare that night, he would have nothing of consequence to repeat.

Once inside the terminal they darted to the restroom and cleaned up. After O'Bryan's call to the car rental agency, they went in search of coffee. Neither was hurt, but both were feeling a painful stiffness beginning to invade every joint.

O'Bryan was still rattled. "It couldn't have been a set-up, Justin," he said over a steaming mug. He spoke in a low, scared voice. "We didn't know we'd be at that railroad crossing. We were lost, for God's sake!"

"Relax, Jack. It's over, and we're okay. Look, whoever was in that car probably had orders to shoot us, but when they were presented with an opportunity to see us crushed under a train, they acted on the spur of the moment, and their stupidity killed them. Lucky for us; too bad for them."

"Who do you think put them up to it? Laufenburg? I'm thinking that just maybe I now know why he didn't destroy all of the pictures when he had the chance."

"Yeah, I think it was Laufenburg. Could be the count is cooking up a little blackmail scheme of his own."

"Good thing it wasn't a Mercedes or a Beemer those guys were in," O'Bryan said, his mind in a whirl as he switched topics. "A car the size of either one of those brutes would have bulled us into the train's path no matter what. Would have been curtains."

"Can't find fault with your reasoning there either, Jack. One last thing, though. Let's not tell Paula about this, okay? I don't want her to worry because she already has enough on her plate just trying to get over the death of her husband. We're alive; we're unhurt; and we're oh so very much the wiser. What do you say, Jack? Mum's the word?"

A still shaken O'Bryan looked at his friend and silently nodded.

CHAPTER 18

Valerie arrived at her office to find a nervous Tom Braddock pacing the hall. She entered without speaking or giving a sign to acknowledge his presence, and left him not knowing what to do. She looked at her desk clock. Eight forty-seven. He could damn well cool his heels and stew in his own juices until nine.

Foregoing the ritual of coffee, she scanned the freshly delivered duty summaries, noting that there had only been one homicide in the past forty-eight hours. Wow! That was a first for the year. Then she tackled an Everest of paper scutwork. Schedules had to be approved, transfer requests mulled, disciplinary recommendations vetted, plus a zillion other tedious tasks that only she could do.

Finally, she knew she had to face him.

"Lieutenant Braddock," she called out.

He entered, then stood just inside the doorway.

"Close it, and sit down," she commanded, noting that he looked none the worse from his weekend hijinks. But, she reminded herself, his conduct could hardly be placed in a category one attributes to the misdeeds caused by the exuberance of youth.

His suit was immaculately pressed, his shirt and tie probably brand new, his shoes polished and shined to do a drill sergeant proud. He could have easily passed for a manager-on-the-move at IBM, or any other Fortune 500 company.

She tossed down her pen. "I guess you won't be happy until you're fired and you've taken me down the crapper with you," she began, willing herself to appear every inch the no-nonsense superior she wanted him to see. "Well, you can self-destruct for all I care, buster, but I'll be damned if you're going to try to blame your troubles on me, or anyone else in this department for that matter."

He sat ramrod straight on the edge of his chair; desperate not to reveal the fear he felt within. He fully realized she had the power to fire him, and because of Atlantic City, he didn't doubt for a second that she could make it stick.

"Val ..."

"Inspector Tobias."

"Yes ma'am. Inspector Tobias ..."

"You speak when I tell you to speak, and not until."

"Yes, ma'am."

The adrenaline was now flowing freely, and she no longer had to force herself into a state of agitation. She wasted no time laying into him. "You're out of control, Braddock. You've become a menace to yourself and everyone around you. I sure as shit don't feel that I can count on you anymore, and God forbid one if my officers should ever have to depend on you for backup on the street. You flat-out wouldn't be there, and that poor, unfortunate somebody would be very dead. Well, I've got a news flash for you, pal. *I am not about to let that happen*!"

She got up and began to storm around the room, hammering away at him unmercifully for another five minutes, throwing in his face a veritable litany of his transgressions—some known, some guessed. And when she finally ran out of words, she just glowered at him for another minute, using the time to burn off steam. Then she eased her way into her chair and asked in a suddenly subdued voice, "What am I to do with you, Tom?"

"Permission to speak?"

"Speak."

"First off, Inspector, I'm mortified by my conduct. Being drunk is a pathetic excuse, and I won't patronize you by using it. I've done a lot of thinking over the last twenty-four hours, and you're right. I've reached the same conclusion you have. I'm a runaway roller coaster, and I need help." He took a deep breath, and plunged on. "So, for starters, I'm going to join AA. Like today. I mean, tonight, right after work. Also, no more gambling. No casinos, no penny ante card games, no sports betting, no horses. That's history. It's got to be. I can see that if I don't get a grip, then I'll be out of here on my butt. No twenty, no retirement, no future. If I keep this up, I'll be on skid row in six, dead within twelve. I'm scared of what I've become, Inspector, and I beg you, please, give me a chance to win back your trust." He opened his arms, a pitiful, pleading gesture. "Being a cop is all I know. To lose this is to lose everything. Just let me prove to you that I can be the officer I once was."

She reflected on his plea. She appeared at war with herself, weighing carefully his promises. It was time for her verdict. She began by telling him of the personal check he was to make out to the American Cancer Society, informing him of the amount expected. One week's gross pay, not a penny less.

He only nodded.

Then she explained how she intended to monitor his every move for the next six months. If he screwed up even once, then it was to be curtains. No begging for another chance, no whining about getting in his twenty. Those pleas would fall on deaf ears.

He continued to nod, brushing a hand across his eyes. He did not need to be told how perilously close he had come to termination, and he found himself truly grateful for her compassion. "I won't let you down, Inspector. I promise."

She dismissed him with the reminder to have a check on her desk by the end of his duty day.

Valerie slumped low in her chair, physically and emotionally spent, suddenly shaking from the encounter. "God help me!" It was as much a prayer for divine guidance as a lament for herself. Because if Braddock screwed-up again, then her covering for him would soon become public knowledge, which meant she would in all likelihood sink into the abyss alongside him. Suddenly, she saw her future inexorably intertwined with his, and it made her shudder. How could she have allowed it to happen? Her own job security now hinged on the promises of a drunk. She wanted to cry.

* * *

"Surprise! Look what the cat dragged in." Paula was all smiles as she spotted Justin and O'Bryan entering the conference room.

They wore rumpled clothes and in need of a shave, but their eyes were alert and full of excitement.

"What are you two guys doing here?" she asked. "Sit, sit, tell me what's going on. How come you didn't call?"

"Don't want to even look at a chair," Justin replied. "Been sitting all night. Need to stand and stretch for about four days. Sure could use some coffee, though."

Fifteen minutes later Paula could wait no longer. "Okay, Justin, what gives? Why didn't you call?" she repeated.

Justin, still standing, rolled his eyes as if exasperated at the question. It was strictly for show. "Wanted to, but it seems Miglianico has yanked Jack's diplomatic credentials. We were tossed out of the embassy last night when we tried to phone. Looks like the crowd in Rome has decided to play hardball."

"I've also started to feel their pressure on this end. What else have you got?"

Justin described their meetings at *Ibel & Laufenburg*, lending a personal touch which no written report could duplicate. Next, he told of their chance encounter with the Steiners, and the bombshell the women had dropped about Lieutenant Tom Braddock being in Switzerland several weeks before the murder. He finished by whistling the opening bar of Notre Dame's fight song.

But said nothing about the attempt made on their lives.

* * *

The three studied their folders, and in particular, the pictures of Lieutenant Tom Braddock.

Paula was the first to comment. She peered over the top of her half-frames. "It just doesn't make sense, Justin. To place him there *after* the fact, okay, that I can understand. He's a homicide detective, but *before* the murder?" She was shaking her head. "There's got to be some mistake."

Justin's eyes darted from Paula to O'Bryan, then back to Paula, his face radiating pure joy. "*Mistake*? This is the break we've been waiting for."

"Are you saying that Lieutenant Braddock is the murderer?" Paula asked.

"Heck, no, I'm not saying that at all. The man could have had a very good reason for being in Switzerland before the murder."

Justin didn't wait for the obvious follow-up question. "Let's just say for argument's sake he could have gone there because of another killing in the District, and the evidence led the police to suspect Kettering. He'd have to dig into the cardinal's background, right? So he'd have a very valid reason for being there. Maybe not the best example, but I'm sure you all see what I'm saying."

"Then maybe we should just ask the metropolitan police department if Braddock had been sent to Switzerland on assignment. That would save us a whole lot of time," Paula suggested.

Justin shook his head. "And blow our cover if they came back and said the guy's not been out of the District in years? Not a good move. Braddock would hear about it through the grapevine, and if he were guilty of anything, he'd destroy any trail that could lead to him as the killer. I know I would. No, I recommend we tread lightly, and I think I've got an idea as to how we should proceed."

"Shoot," O'Bryan said.

"We need to put Braddock under a microscope. I want to dig deep into his background going all the way back to his high school days—and beyond—if necessary. I want to get a rundown on all his foreign travels over the past few years. I also want to know how much money he's got. I want to know if he's supporting a mistress, or has any other bad habits. In other words, I want to know everything there is to know about the guy. And once I have all that, I'll want more."

"Sounds like a mighty tall order. How do you propose to do it?" O'Bryan wanted to know.

"Jack, we're going to need help. I'd like your okay to approach a firm in New York called *The Industrial Management Consulting Group*. Don't let the name fool you. This is the best outfit in the world when it comes to solving problems involving industrial espionage, individual surveillance, background checks, murder investigations, what have you. They're all retired FBI, Customs, and DEA types. Hell, they even have a couple of former CIA spooks on the payroll. And I know for a fact that the government contracts with them on special cases. They're the *crème de la crème* in their field, with the exception of yours truly, of course. But most importantly, Industrial Management is the only outfit I'd trust with something as significant as this."

"Are you talking round-the-clock surveillance on Braddock?" Paula asked. "If so, you're talking big bucks."

"Right, and right again. But it's the only way. Without these guys to help us, we'd simply be spinning our wheels. They can be rolling within twenty-four hours, and have information flowing back to us within forty-eight. They know which buttons to push, which rocks to look under. If we see it's going nowhere fast, we can always shut it down and try something else."

Both sets of eyes turned to O'Bryan.

"Justin, I don't want you to think I'm holding your feet to the fire, but what sort of money are we talking about? A ballpark figure will do fine." O'Bryan didn't sound happy.

Justin scrunched up his face and ran both hands through his thick, graying hair. "Jack, it could go a hundred thou. Maybe more. I'm hoping we won't need to go more than fifty K." He shrugged. "Sorry, but that's the best I can do."

"How soon can you contact them?"

"How about now?"

"Let's roll!"

Justin looked at O'Bryan, and allowed a grin to spread. "As soon as I've called New York, I'm hitting the hay for the next eighteen hours." he turned to Paula. "I'm beat. You have no idea what it's like partying with O'Bryan every night. The guy doesn't know when to stop."

They all laughed.

"Good work, Justin, you, too, Jack," said Paula with pride, then clapped her hands in a spontaneous manifestation of support and appreciation for a job well done.

Justin took an exaggerated bow then held up his hand. "One last thing. From now on when we talk or write about this part of the investigation I want us using a code name." Again he looked at O'Bryan, then winked. "Jack suggested, *Dies Irae*, but only after I patiently explained to him what it means, and where it comes from. Jack, do the honors and enlighten the lady. She'll be impressed that I'm so smart." On that whopper he left.

* * *

The next morning Justin sat alone at the conference table writing checks. Bills had come due, and he watched in alarm as his bank account hemorrhaged money. The expenses of just this first month were formidable, and he suspected Cardinal Miglianico would turn a deaf ear to any request for a transfusion. He thanked his lucky stars that the Vatican had advanced the amounts he had originally demanded, but at this rate of depletion, there would soon be nothing left. And they were still months away from trial.

At noon he visited Kettering and immediately noticed that the cardinal did not look well. He excused himself and went in search of Capelletti.

"I, too, am concerned, Mr. Scott," Capelletti said, and indeed he looked as worried as he professed. "Cardinal Kettering's eating like a dying bird, and he's spending too much time alone. Yet, he has not uttered a single complaint to anyone at the legation."

"I think it's time I bring a doctor in to examine him," Justin said quietly, chastising himself for not having thought of such a move sooner. "I'll do it today."

"You know, Mr. Scott, the cardinal had a mild heart attack a few years back. It was kept very hush-hush by the cardinal, but it seems he made a full recovery because he was given a clean bill of health by the Vatican's medical staff before his present appointment. But still, I fear the stress of the last month has taken its toll."

"I wasn't aware of any heart problems, Monsignor," Justin replied. "Thanks for filling me in. I'll see to it that he gets a thorough checkup. I'm sure he'll object, but I can be pretty persuasive when I have to be. I'll keep you in the loop."

Kettering was unable to shed any light as to the identity of the four unknown men in the photographs Justin had brought along. He studied the prints intently, holding each close to the upturned lamp on his desk and using a small magnifying glass, but was forced to shake his head every time he looked at a new picture.

Justin kept his eyes glued to the Cardinal's, and had to admit that if Kettering was holding back information, his impassive face betrayed nothing.

"I wish I could say yes, or even a maybe, to at least one person shown, but I can't. I'm sorry."

"Not to worry, Your Eminence. We'll get an answer soon enough. It was a long shot at best." He took the photos and placed them in the safe beside Kettering's desk, then briefed the cardinal on the latest. Kettering listened intently, his hands loosely clasped and resting on his tooled leather writing pad cover. As he spoke, Justin noticed that the hands seemed frail and translucent; truly an old man's hands. He studied the cardinal's face, and saw the same fragile quality.

When Justin was finished, Kettering smiled. "In so many respects my fate rests in your hands, Mr. Scott. You have the singular, yet difficult task of unearthing the information you need to defend me. I'd be less than human if I didn't admit that with any other investigator I might have cause to worry the task was beyond his capabilities. But for some reason I don't have that concern with you. Am I being naive?"

Justin shook his head. "Nope, and I'm not just saying that to make you feel good. I truly believe in you, and I'm counting on my many years of experience with the FBI to see this thing through to total exoneration."

"Thank you. That goes a long way to making an old man feel better."

The last subject broached dealt with the cardinal's health. Kettering stoutly insisted he was well, but Justin was not about to be dissuaded from his task. He informed the cardinal that he would be examined by a cardiologist within the next day or so. "No arguments, Cardinal. I'm the boss, and this comes under the heading of the attorney wanting a healthy client who can fully participate as a partner in his own defense."

Kettering capitulated diplomatically and with a smile. "Mr. Scott, you're the boss. I will obey."

"Thank you, Your Eminence." Justin stood and shook hands, being deliberately gentle with his grasp. "I'll stop by tomorrow. Just keep the faith, Your Eminence, and try to do better in the eating department. You're going to win the day, and win on your own terms. I guarantee it. *Auf Wiedersehen.*"

Bowing to a lifetime of habit, the cardinal blessed the investigator as he made his way to the door.

Justin sprinted to his replacement rental Jaguar and set off for his next appointment. Keep your cool, no matter what they might do to goad you, he lectured himself, as he bobbed and weaved his way eastward toward the heart of the city.

* * *

"Thank you for coming," Attorney General Jane Renfrew said in her greeting to Justin. It was a gracious welcome in that it had been he who had requested the meeting that morning. She had said she would rearrange her schedule to accommodate his.

She guided him to the conference table and introduced him to the director of the FBI, a man who'd taken over running the bureau since Justin's retirement. Next came her deputy, and lastly, the United States Attorney for the District of Columbia.

She waited till he was seated then opened the meeting by asking him how she could be of help.

"First, let me express my thanks to you for clearing your calendar on such short notice, General. I appreciate it."

She nodded. She had yet to feel at ease being addressed as general, but because she did not know her guest, she felt it would somehow come across as condescending to suggest using her given name. She said nothing, instead replaying the events of the last several days in her mind while she waited for Justin to continue.

The federal grand jury for the District had handed up a bill of indictment against Cardinal Kettering. It was a carbon copy of the one Justin had squashed, and the attorney general had indeed confirmed that she would personally take charge of the case.

Her announcement was not categorized in the media as political grandstanding, possibly because she had spent almost two decades as a prosecutor in Atlanta, and felt personally challenged by this rock solid man who had been hired to defend the cardinal. But she was secure in the knowledge that she could more than hold her own in this highly charged legal arena.

"I received the initial discovery package from your office, and I thank you for turning it over before you really had to. I only can ask that as more requests for discovery materials are made, you continue with your excellent cooperation," Justin said.

"Just keep in mind it's a two-way street, Counselor," the director of the FBI interrupted, his feelings of ill will bubbling to the surface along with his words. Judge MacAllister had made several pithy statements to the press about the case, and though he liked to reiterate during every encounter that he had formed no opinion whatsoever, all knew exactly where he stood. He was the one man in the government who really wanted a trial. He wanted to see Cardinal Kettering crucified.

Justin answered pleasantly. "Yes it is, Judge, and I fully intend to do my part." He turned to Attorney General Renfrew. "My client would very much like a speedy trial, ma'am, and I'm suggesting the defense will be ready by late winter, early spring at the latest."

"I don't think the government has any problem with your timetable, Mr. Scott. I don't yet know which judge will be assigned the case, but as soon as I do, I'll inform the court that we'd appreciate a fast track." She paused, toying with a fountain pen, carefully formulating her next words. "Frankly, the four of us had speculated that you were coming to iron out the particulars for your client to enter a guilty plea to the government of the United States. I admit I was hoping for such, but I see we all jumped to the wrong conclusion."

Justin returned her smile. "General, what I say publicly, I'll say privately. We have every intention of proceeding to trial. I will also state for the record that I'm confident my client will be proven innocent beyond a shadow of a doubt long before that event comes to pass. Not innocent just beyond a reasonable doubt, but total vindication on all charges," he added with emphasis. If there had been a jury present he would have had their undivided attention.

"Have you not had a chance to look at the discovery we've sent over?" the deputy A.G. asked. The evidence so meticulously gathered by the bureau was as solid and as damning as any he had seen in over twenty-three years handling such cases. What Justin had just said flew in the face of the facts.

"I have. I did so before leaving for Europe on related matters, and have done so again since my return," Justin said. "I commend you on the thoroughness of your work."

"Then I don't understand the reason for this meeting," the deputy responded, genuinely at a loss. He quickly glanced at his colleagues as if looking for confirmation that he was not out on a solitary limb with his analysis. Three slightly nodding heads telegraphed to the deputy that he was indeed speaking for his peers.

Justin looked the man squarely in the eye. "I came here to ask for samples of the blood taken from all the parties; the cardinal, the victim, and, of course, the fetus. I need enough material in order to run some pretty sophisticated tests of my own. I have a duty to the client to do so."

"You've got Kettering," the director retorted, testily, "so I don't understand why you can't draw all the blood from him you want. The facts are the facts. Your man was pissed to the gills, and preliminary DNA tests tell us he fathered the child. The more sophisticated analysis will only confirm what we already know." The director paused for effect, then added, "Unless you really think you can convince a jury otherwise." His reddening face reflected his building anger. "In all of Western thought, there's only been one claim of a virgin birth that I'm aware of, and I don't think you can sell a jury on a second. At least not in this town."

"*Judge MacAllister! That's quite enough,*" the attorney general shouted. Embarrassed by the spurious remark to her visitor, she demanded heatedly, "I insist on an apology this very instant."

The director glowered belligerently, his eyebrows seemingly darting all over his forehead like two demented caterpillars. He slammed his fists onto the table, causing the untouched decanter of ice water to splash over its rim. "*The hell I will!* and to think this lowlife of a lawyer used to work for my bureau!"

Jane Renfrew jumped to her feet. "Judge, you will apologize, or I will have your resignation before you leave this room. Make no mistake, I shall phone the President from where I stand, and I assure you, I will secure his approval for such an action."

Judge MacAllister was equally furious. "The man's implying that the bureau might have doctored the evidence. Well, I'm not about to sit idly by and see my agency pilloried. And I won't be a party to a circus such as we were all a witness to several years back in Los Angeles. The bureau's forensic scientists are recognized as the world's best, and they do not resort to tampering with evidence, in spite of the recent bullshit we've all seen in the press."

"I didn't hear even a hint of such an accusation in any of Mister Scott's words," replied the attorney general. "The defense is entitled to the evidence, and they shall have it. Now, if they feel it necessary to duplicate your work, then so be it. That's my decision, and it's the only one that counts. So the next words out of your mouth better be the ones I want to hear."

MacAllister swallowed the bitter bile of defeat. "I apologize for that comment referring to a second virgin birth and the lowlife bit. Both were uncalled-for, and I had no intention to cast a slur on any religious beliefs. But as to my suspicion for the reasons I think the defense wants to run duplicate tests, I stand by my convictions."

"You can hold those convictions till hell freezes over, Judge. My displeasure was directed at the intemperate remarks for which you've apologized." She looked at Justin. "Do you accept the director's apology?"

"Yes, ma'am, I do. I'm sure it was a slip of the tongue in a moment of frustration rather than a reflection of the director's attitude towards any religious beliefs. As far as I'm concerned, it's forgotten." He turned to the director and added, "Please remember, Judge, the woman did have a husband, and it's our fast held contention that conception occurred within the bond of holy matrimony."

The attorney general sat, thankful that a nasty crisis had been averted. "Thank you, Mr. Scott. You will definitely get the samples you've requested. Is there anything else?"

"No, that should be all. I know I could have sent a letter detailing my request, General, but I felt that I should meet face to face with you before too much more time passed. I fully realize you are committed to a marshaling of all the resources at your disposal in prosecuting this case, and I expect nothing less from you as the peoples representative."

Jane Renfrew laid the pen down beside the pristine yellow legal pad in front of her, then leaned forward, shoulders hunched. "May we speak off the record for a moment?"

"Yes, of course."

"We've given a summary of our findings to the secretary of state for transmittal to Rome. It's my understanding that Cardinal Miglianico has now expressed more than a little reluctance to continue to support the position you've steadfastly maintained.

My conversations with him convince me that the Vatican would now like nothing more than to recall the ambassador, and make a formal apology to the people of the United States for his conduct." Her owl-like gaze was unwavering as she continued to voice her misgivings. "However, it's been suggested that it's on your advice that the cardinal has refused to entertain such a course of action, and that he has made it clear that he will disobey any such command from Rome. The word is out that it's you who's persuaded the cardinal to remain in this country and stand trial."

She hurried on. "Forgive my boldness, but I'm convinced that your continued intransigence in the face of the facts can only end in disaster. It's a no-win situation for everybody. Once Cardinal Kettering is found guilty—and he will be, he can always change his stance and clamor for the protection of the prematurely discarded cloak of diplomatic immunity. I suspect you feel when all else fails, then *ex-post facto* will win the day.

"I've taken the liberty of speaking to the Chief Justice of the Supreme Court," she hurried on, "and informed him of my misgivings. He agrees. The problem of the cardinal standing trial is fraught with perils, both political and religious. Such an event will polarize the country. As you know, sir, you're entitled to petition the case to go directly to the Supreme Court because it involves an accredited ambassador. The court would have to accept it. However, it would have to be heard piecemeal, around all the other business coming before the court. It could take over a year for a decision to be handed down. Needless to say, the chief didn't like that specter one little bit." She paused for her words to sink in.

"What I'm leading up to is this: My door is always open, and I'm available on a moment's notice should you want to discuss a settlement, which is what I sincerely recommend. I'll end by just asking that you keep my offer in mind. I repeat: we *will* win our case. But I'm afraid the cost will simply be too high. That's the end of my sermon. Thank you for hearing me out."

Justin walked over to her and extended his hand. "I promise to keep your offer in mind. When I've gathered my evidence and share it, hopefully I can convince you to drop all charges." Justin could see from the look on her face what he was suggesting was the stuff of fiction.

Justin was pleased with himself as he left the Justice Building. He would get his blood samples, and felt confident that no suspicion had been raised as to his need for all three. He had not divulged a motive or a reason for the bureau to suddenly decide to perform its own DNA profile on Maritha von Snellenberger. The director had played beautifully into his hands. But pleased as he was, he couldn't avoid an inward shudder at a sudden passing thought. Supposing there was no genetic link between Maritha and the cardinal, but only one between the cardinal and the child? What then? He shuddered again, then sternly willed the thought from his consciousness. Because if that's how it played out, and Kettering was found guilty as charged, there wouldn't be a person alive in a position to stop the deluge. But if he could prove Kettering's innocence *and* deliver the murderer, well, kudos would pour forth from every corner of the earth.

It was the substance of fantasy and dreams.

CHAPTER 19

A thief called October snuck in, stealing any hope of relief from the oppressive heat. Everyone offered an opinion on the weather, and grumbled at still-soaring electric bills. Tempers were frayed, but crime was down. Washington was a city under siege, and its citizens prayed for the Canadians to lob a cold front their way. As of today, no one in Canada was listening.

But the sweltering morning brought with it unbelievably good news for Justin.

Five days earlier the promised blood samples had arrived from the FBI, and had been immediately forwarded to *CellTest Laboratories,* in Bethesda, Maryland. Justin held the refrigerated package long enough to include a control sample of the cardinal's blood which had been drawn by the cardiologist sent to examine him. The physician had reported Kettering's heart to be sound, but recommended a complete workup be done by an internist. Justin assured him he would follow-through on the suggestion.

At a couple of minutes past nine a call from *CellTest* was routed to Justin.

"Dr. Singh here, Mr. Scott. I hope I'm not disturbing you." Singh spoke with a clipped, Indian accent.

"Not at all, Doctor." Justin was confused. It was impossible for the lab to have completed the tests. Preliminary results had been promised in about ten days; final analysis within eight weeks. But certainly nothing this soon.

"We have a problem with the cardinal's blood."

Justin felt his heart skip a beat, and immediately thought the worst. Kettering was harboring some dread disease. He gave voice to his misgiving. "He's dying, isn't he?"

"Oh, my goodness gracious, no," came the reply. "Your man is as fit as a fiddle. We know that from a quick examination of the blood drawn by your doctor a couple of days ago. No, no! The problem is with the sample sent from the FBI. That's why I thought I should call you right away."

"Tell me what you've got, Doctor."

"It's been tampered with, plain and simple, Mr. Scott."

Justin bolted up from his chair. O'Bryan, seated across, stiffened, but because he couldn't hear the other end of the conversation, he had no idea what had been revealed. Justin caught a glimpse of his worried look, shook his head, leaned over and transferred the call to the speaker box.

"Dr. Singh, I've put you on the speakerphone. I want Monsignor O'Bryan to hear this. Could you repeat what you just said?"

"Certainly. I said the cardinal's blood sent from the FBI has been tampered with. There's no doubt about it. I suspect it was accomplished by a rather good chemist, but we caught it just the same."

Justin could barely hear. His heart was pounding, coursing a torrent of blood into his ears. "What exactly has been done to it?" he managed to ask.

"Someone introduced alcohol soon after the blood was drawn from the cardinal on the night of the murder. As I said, it was skillfully done. Whoever did it would have needed a sufficient quantity of blood to work from in order to get the chemistry just right. Anyway, I knew you'd want to know."

O'Bryan asked, "Will that in any way invalidate the DNA tests you'll be doing?"

"Not at all. We have a clean sample as a control, and alcohol doesn't change DNA. I see no problems."

"Do you think it was contaminated by the FBI, Doctor?" Justin asked.

Singh was silent for a long minute. Then: "I don't know. But you tell me: Who else had the opportunity?" Another long pause. "Or a motive?"

Justin and O'Bryan just stared at each other.

"Hello. Hello. Are you still there?"

They snapped out of their common trance and answered in unison. "Yes, Doctor, we're here."

Justin continued. "Doctor Singh, that's fabulous news. Please stress to your technicians the need for absolute secrecy about this. Nobody must know what you've just told us."

"Even the FBI?"

Justin jumped like a scalded cat. "*Especially not the FBI*! Stay in touch, Doctor. Call me day or night if you find anything else."

O'Bryan allowed a smile to spread slowly across his face as he sat back and pondered the enormity of what he'd just heard. "You think the bureau could have actually done this?" he finally managed to whisper.

"Apparently so."

"And to think they had the audacity to send us a report they knew was false. They doctored the blood evidence to make it corroborate their contention that the man was drunk. And all because the arresting officer said he *thought* he smelled alcohol. It was perfect for them. No wonder the director was miffed about us getting blood samples for ourselves. That son of a bitch lied to us!"

"Tsk, tsk. Such language. And from a man of the cloth no less."

They broke out in howls of laughter.

"Come on, Jack," Justin finally said, "we've got to tell the cardinal right away. Can you believe this shit?"

* * *

"Do we tell the cardinal?" Paula asked, after hearing the news.

"Darn tootin' we do. Kettering deserves to hear something positive. It's just what the doctor ordered," said Justin.

"Actually, I was thinking about the other cardinal," she replied. "The one in Rome."

That made Justin jump. "*Absolutely not*! I have come to the conclusion that I no longer trust Miglianico, neither does Jack, and I dare say Kettering doesn't either. No, Cardinal Miglianico should be the last to hear."

"Sad to say it, but Justin's right," said O'Bryan. "This whole affair is starting to take on the look and feel of an onion. The top layers have finally been exposed, but as we peer into the mass, we see nothing but more and more layers."

Justin broke in. "Paula, I think it's time we give the good news to Kettering, so my plan is to shag on over to the embassy and take O'Bryan with me. He winked at the priest. "I think you've become something of a favorite."

Paula laughed. "Tell you what. Seeing how you're also a fair-haired boy, maybe you can get the cardinal to talk about his time with Maritha's mother. He might be more forthcoming if it's the two of you there." She squirmed uncomfortably, then added, "The more we know about that relationship, the better prepared we'll be if there comes the need for damage control somewhere down the line. You might have to take his sin public in order to remove the last vestige of doubt from his most vitriolic detractors. I hope not, but in case you do, see what you can come up with. Because, when all is said and done, Kettering really does trust the both of you."

Justin looked admiringly at the woman. "You're right, as usual, Paula."

* * *

When Justin explained to Kettering the significance of what Dr. Singh had told him, the cardinal wept unabashed tears of joy. "I know I'm not yet clear, but I couldn't be happier. Hopefully, this is a major step in the right direction to our finding Maritha's murderer."

Justin assured him that it was. It took a few minutes for Kettering to compose himself, and that's when Justin gently steered the discussion to his younger years and his relationship with Maritha's mother.

They were in the sitting room just off the cardinal's office, all three truly relaxed in each other's presence. It was a watershed event. Kettering had invited them to join him for lunch, and they had eagerly accepted. And, for the first time Kettering used their given names.

"Justin, Jack, let me begin by saying that I loved Catherine with all my heart and soul, but I loved the Church more. It always sounds so trite, even to my own ears more than thirty years later. But try to follow with an open mind what I'm about to say." He glanced at O'Bryan. "Maybe only another priest can fully appreciate what I did. My love for the Church overshadowed my love for a woman, and it has caused me never-ending pain. I denied Catherine in her hour of want, but thank God I managed to salvage some semblance of self-respect before irreparable harm was done. Of course, I need not tell you how I felt towards Maritha. But I'm getting ahead of myself.

"I met Catherine Ibel when she was twenty-two and I was twenty-seven. My family had moved to Germany from Vienna at the beginning of the war. My father had been offered a position overseeing a huge bakery in Munich. He was never a party member, but I'm ashamed to say I think he approved of much of what the 'New Germany' was about. We spent the entire war in that city, father eventually becoming a deputy something-or-other to a deputy of Albert Speer, who placed him in charge of all bread production for the Third Reich. Although Speer was a brilliant architect, Hitler made him the Armaments and War Production Minister, and for some strange reason, it seems that all bread output in the Reich fell under his bailiwick. At least that's what I remember being told. Anyway, there were five of us: my parents, my brother Alphonse, my sister Kristin, and me. I was the youngest, a toddler at the time.

"After Germany surrendered in 1945, life became a desperate struggle to survive for everybody in Europe. Millions were displaced, and those in the East were frantic to find sanctuary in the West. As you know, the Russians controlled much of the continent, including my native Austria, so there was no talk of us returning there. Anyway, in early 1946, the Allied High Command approached my father to reopen the bread factories. The Americans came in, and as only they know how, got many of the huge bakeries up and running in no time. They also provided the flour, and soon father was producing bread at a level not seen even at the height of the war. Those factories went a long way in feeding a significant sector of the population of postwar Germany.

"Rather than bore you with everything about our lives in those days, let me just say that when the Russians finally left Austria in 1955, my parents returned to Vienna, and reopened the bakery they'd sold fifteen years earlier. The family prospered, and in due course became very wealthy. At one time my parents owned six bakeries. My brother runs the business now, but he only has two. My parents and sister are dead, God rest their souls.

"I was able to attend university where I studied philosophy, and earned my doctorate. After graduation, my mentor secured a position for me on the staff of the University of Bonn, and that's how I found myself back in Germany. And then I met Catherine. She was a third-year student, studying Latin and Greek. Not wealthy, but not poor, either. We fell in love.

"But all was not well within me. I knew I wanted to become a priest, yet here I was falling in love. Maybe I was a coward, maybe it was because my parents didn't approve of the idea, maybe it's a million other things, but the point is I was sitting on a very comfortable fence. My time for decision-making was slipping by. I was getting to an age where I would be considered too old for the seminary. So, I courted Catherine, and prayed halfheartedly for guidance. Alas, no intervention came from the Almighty for this Saul of Tarsus. No answered prayers like those of St. Monica for her wayward young son Augustine. No, God made sure I came to my own decision, and in my own time. I was in love, but I was not happy. I was trying to serve two masters.

"One spring evening, the weakness of my flesh won the day. Suffice to say, when I returned to my rooms that night I was no longer chaste. Catherine saw the event as but a prelude to marriage, and she was very happy. For me it was a disaster. I was overcome with confusion and guilt. But I recovered. Less than two months later I shattered her world by informing her of my decision to enter the clergy. She wept bitterly, and begged me to reconsider, but I wouldn't change my mind. I apologized for my conduct, and even asked for her forgiveness. I was such a coward. I wanted everything neatly in its place before my departure. Soon after, she simply disappeared from my life. And she never uttered a word about the child she was already carrying.

"I didn't see her again until about fourteen years later, when she appeared on the steps of my church in Vienna. She'd come seeking help for Maritha. She was destitute. Her parents had disowned her when they discovered she was pregnant. Just before she gave birth, she accepted a marriage proposal from a Heinrich Furstenburg, a schoolteacher many years her senior. Of course, I learned all of this much later from Catherine. He was a good man, and accepted Maritha as his own. He allowed his name to become her name, and the child never knew any other father. Maritha adored him.

"He died of a stroke one morning in front of his students, and left his wife and daughter penniless. He was employed by a small, private Catholic school, and had no pension, no insurance. Of course, Catherine had never finished her education, and she had not been employed during her years of marriage. Now she found herself with nothing except her beautiful daughter to raise by herself. Germany was mired in a deep recession, and work was impossible to find.

"She had kept track of me, knew of my ordination, and various postings through the years. That's how she came back into my life. And in her hour of greatest need I almost turned my back on her. So much for Christian charity. It's no wonder they call me the Nazi behind my back. I was so impressed with my position that all I wanted was to brush aside this uncomfortable reminder of my past. In a last, desperate plea, she begged me to at least help my daughter. And in return, she promised to disappear forever.

"*My daughter*! I immediately thought she was trying to blackmail me, but the moment I laid eyes on the child, I knew the truth. She was the image of my own mother.

"I had to face my harsh reality. I was paralyzed with fear. Suppose Rome found out about my past? What then? In all likelihood I would be shipped off to the foreign missions, and live out my days on some awful atoll. And I had such plans. But here was my flesh and blood. Thank God, some spark of goodness arose in me, and I did what I had to do.

"I used my influence and secured a place for them to live. I found a good job for Catherine, and made sure Maritha attended the best Catholic school in the city. Catherine told her daughter we were old friends from our college days, and the child accepted her mother's explanation without question. Of course, I had a moral and legal obligation to help. It was not only my duty, but I also truly wanted to. I had my own money from when my parents had died, so I didn't have to divert funds from the Church. I can't imagine what I would have done had I not been blessed with my own resources.

"Anyway, I was eventually consecrated a bishop and posted to Rome. They followed. Maritha was an excellent student, so she had no trouble gaining entrance to the university on merit alone. Her mother worked, and we all remained close. Think back on the times. Those were still the days of innocence, and no one for a second thought there was any more to the relationship other than friendship. Maritha looked on me as an uncle. She trusted and confided in me. I was so proud of that child. The rest you know."

The cardinal sat silent, lost in thought.

Justin gave him a minute before asking quietly, "What became of Catherine?"

Kettering, still gazing at nothing, shrugged. "I don't know. Shortly after Maritha's marriage, and my return from Australia, Catherine came to me one last time to inform me she was leaving Rome. Her explanation was that her duty was done, and she thanked me for all the help I had rendered over the years. She said that she was finally removing herself from my life. Maritha told me later that her mother had moved to Saltzburg. By then Maritha was a wealthy woman, so she was only too happy to provide for Catherine's needs. That's been over a year, and I haven't spoken to her in all that time." He turned and stared at O'Bryan. "I don't know if she's alive or dead. But if she's alive, then what must she think about all this?" He hung his head as though carrying the weight of the world on his frail shoulders.

"Do you want me to find her, Your Eminence?" Justin asked. He was not about to tell the cardinal that he feared Catherine, too, was dead.

Tears welled in the Cardinal's eyes. "Yes. Catherine *must* be told the truth. Please, find her for me, Justin." It was the silent beseechment of a tired, worn out soul.

"I will do my best, Your Eminence, I promise."

Kettering sighed deeply, and lifted a trembling hand to wipe his tearing eyes. His lips quivered uncontrollably. When he finally spoke again his voice was low and weak. "Maritha came to Washington because she feared for her own life as well as her husband's. She was expecting their first child, and she truly believed she would never live to see it born. She was desperate, so she turned to me for help. I was the only priest in a position of power she felt she could trust."

Now huge sobs wracked his body. "Certain people had discovered Maritha knew what they had planned, and decided they had to stop her. However, they aren't yet sure whether or not I too know the truth, so I'm certain they'll try to kill me just to be safe. I am the last link in their chain of containment, but I have no clear memory of what it is I'm supposed to know. The only thing saving me so far is the fact that I am a prisoner inside this legation." He waved a feeble hand in the air. "I don't care for my own life, Mr. Scott, but I must be cleared of these charges so that I can first learn, then expose, whatever it is that cost my daughter and grandchild their lives. That's the real reason you must help me. You are my only hope."

"No wonder you didn't trust O'Bryan," Justin murmured. "In your shoes, I'm not so sure I would have either."

The cardinal managed a weak smile as he turned to O'Bryan. "I hope you've forgiven me."

"Long ago, Your Eminence."

Justin spoke up. "No matter what's unfolding within the Church, and, trust me, I believe what you've just told us, we must stay focused on the task at hand. As your lawyer, I insist on it. That's our priority. And as much as I'd like to know the particulars of what it was Maritha came to warn you about, that will just have to wait. Once you're a free man you can use your restored prestige to convince the Holy Father that there's a spreading cancer inside the Church. And, yes, Cardinal, I'm persuaded it's that serious. So is Jack. But I repeat: it's just going to have to wait. First we must clear you of all charges."

Having said that, Justin decided it was enough for one day and deliberately changed the subject. "How about that lunch you promised us, Cardinal Kettering? I've always wanted to experience how the pooh-bah's live," he added with a mischievous grin.

"Then I'm afraid you've come to the wrong place, Mr. Scott," came Kettering's quick-witted reply.

CHAPTER 20

Justin introduced Paula and O'Bryan to his friend Steven Mannix, from *Industrial Management*, then invited everybody to take their seats at the conference table. Each place had a file before it, prepared by Mannix and labeled *Dies Irae.*

"Steve's the lead on *Dies Irae*," Justin began. "All information flows to, and stops with him, and it's his job to separate the wheat from the chaff. Suffice to say, there's been a lot of both. Anyway, you aren't here to listen to me jabber, so let's find out what Steve's got for us." He nodded to Mannix.

Mannix used the console by his side to dim the lights and start the video system, bringing Braddock to life on the silvered screen. It was a montage of clips, taken at various times, and in different settings. "Just want you to get a feel for the guy," Mannix explained. "He's mid-forties, almost a twenty-year cop, kind of a loner, but not disliked by his peers. Got an ex-wife and a twelve-year-old daughter, but resents the hell out of paying alimony and child support. The ex-Mrs. Braddock lives in the city, but keeps threatening to split for Oregon and join a tree-hugging commune out there. Braddock couldn't-care-less. He just wants to see her get married so he can keep more money in his pocket. They don't communicate much with each other." He paused to study the footage along with the others. A minute later the screen automatically went blank, and Mannix reset the lights. He rose from his chair, and stood in place.

"We've gathered a ton of information on this cop and it all boils down to this: Tom Braddock is in deep shit, and, yeah, he's capable of murder. I'm not saying he *has* killed, mind you, I'm just saying he's capable. And he's got motive up the wazoo."

"Motive?" O'Bryan asked, as if he hadn't heard correctly.

"Motive," confirmed Mannix. "The guy's gone through a truckload of money in the last couple of years. He gambles on anything and everything, and from what we can tell, he ain't too good at picking winners. He's had markers out for weeks at a time, both in Vegas and Atlantic City. Braddock's considered a good client, and they probably know he's a cop, so they don't lean on him too hard. And he always seems to come up with the money at the last minute."

"How much are we talking about here?" Justin asked.

"Fourteen thousand was the last payoff made in Atlantic City a week ago. Also, it seems he got into some kind of a pissing contest with the local gendarmes at the time and they've let him know he's no longer welcome in their town." Mannix paused to let that sink in, then continued. "He also lays off some heavy bread with the local bookies, playing the Vegas spread on a potful of sports events damn near every weekend. I'm talking thousands. Which begs the question: Where does a cop making eighty-seven-five a year come up with that kind of change? and as if that isn't enough, the guy's got a serious drinking problem. Betting and booze. Not a good combination," he observed, dryly.

"So, where does a cop get that kind of money?" O'Bryan wanted to know.

"If you're a dirty cop, lots of places. For starters, you can steal drugs from the evidence locker; you can become a tipster to the drug gangs and organized crime; or you can shakedown street pushers, pimps, and prostitutes. There's no shortage of people out there to strong-arm. And if you're a lieutenant running a homicide division, not too many folks are going to cross swords with you. Your superiors probably wouldn't suspect a thing. My guess is Braddock's been dirty for a hell of a long time."

Justin spoke up. "All you've presented so far could be considered circumstantial. Any lawyer worth his salt would stop you in your tracks if you tried to indict on what we've just heard. Don't get me wrong. I'm impressed with what you've uncovered, but it's a long way from being enough."

"You're right," replied an unfazed Mannix, "but I've got more." He dug into his folder and pulled out a handful of documents. "This is his travel history, courtesy of the passport section at State. It seems he's been abroad several times in the last eighteen months. Three trips to Europe; one to Hong-Kong; and two to the Cayman Islands. Each time he re-entered the country he had nothing to declare. One trip lasted ten days; another, two weeks. The rest were just quickie jaunts."

"Was he in Europe in late June, early July, of this year?" asked O'Bryan, looking up from his folder.

Without checking his papers Mannix replied. "Yup. Ten days. Departed Kennedy on the twenty-fourth of June, arrived back at Kennedy on July fourth."

"What about bank accounts?" Justin asked. "Have you been able to take a peek there?"

"We have, but we're not finished. His local accounts are what you'd expect. The guy's smart. His checking account dips to almost zilch twice a month, and his savings account has forty-four-hundred and change. He pays his alimony and child support, but usually only after a nasty call from his ex. We're still trying to get close to his bookies, and when we do we'll know just how he pays the locals, but it's my guess the guy has some serious money stashed away in Europe; possibly the Caymans. If he does, we'll find it. Meantime, I have him covered round the clock. Funny thing. We taped him showing up at two different Alcoholics Anonymous meetings, but both times he only stayed a few minutes. It makes me wonder if he's meeting someone there, but that's only a guess."

"How about his boss?" asked Paula, peering into her folder, searching for a name. Her index finger found what she was looking for. "Inspector Valerie Tobias. Could she be in on it, too?"

Justin held his breath, taken aback by the question.

Mannix shook his head. "We looked at her, but she's clean. The woman's been married to the same man for a dozen or so years. He runs a small, successful computer company called *Bytes & PCs*. They have one child, a daughter who's got Down syndrome. From what we could find out, they're a close-knit, salt of the earth type family. Bottom line? The woman's okay."

Justin, flooded with a sense of relief, then looked over at O'Bryan who was stroking his jaw, obviously mulling over the cost of this operation. Four teams of investigators for round-the-clock surveillance, plus an untold number of others digging into other aspects of Braddock's life. This was hitting-up the defense for some heavy-duty cash. "So, where do we go from here, Mr. Mannix?" O'Bryan wanted to know.

"Something will break soon with Braddock, Monsignor," Mannix replied. "He'll tip his hand by showing up with somebody he shouldn't be seen with, and when he does, we'll have it on tape. Also, within a couple of days I should know for sure if the man's got money stashed away in some offshore hideaway. We'll get the goods for you, I promise."

"Thank you," O'Bryan replied. "Justin insisted you were the best, and you've proved him right. It's the waiting that has us all on edge."

"Understandable, given what's at stake. But let me leave you with this thought." He turned and squarely faced Justin. "If we get Braddock, there's only so far we can take it by ourselves. At some point you'll have to consider telling his boss, Inspector Tobias, and have her get metro's Internal Affairs involved. Those folks can get the dirt from the inside to corroborate whatever we come up with. Also, they can approach a judge for a wiretap, or even a search warrant for a covert entry into his premises, so long as we specify *exactly* what we're looking for. No judge will allow a free-for-all search party, but would probably look favorably on issuing a very narrowly constructed warrant, as long as the facts presented indicate a felony crime has been committed. But, hey, you're the lawyer," he smiled. "Didn't mean to preach to the choir. Anyway, keep it in mind, because we might have to move fast when we do."

"We will. Again, thanks for coming on board."

"My pleasure, Justin."

* * *

"Heads up, partner. Look alive. Our man's on the move."

The words came from inside the Ford Bronco parked across the street from Braddock's apartment building. It was Sunday morning, not quite eight o'clock, and he was taking the steps two at a time, hitting the sidewalk, and heading north on foot.

"Who's relieving us?" asked the man behind the wheel, eyes boring in on Braddock's departing back, but making no attempt to start the engine. Traffic was still extremely light.

"Conyers and Morgan," came the reply. "In fact, they're already late."

"Call and tell them to hang back," said the driver, starting the engine, but not putting the Bronco into drive.

They saw Braddock stop at a newspaper rack on the corner, feed it a pocketful of change, open the plexiglass door, and extract a fat Sunday paper. They watched as he rifled through the many sections, tucked two under his arm and left the rest at the foot of the box. He continued to walk.

As the Bronco eased away from the curb, the passenger was already relaying instructions to another car on his encrypted cellular phone. "The subject's on foot, probably just going out for breakfast. When he plops his butt down, you guys swing in and take over. Hang loose. Out."

But Braddock was not going to breakfast. He continued heading north for two more blocks, then abruptly turned east. Ten minutes later he entered the newly opened West Meridian Hill Park, and strolled towards the lone handball court.

The Bronco eased into a parking place a hundred yards away, its tinted windows obscuring any view of the occupants.

"That guy's a regular walking billboard for *Notre Dame*," observed the passenger as he began fiddling with a camcorder.

Braddock was wearing a windbreaker and sweatpants, each emblazoned with the university's name. "Damn near got to be eighty degrees out there already. What's the man thinking? We're going to get snow?"

They phoned their position to the other team, and two minutes later a Chevrolet mini-van pulled in, and parked at the opposite end of the lot.

Braddock had chosen a bench well apart from any other. Situated in a clearing where he could only be approached from one direction, he made himself comfortable, and settled in with the paper.

Both teams began to record.

"Company's coming," the driver of the Bronco alerted the duo in the Chevy about five minutes later.

A solitary male was making his way casually towards Braddock's bench. The man stopped by the handball court, and watched the middle-aged foursome chase the rock-hard India rubber ball all over the concrete pad. He stayed about two minutes, then seemed suddenly to decide he'd seen enough, and headed for Braddock's bench, but not before first stopping at a bubbler for a quick drink. Straightening up, he wiped his chin with the back of his hand then meandered over to Braddock's bench and plopped himself down on the opposite end. Braddock kept his face buried in the paper.

The men in both vehicles saw immediately that the newcomer was starting to talk, but couldn't hear what he was saying.

"Damn! This is a prearranged meet." The driver of the Bronco was peeved. "You getting everything?" he snapped at his partner as he studied the men through binoculars.

"Roger, that. Now will you just relax."

The visitor continued to talk, but refused to look at Braddock, whose face remained hidden behind his newspaper.

"Put that frigging newspaper down, Braddock," the driver commanded testily.

It was as if he heard. Braddock lowered the paper, seemingly in mid-sentence. After a moment or two he appeared to be getting agitated. He began shaking his head, slowly but emphatically at first, then he picked up the pace.

"Braddock's not a happy camper," observed the man behind the camcorder. "He's pissed about something."

The visitor cut Braddock off by seemingly giving an ultimatum to the detective. He then heaved himself clumsily to his feet and set off down the narrow path without a backward glance.

The Bronco driver spoke rapidly into the phone. "You guys take the walker; we'll stick with Braddock. Anyone have a make on the visitor?"

He received three negative replies, then made a quick decision. "Okay, I'm calling Mannix to tell him I want us all to meet as soon as possible. I'm also going to request another team take over baby-sitting Braddock. Any questions?"

"Just an observation, Jim," came a voice from the Chevy. "I'm thinking Braddock was decked out in his *Notre Dame* formal wear for recognition purposes. And I'll bet that's why he was wearing the sweatshirt the day he met that lady in Switzerland. He was definitely in that town square to meet someone."

"Makes sense, Morgan. Okay, see you guys back at the barn. Out."

* * *

It wasn't until one o'clock that the teams assembled, with Mannix running the show. There were six of them crammed into his motel room. Two were sprawled across the bed, two scrunched down in chairs, one stretched out on the floor, and Mannix standing. They had coupled the recordings to play on a monitor with a split-screen, allowing them to study both images at once, and to select one over the other at will.

Braddock had returned to his apartment, and as of five minutes ago was still there. The 'walker' had flagged a taxi outside the park and had gone straight to Ronald Reagan National Airport where he'd retrieved a suitcase from a locker, then dashed onto a departing shuttle bound for New York. Mannix had been able to get an investigator out to Kennedy in time to intercept, then tail the man to the American Airlines concourse where he paid cash, and boarded a flight to London. Grass didn't grow under Mannix's feet. He arranged for the man to be followed once on the ground in England.

The group studied the videos intently. Both camcorders were state-of-the-art, and the picture quality was excellent. Even from a distance of almost four hundred feet, the zoom capability had presented the subjects in sharp detail, greatly aided by the machines' self-stabilizing imaging feature. But they had no sound. Everybody added their comments, but when all was said and done they really didn't know where to go next with what they had.

Mannix took multiple sips of a Pepsi as he pondered. Finally, he shrugged his shoulders and picked up the phone.

He spoke to Justin and told him what they had. Justin asked a couple of questions, then informed his friend that he'd drop by in an hour to see for himself.

Mannix told his men to shove off, reasoning that they had better things to do, like sleep, or just plain relax. He waited alone.

Justin came with a man in tow. "Steven Mannix, Paul Sinclair," he said by way of introduction, and the two shook hands. "Paul's a speech professor, and he's agreed to see if he can help."

"Justin, forget it. I guess I didn't make myself clear. We don't have any sound."

"We don't need sound. Paul teaches at Gallaudet, you know, the university for the hearing impaired. He's a master at lip reading."

"Son of a gun!" Mannix's face lit up. He scrambled to reset the machines, at the same time offering sodas to his guests. Both declined, and positioned themselves in front of the monitor.

The split-screen came alive playing both tapes simultaneously, but after a couple of seconds Justin called out: "Stop. Dump one or the other of those images, Steve. Give me a full screen."

Mannix obeyed and Justin peered intently at the monitor. "Yes." he called out excitedly. "Yes. That bugger's one of the guys in the photos from Switzerland."

"You sure?"

"Is the Pope Catholic? Hell, yes, I'm sure!" he waved his hand in the air. "Let's do a clean run-through with no more stops so Paul can get a feel for it."

Fifteen minutes later both investigators awaited the professor's verdict.

"No problem, gentlemen. At least not with the man whose face we can see at all times. However, as far as the one playing peekaboo behind the newspaper, I can only give you what I see after the paper comes down."

"Shoot," commanded Justin.

"The one we can see clearly doesn't speak English as his native language," Sinclair began, "that's obvious from the slow, almost exaggerated way he moves his lips. He's thinking in one language, speaking in another, thus he's very careful with his pronunciation.

"I hope what he is saying makes sense to you gentlemen," he continued. "The foreigner is telling the American that people in Italy and Russia are not happy. He says that the money paid to get rid of the woman was not value received. Those are his exact words: Not value received. And, he adds: You should have eliminated the old man when you had the chance."

"Go on," encouraged Justin. "You're doing great."

Sinclair continued. "This is where I only get bits and pieces of what the man with the newspaper says. Basically he challenges the other guy, telling him he was only contracted for the woman, and nothing was said about the Nazi. He wasn't part of the deal." Sinclair looked at Justin. "Making sense so far? I'm pretty certain Nazi is the word he used."

"Heck, yes, Paul, keep going."

"Well, the foreigner says it should have been taken care of months ago in Europe. 'If you had done your job properly *then,* I wouldn't have to be here *now,*' are his exact words. Apparently there's a cat loose from a pretty nasty bag, and certain people are laying the blame squarely at this guy's feet. Then the European suggests that the American is trying to hold them up for more money. That's where you see the guy shaking his head, denying it. The other man really gets mad and tells him to fix the problem and fix it fast, because if he doesn't, then he, his mother, and his daughter can expect very unpleasant, very painful, accidents. Odd, but he definitely doesn't say wife and daughter."

Sinclair paused long enough to take a breath. "'You understood that the woman had to be eliminated because she knew too much, and that the Nazi had to be implicated and thoroughly disgraced so as to never be in a position to threaten what has already been set in motion. You assured everyone you could do what needed to be done. Well, the orders now are for you to get rid of him. I'm instructed to tell you there will be no further warnings.' Then he just ups and leaves without so much as a good-bye. And that's it, gentlemen."

The three men stared at one another. Finally, Justin said, "*Dies Irae.*"

"Pardon me?" said Sinclair. "I didn't catch that, Justin."

"Judgment Day has finally arrived, Paul. As of this second I've just hired you for the rest of the day. A thousand dollars sound fair enough?"

"I don't understand ..."

"You will. I need you for a few more hours. You've just blown the cover off something with major international ramifications, and I could sure use your help to bring it home. Okay?"

"Of course, Justin, glad to."

"Good." Justin studied his watch and frowned. "I want a meeting at my office," he told Mannix. "I'm going to make some calls and set it up for six o'clock, and I'm inviting some new players to join us."

Justin then pounded on the table, making the machines dance. He shook his fist at the frozen image of the police lieutenant staring defiantly back at him from the screen. "*Braddock, I'm going to nail your hide to the wall, you miserable, damn, murdering son of a bitch*!"

CHAPTER 21

Justin escorted Chief Tuchmann and Valerie from the underground parking garage up to his law offices on the fourth floor of the huge Watergate office complex. Both carried police radios into the conference room, and both were at odds to fathom a reason for why they had been summoned. But they had come nonetheless.

"This is Chief Matthew Tuchmann and Inspector Valerie Tobias," Justin said by way of introduction, then quickly added, "Valerie and I have had occasion to work together in the past. Good to see you again, Val."

"Likewise, Justin."

At that moment the chief's radio began to squawk. He'd just put it on the table, but hastily snatched it up and lowered the volume. "Sorry about that," he mumbled. Taking a cue from her boss, Valerie turned hers completely off, reasoning that one radio tuned to the command channel was enough.

"Chief, Inspector, I must ask if either of you told anyone you were coming here?"

Both shook their heads, puzzled. They knew this group represented the defense team for Cardinal Kettering, but had no idea why they had been summoned. Both thought that maybe there was something a little improper about it, but weren't really sure.

"Central knows I'm on the brick," explained Tuchmann, pointing to his portable radio. "That's standard operating procedure. Ditto for the Inspector. So, what gives, Mr. Scott?"

"Let me be more specific," Justin pressed. "Have either of you spoken to Lieutenant Braddock since I called?"

The chief shook his head, but Valerie jumped slightly in her chair. Justin's eyes were riveted on her. She recovered and shook her head.

"Good, because this meeting is all about Braddock."

For the next twenty minutes Justin methodically walked both officers through the evidence chain the team had uncovered linking Braddock to the murder of Maritha von Snellenberger. He ended by introducing Paul Sinclair who gave voice to the silent videos shot earlier in the day.

The chief sat impassive throughout, but Valerie was in shock, and it showed. She continuously shook her head in disbelief at what she was hearing and seeing, but listened intently to every word.

"Run the tape again," said the chief, unbuttoning his collar and loosening his tie. His movements were slow and deliberate, his face still betraying nothing.

Justin obliged.

Tuchmann sat back in his seat at the end of the second showing, and massaged his temples with both hands. The group waited for him to speak.

"First off, I'm troubled with what I've just seen and heard. It looks as if I've got a bad cop in my command. My bigger problem though, is the evidence against Kettering. The facts of the case are in conflict with what you're suggesting about Braddock. Unless you think Braddock and Kettering were in on it together?"

"No, we don't think that, Chief," Justin replied. "Tell you what. Let's go through the parts that trouble you, okay?"

The chief leaned forward. To give his hands something to do, he picked up his radio and began playing with its stubby rubber antenna. "Fair enough. For starters, the ambassador was drunk. His blood workup proves it."

"The blood was tampered with. Alcohol was introduced shortly after it was drawn. We have irrefutable proof of that."

"You saying the bureau tainted evidence?" Tuchmann said.

"I'm saying the evidence was doctored. I'm not accusing anyone at this point. Next?"

"The murder weapon. It belonged to Kettering and had his prints plastered all over it."

"We've examined the candlestick. We agree it belonged to Kettering, so it's not unexpected that his prints would be on it. Believe me, Chief, that piece of evidence doesn't cause me too much alarm. I'm by no means downplaying its significance, but it can be explained."

"Well, how about motive? The whole world knows the cardinal had been having an ongoing affair with the victim for years. She was pregnant. A scandal was about to erupt, and it was more than he could bear. People go over the edge in times of crisis. They do stupid things. Things like murder. Even priests. The DNA tests will prove paternity. What then? How do you get around that?"

"Chief, there was no affair." Justin paused for a second before coming to the decision to tell all. "The woman was the cardinal's daughter."

"*What? Come again?*" The chief dropped his radio with a loud crack on the marble-topped table. "*His daughter*!"

"That's correct. She was born before Kettering became a priest. We have all the information to document that fact, and we'll gladly share it with you."

"Have you told this to the FBI?"

"Not yet. When we go to the bureau it will be to have the charges dropped. We have no intention of presenting evidence piecemeal. And frankly, we're still not a hundred percent sure where the bureau stands on this. I repeat, I'm not accusing it of misconduct, but we have good reason to be cautious. We're doing our own DNA tests at *CellTest*, and we'll prove that the cardinal and the victim were father and child. The FBI hasn't even thought of that possibility, because it doesn't fit their theory of what's happened. They're only looking at the cardinal and the fetus."

Tuchmann's mind was racing. "So you want me to go out and arrest Braddock, is that it?"

"Absolutely not. There are still some pretty important questions we need answers to before that day comes. We need to get to work on finding those answers right away, and that's where you can help."

"Internal Affairs?" It was the first time Valerie had spoken.

Justin nodded. "Yes, but I suggest that only those who have an absolute need to know get involved. There's more at stake here than Mrs. von Snellenberger's murder. She was silenced, but not for the reasons everyone thinks. She was in this country to warn the cardinal about a much larger issue, one involving the Vatican and several foreign governments. That issue is still very much unresolved. What we decide here can impact dramatically on what I've just alluded to, and if we're compromised, then a lot of people could die. I know you're skeptical, but I ask you to believe me."

"What exactly are you looking for, Mr. Scott?" Tuchmann asked. "I mean, we can and will have him covered twenty-four hours a day. Other than that, just what do you think he'll do?"

"I suspect he's going to make a run on the cardinal. Not him personally, but I think he'll hire the necessary talent. The man's been given an ultimatum. He's got to be scared."

"What else do you need?" asked the chief.

"Personnel records. Vacation sheets. For example, when was he on leave? Did he mention he was going abroad when in fact we know he did? Official reprimands. Missing evidence. Complaints from street people of being squeezed by a lieutenant. That sort of thing. Things you would normally do in an investigation of a bad cop."

Valerie interrupted. "Chief, Tom works for me, and he never said a word about foreign travel. In fact, in June he told me he was taking a driving vacation out west. When he got back he said it was the best holiday he ever had. Highly recommended the same trip for my family. 'You've just gotta see Yellowstone and the Grand Tetons, Val,'" she mimicked. A second later she added in hushed voice; "The man flat-out lied to me, Chief."

At that moment Tuchmann's radio came to life. "Echo One, Central."

Tuchmann picked it up and keyed the mike. "Echo One. Go."

"Echo One, call Rainbow."

"Roger. One, out."

Tuchmann grinned sheepishly at the group. "Rainbow's my wife. I told her I'd be home in an hour."

Justin smiled as he stood up. "Sorry for the inconvenience, Chief, and sorry for the bad news about Braddock."

Valerie cleared her throat. "Chief, I'm going back to the office and get things moving. Tom was the duty officer the night the woman was murdered. He gave the briefing, remember? I want to go over those reports and his duty log for that night. I want to know if he was out of the Daly Building at any time. Things like that. I can get a lot done because Sunday's traditionally the quietest night of the week. Might as well. There's no way I'll be able to sleep tonight."

Tuchmann agreed. "But I'd better not go with you," he added. "If I show up, everybody at headquarters will know something's going down. Meet me in my office at seven in the morning, Inspector, and we'll get Internal Affairs moving then." He looked around the room, eyes finally coming to rest on Justin. "That about do it for now, Mr. Scott?"

"Yes, Chief. We'll keep you posted."

"Likewise. Goodnight."

Justin's small group remained in the office for another hour, but by eight o'clock all had left except Paula who said she wanted to stay a while longer to copy some files, and the latest photos into the computer. "I'll be done in less than an hour. See you in the morning."

* * *

Justin and O'Bryan drove Sinclair home, with Justin cautioning him to say nothing about what he had heard this day.

"It never happened," replied Sinclair. "Isn't that what they say in the movies?"

Justin smiled in the dark. "Yeah, I believe it is."

But Justin's day wasn't done. He and O'Bryan headed for the embassy to meet with Doctor Brosnan, the internist he had called a few days before. This was the only time the doctor could fit Kettering into his busy schedule.

* * *

At one minute past nine, the office fax came to life and spat out a document. The message took twelve seconds to transmit. And like the two before it, there was no recipient named, nor any sender's identification block included.

* * *

Valerie stopped for a Big Mac, fries, and a soda before heading to work. She called Danny and told him she'd be late and not to wait up. "Give Dania a kiss and a hug from mommy. Love ya."

She sat at her desk for a moment, wondering where to begin. One thing was for sure: she'd have to come clean with the chief about Braddock's run-in with the Atlantic City cops. God only knows what the man would say about her cover-up.

"Okay, hotshot, start with Braddock's report from the night of the murder," she said out loud as she walked to her file cabinet and zeroed in on the folder in question.

It took her ten minutes to read it twice, and as she settled in for a third reading, a thought popped into her head. The murderer had to have known which car Kettering would use that night. Had to, because he had gone to great lengths to switch tags with a car of the same make and color. And he'd located a vehicle with only a one-digit difference in the VIN number. How was that possible? Then it dawned on her.

She began clicking away at her computer keyboard. Following the instructions on the screen, she worked her way into a data bank maintained by Ford Motor Company, in Dearborn, Michigan. Once in, she typed the serial number of the car bought by the Vatican.

A few seconds later Ford's Dearborn computer came back with an answer. She learned the car had been manufactured on May 15 at a plant in Ontario, Canada, then shipped to a dealer in Fairfax, Virginia, two days later. It was not a special order item. When she tried to ferret her way deeper into the computer, she hit a brick wall. Without special passwords there was no information available about who the vehicle had been sold to. Okay, she could live with that. It didn't take a rocket scientist to figure which car the cardinal would leave the compound in for a midnight ride. Certainly not one with diplomatic plates requiring a chauffeur.

Next, she asked herself: How did Braddock lure the ambassador out that night?

She asked the computer for a listing of the ten cars manufactured immediately before and after the one sold to the embassy. Instantly came a summary of twenty vehicles. And there it was! Same make, model, exterior, and interior. A veritable clone. In fact, she scanned the list and discovered that out of the twenty units listed on her screen, four were identical. *Must be a popular combination*, she concluded, fingers tapping rapidly across the keyboard.

The car had been delivered to a dealer in Baltimore, then sold to a couple in Gaithersburg, Maryland. The buyers' entire credit history was flashed on the screen for her to peruse at her leisure. She chose not to, since she already knew all she needed to know.

She went back into the computer for the identification numbers of the Vatican's car, and asked for the warranty history.

The car had been serviced twice. Once, for a broken seat belt extractor, the second time for a major problem with the air conditioner. The report in front of her showed Ford had been billed by the dealer for twelve hundred fourteen dollars for a new compressor, evaporator-dryer, refrigerant, and, of course, labor. The job had been approved by the area service rep. The car had twenty-one hundred and four miles on the odometer, and it had been released back to the owner the day before the murder.

She sat back, a look of satisfaction spreading across her face. But, if she could do this, then of course, so could Braddock. And in all likelihood that's exactly what he did. She reminded herself to make sure Internal Affairs went over all the logs from his computer station to see if he'd keyed in on the vehicle in Gaithersburg. Nothing was sacred or secret any more. Braddock could have switched tags at the dealership; but how would he have really known the car would be there for service? She realized this called for a huge stretch, a forcing of events to fit a wanted result, but at least she was thinking. Everyone left a trail. She allowed herself an additional second or two to mentally review what she had done so far, then pressed on.

Tom had been the shift commander that night, responsible for all the detectives on duty in the city for a twelve hour period. She rummaged her way rapidly through his daily logs, stopping at the day in question. She studied the screen. Braddock had come on duty at 6:00 p.m. He'd left the building at eleven, logging out for the second district. He'd returned at 2:55 a.m. He'd certainly had enough time to get into mischief. Still, she was not unduly excited with this tidbit of knowledge. Braddock hated the office, and often spent hours on the street. She'd do the same if it weren't for the mountain of paperwork ever-present in her in-basket.

Then all hell had broken loose. Braddock had remained on duty throughout the day running down leads, until finally a Red Flag had been declared by the chief, and the lid slammed shut. No more computer entries. Indeed, nothing to even indicate the nature of the Red Flag. Any information after this point was entered into a restricted area of the computer, and even she couldn't access all of those files. No big deal. She knew the rest anyway.

Braddock must have been really wired to the wall that day. If he'd killed the woman, he knew it would only be a matter of time until the body was discovered in the trunk. And who had responded to the call from the police yard when it finally came? Braddock. And who had had the opportunity to plant a murder weapon? Braddock.

She felt her flesh crawl. Her breaths escaped in short, ragged bursts as she contemplated the enormity of what had apparently happened. But why? she kept asking herself. What was the connection between Tom Braddock and Maritha von Snellenberger?

As she sat staring into nothingness, a thought bubbled up from the recesses of her mind, then slammed into her consciousness. It made her cry out involuntarily. She jumped off her chair with such force that it toppled over behind her, spinning on one armrest before slamming into her leg. She didn't feel a thing.

"Oh my God! Oh, sweet Jesus!" Her voice was a rasping, atavistic strangling sound even to her ears. She grasped the edge of the desk to steady her suddenly-jellied body, and began to shake like one possessed. She moaned. When the chief heard this he'd have her head.

* * *

"No rest for the weary, Justin," O'Bryan joked, pretending to sag as they stood at the embassy's front door. "Hopefully the cardinal's check-up won't take too long, and we can all hit the hay."

They were led into a sitting room and a waiting Monsignor Capelletti who asked if they would care for some refreshments.

Both declined.

At that moment a young priest entered and informed Monsignor Capelletti that there was a call for Mr. Scott.

Justin took it on an extension in the room.

"This is Doctor Brosnan, Mr. Scott. I was supposed to meet you at the embassy at nine, but I've been involved in a fender-bender. No one's hurt, but by the time the cops are through with all the paperwork, it'll be too late. I'm really sorry. Could you call my office in the morning to reschedule?"

"No problem, Doc, thanks for the call."

Capelletti looked ashen. "That was Doctor Brosnan on the phone?"

"Yeah, he has to cancel because of a car accident."

"But that's impossible. Doctor Brosnan's upstairs with the cardinal right now. There must be some mistake."

"*Holy Mother of God*!" Justin grabbed Capelletti's arm. "What room are they in? Take me there, now."

The three men flew up the stairs, their singular prayer being that they weren't too late. Capelletti pointed to a door, and Justin turned the handle with all the strength he could muster. Locked.

He took a step back, raised his leg, aimed at the handle and lashed out. The violence of the kick tore the lock from the wood, and with continued momentum he shouldered his way into the room, eyes sweeping the scene.

"See here. What's the meaning of this?" The doctor was holding a syringe, frozen in mid-air, inches from Kettering's exposed upper arm. The surprise and shock on his face spoke volumes.

Justin covered the distance between them by launching himself into the air, feet first, striking the man hard in the chest. Both crashed heavily to the floor, Justin managing to land on top. He bounced to his feet in one fluid motion, but a second later he was back on top of the man. He grabbed a handful of hair in both hands and slammed his face down. They all heard the nose break, and saw the blood spurt onto the carpet. The man yelped once, then lapsed into unconsciousness.

Still riding the charlatan's back, Justin studied Kettering. "You all right, Cardinal? Did he have a chance to give you anything? Pills? Another shot, perhaps?"

"N … n … no," Kettering stammered. "Nothing."

"Thank God!" Justin issued orders to Monsignor Capelletti. "Get me some strong rope for this dirtbag."

Five minutes later the 'doctor' lay trussed, alert and moaning, while Justin expertly went through his things. He was carrying a standard medical bag, crammed with items unfamiliar to Justin. He recovered the syringe from under a chair, miraculously intact, and gingerly placed a rubber cap over the needle. "God only knows what's in here," he said. Then he roughly searched the doctor, uncovering a .25 Beretta in a holster secured to the middle of his back.

"Ain't you a regular Marcus Welby." He glared at the man, wondering what he was going to do with him. An idea hit home. He scrambled to the phone and, with three sets of eyes following his every move, dialed a number.

His call was answered on the second ring. "Mannix, it's Justin," he announced. "Get some backup, and hightail it over to the Vatican Embassy. Somebody posing as a doctor just tried to off the cardinal. Kettering's okay, but there's a phony doctor here who's somewhat worse for the wear. I want you to put this clown on ice for a couple of days. See what you can squeeze out of him. Also, I need you to have your lab run a test on what the son of a bitch damn near injected the cardinal with, and I'll need the results like yesterday. Needless to say, the whole operation stays black. The last thing I need is for the cops to hear about this little escapade, because something tells me if our pal Braddock finds out, he'll get spooked and bolt. See you in a half-hour."

A very shaken group waited for the duo from Industrial Management to arrive. Justin realized it had been a close call. A few seconds later and Kettering would have been dead.

* * *

"Are you out of your frigging mind, Tobias? You're telling me you not only knew that he stashed a vial of blood in his refrigerator, but that you actually approved?" They were in Tuchmann's office and the chief couldn't believe what he'd just heard. "But you never thought to shag your ass over to his apartment and bring the evidence back? Evidence in a murder case?"

"Chief, at the time it seemed like a good idea," Valerie said, lamely, knowing how it must sound. "We were being steamrollered by the bureau. Those guys came in and took charge of our case, and it hurt. So when Braddock told me what he'd done, I admit I was pleased. I didn't know exactly what we'd do with the blood, but then I just plain forgot about it."

"You think it's still there?"

She shrugged.

"Why in the hell would he want to keep a vial of blood?"

Another shrug. Then a thought. "Chief, Braddock admitted to me that he'd picked the blood vials up from the hospital's lab. Knowing what we know now, he definitely had the time to take it somewhere and have it altered. I'm thinking that was his plan all along. It was part of a setup. Maybe the FBI didn't do a thing to their samples. Maybe they just did a quick and dirty look-see for alcohol because the main thrust of their testing was going to be in the area of DNA. They expected to find alcohol, and bingo, they found alcohol. And they moved on. Not the FBI we've come to know and admire from training tapes and slick PR commercials, but shit happens."

"I'll certainly give Braddock credit for having a humongous pair of brass ones." Matthew Tuchmann let loose a sigh of surrender. "All right, Tobias, take it from the top."

For the next hour they sat undisturbed, reviewing the case, and the evidence that could link Braddock to the murder. Tuchmann made some cryptic notes on a legal pad as they painstakingly dissected what they knew. He had calmed down considerably, but Valerie could see he was still fuming beneath the surface. One of his ranking officers was not just dirty, but very likely a murderer as well. *Bad medicine for any police chief to have to swallow*, she admitted.

"Okay," Tuchmann finally said. "Here's the drill. I want to meet Justin, ASAP. Set it up for you and me to go to his office because I sure as shit don't want him seen around here. We'll draw up a writ for a search warrant on Braddock's apartment, and I'll hand carry it to Judge Harvey Tanner at the federal courthouse."

He glanced at his notes, placed a check mark beside an entry and pressed on. "We're definitely going to specify that we want to recover the vial of blood, but I'm sure Justin's got other things he's looking for." Again he studied his notes. "If his requests aren't off the wall, we'll add them. And, lastly, I'll be asking the judge to authorize a phone tap." A final check mark appeared on the sheet. "I want this signed, sealed and delivered by noon, and I want to have a team in and out of Braddock's place by the end of the day." He looked up at Valerie. "Arrange for Braddock to disappear for several hours. Send him out of town on an errand. Use your head. Think of something."

"Yes, sir."

"Okay. I meet with Captain Gardner from Internal Affairs in ten minutes to give him his marching orders. Anything special you want me to tell him?"

She shook her head, then took the liberty to change the subject. "Do you think Justin's giving us the straight skinny about there being a crisis unfolding in the Vatican? I mean, well, if he is, then how in the name of all that's holy could Braddock be involved?"

The chief snorted. "I think putting out fires is a way of life in the Vatican. Even so, something tells me this one's a real dilly, and yeah, I do indeed believe Braddock's involved. Something big is going down alright, something with an international twist, but I guarantee you this: We aren't going to be privy to whatever it is. I'm no Catholic, but I know that the Church knows how to conduct damage control. It's had two thousand years' of practice." He snorted again. "Come to think of it, I don't *want* to know about the Vatican's troubles because I've got troubles enough of my own. You got anything else for me?"

Valerie shook her head, deciding this was not the time to tell the chief about Braddock's escapade in Atlantic City.

Five minutes later she was on the street, tired from only three hours of sleep, but wired and flying on an adrenaline high. Shit was happening, and happening fast. It felt weird to be working so closely with Justin again after so many years, and she found herself flooded with nostalgia. *Where would this take them*? she wondered, but in the recesses of her cortex the bigger question begging an answer was a simple variant: *Where would it end*?

CHAPTER 22

Paula handed Justin the fax. "This came in after I left last night."

> SEE PAGE 4 OF LAST SATURDAY'S INTERNATIONAL TRIBUNE. CERTAIN PEOPLE ARE GOING TO PROTECT THEIR INTERESTS AT ALL COSTS. BE CAREFUL. YOU ARE ALL TARGETS.

"I retrieved the article off the Internet," she said, passing a second page to Justin.

> COUNT MURDERED ON BUSY STREET
>
> GENEVA, SZ- (AP)-
>
> A man identified as Count Rudolph Laufenburg, 39, of Lausanne, Switzerland, was murdered Thursday afternoon on a busy Bern thoroughfare. At first it was believed he had suffered a heart attack. He was rushed to St. John of God Hospital where doctors declared him dead shortly after arrival. However, it was only after

an autopsy was performed that authorities learned the true cause of death. Laufenburg had been struck in the neck by a small, hollow pellet filled with Pyrolene, a highly toxic nerve agent. According to police sources, Pyrolene, a derivative of Sarin, is so deadly that less than one one-thousandth of an ounce can cause death within a matter of seconds. It has the characteristic of leaving no discernible trace once in the body. However, residue from inside the pellet was recovered, and positively identified as Pyrolene, a substance which when dried, forms a unique, vermilion colored crystal. This is what alerted the medical examiner as to the true cause of death.

Authorities noted a similarity to a case two decades ago in London where a diplomat was killed in like fashion, but with a slower acting poison called Ricin which is extracted from the castor bean plant. Like Ricin, Pyrolene is known to have been manufactured by both the Russians and the Bulgarians, but has never been produced in the West.

Count Laufenburg was a partner in *Credit Lausanne*, a private bank operated by his family for over eighty years. He also was a director of *Ibel & Laufenburg*; an investigative firm owned by the bank.

Mr. Klaus Furlan, managing director, expressed feelings of shock and disbelief, and stated that there was no reason why anyone would want to murder the count. He did admit that their offices had been broken into and ransacked in recent days, but discounted any connection between that event and the death of his partner. He also insisted nothing of value was missing.

> Count Laufenburg is survived by his wife, Helga, and his mother, the Dowager Countess Sabrina Laufenburg, both of Vienna. He also leaves a sister, Mme. Jacqueline Pompidou, currently a resident of Versailles. Funeral arrangements are incomplete.

O'Bryan walked in while Justin was still reading, and when finished handed the pages to the priest. They made eye contact, and Justin made an almost imperceptible shake of his head, a reminder to O'Bryan not to comment about their experience the night they had flown out of Switzerland.

O'Bryan read the fax and accompanying article. "I'd sure like to meet our *Deep Throat* because his information always seems to be top-notch." He waved the sheets in the air. "This confirms good old Count Laufenburg knew more than he was letting on. Same goes for Furlan. In fact, if I were in Furlan's shoes now I'd be planning on making myself mighty scarce."

"Yeah, I'd say that would be the smart move," Justin agreed.

"Then couldn't the same be said for us?" remarked Paula, her face fully reflecting her concern.

Justin looked at them both. "Valid point. But let's face it: if a U.S. President can be considered fair game regardless of his elaborate protection apparatus, what chance do we *peons* really have?" He shook his head. "The answer of course is none. So, if we want to keep our collective sanity, we continue on with our lives, and hope that certain people will come to the conclusion that we really know nothing of value, and simply leave us be." He didn't for a single second believe one word of it.

"I hope you're right, Justin," said Paula, sensing that Justin did not relish the thought of continuing on the topic, if only for her sake. She made the task easier by changing the subject. "I got a call from Inspector Tobias a few minutes ago. She and Chief Tuchmann want to come over here to draft a search warrant to enter Braddock's apartment. The chief wants to have a federal judge sign it today along with authorization for a phone tap. Tobias said they'd be here at ten unless I called to cancel."

"Then let's do it," O'Bryan answered without hesitation. "In fact, let's make sure we ask them to include the two things we're looking for: a woman's purse—namely Maritha's, and any large quantities of cash." His face took on a frown. "Did the inspector tell you why they've suddenly decided on this course of action? I mean, they only met with us last night, and now they're pressing for a warrant. Makes me wonder what it is they know and we don't."

"Ask at ten, *Padre*," said Justin. "Now, I have a suggestion. I want to strong-arm the chief into allowing me to go in with his boys. Naturally, he'll object, but I think a little friendly blackmail from all of us ganging up on him will go a long way to persuading Tuchmann to see the light. My money says he doesn't want us going public with what we know about Braddock, so he'll fold, and begrudgingly allow me to tag along. You see, I don't want some of the local yahoos screwing with whatever it is that's found. So I'm counting on us all making sure I'm on board, okay?"

Again Paula switched topics. "Justin, have you forgotten that you're supposed to meet with Doctor Mizner at eleven and take him to the embassy?"

"Today? You sure?" The appointment had escaped Justin's mind entirely.

Paula nodded. "Positive. I spoke to the cardinal before coming to work to remind him as well. He admitted he was nervous, but told me he was looking forward to finding out conclusively what happened that night. Doctor Mizner might well be our last hope."

"Who's this Mizner?" asked a perplexed O'Bryan. "How come I don't know about him?"

"*Mea culpa*, Jack," intoned Justin, sounding truly apologetic. "He's a doctor, and Paula suggested consulting with him shortly after you and I came back from Europe. It just slipped my mind to tell you because of all the other things that have been happening. Paula persuaded me to speak to Dr. Mizner because Kettering genuinely can't remember anything of value after he left the embassy that night. He can recall bits and pieces from around the edges; like he knew he was to meet Maritha, yet he does not really remember why. Mizner's a psychiatrist; a leading authority in hypnotherapy, and he's agreed to help."

"How did you get him? What do you know about the guy?" O'Bryan pressed.

"My Uncle Aaron recommended him," Paula answered for Justin. "Aaron's also a doctor, and he's used Doctor Mizner for years when any of his patients have needed help. Aaron swears he's the best in the country, and claims Mizner's the only shrink he knows who's not carrying a lot of his own baggage."

"And I gave the okay, and Kettering said yes," Justin added by way of finishing Paula's explanation. "I'd like you to come with me, Jack to help videotape, because if this works, then a video would be the best proof of all to nail down the cardinal's innocence for once and for all."

O'Bryan agreed. "Okay, but how about keeping me in the loop from now on? Especially now that I'm finding I'm suddenly skittish around medical folks I don't know personally." He was still rattled from the last doctor's visit with Kettering.

* * *

"Do you mind if I call you Francis?" Doctor Mizner was seated across from Kettering while Justin and O'Bryan fidgeted with the camcorder.

Kettering smiled nervously. "No, of course not, that is my name."

"And I want you to call me Thaddeus. Is that not a horrible moniker to have dragged through almost eighty years of life?" Mizner reflected with a chuckle. "Better yet; just call me Thad."

"Thad it is."

"Francis, let me explain what it is I would like to do, and why. There are two reasons why people develop memory loss such as you're experiencing. Trauma, and trauma. Already I've simplified the problem, no?"

He spoke quietly, establishing an intimacy and rapport with the cleric. "Physical trauma, such as a blow to the head, will almost always cause the mind to short-circuit. But, so too will mental trauma. For example, being the witness to a terrible event. You see, the mind protects itself by shutting down when confronted with trauma. But, by so doing, it also protects the physical body in the process. An example of each would be an automobile accident with head injuries in the first instance; and a soldier collapsing in the heat of battle in the second. Our soldier hasn't been wounded, per se, but his mind can no longer cope with the carnage. So, in order to protect itself, the mind simply shuts down. Different traumas; same results. Nature's miracle. But in your case, Francis, you suffered physical *and* mental trauma all at once. Not unusual, but a double whammy, nonetheless."

Kettering nodded that he understood.

"So, Francis, we're going to free your mind of that trauma. And the way I propose we do this is to give you Pentothal. This will help bring to the forefront information which your subconscious is fighting so hard to conceal."

"That's a truth serum, is it not?" Kettering sounded worried.

"Yes, it's often referred to as a truth serum, but I must tell you, what you see in the movies is not an accurate portrayal of how it works. You do not go into a state where you are forced to reveal anything and everything. You can fight the drug and reveal nothing. Many people do. But oftentimes revelation comes because of the subtle manner in which the examiner crafts his questions. The questions are seemingly innocuous, so the patient soon feels secure. He begins to relax. He begins to trust. Then he starts to talk. And as long as there is no frontal assault, so to speak, then the information sought is indeed revealed. Am I making sense, Francis? Sometimes I get carried away with my explanations."

"I understand. At least I think I do. You're saying that I won't be forced to reveal secrets that should remain secret, right?"

"Absolutely. I only intend to focus on the night of your daughter's murder. Nothing more." Mizner paused for a moment, as if to gather his thoughts. "You know, Francis, I can relate to your pain. I, too, lost a daughter to a violent act, so I know how deeply wounded you are. It's unnatural for a parent to have to bury a child. It causes a rent to appear in the fabric of the soul, a tearing which will never fully heal. It's a terrible burden for any parent to have to carry."

"Thank you for telling me that, Thad." Kettering smiled weakly.

"We will clear your mind for once-and-for-all of this trauma, Francis. And afterwards, not only will you remember everything, but you will also find within you the capacity to be able to accept what's happened. Do you have any questions?"

Kettering exhaled loudly to cover-up his nervousness. "No. Let's get started."

Mizner motioned toward the sofa. "Francis, would you be so kind as to stretch out and make yourself comfortable?"

When Kettering was settled, Mizner approached him with a syringe. "First, I want to give you a very small amount of diazepam. You know it as Valium," he explained. "This will put you at ease. Then we'll introduce the Pentothal which will further the process. So, shall we begin?"

Five minutes later, Dr. Mizner addressed the cardinal. "Francis, you should be able to hear me just fine. Mr. Scott and Monsignor O'Bryan are still with us. You can open your eyes and look around if you like, but I'd prefer you keep them closed to better concentrate. Plus, it will aid in forming mental images. Okay, so far?"

"Yes."

"Good. Now let's journey back to the night of Maritha's death. Stay relaxed, Francis, follow my suggestions." Mizner waited a moment, then continued in his quiet, unhurried way. "You mentioned before that you left your embassy sometime after midnight, correct?"

Kettering shook his head. "No, I left about seven."

Justin's face registered surprise. This was news to him. Capelletti had not volunteered this information, but in his defense Justin quickly remembered that was a question he had never asked.

"Tell me about it, Francis. Where did you go?"

"I went to the Italian Embassy to see Donato Rossi, the ambassador. We're old friends, and I had arranged during the week to visit that night. I even told Monsignor Capelletti that if it got to be too late, then I would stay the night. I've done that before. The monsignor wanted to have the driver take me, but I said, no, it was the man's day off, and that I wanted to see if the Ford's air conditioner had been fixed properly. I said that I'd drive myself. Of course, the real reason was I didn't want to be out and about in a car with diplomatic plates."

"I understand. But what was so special about that particular night, Francis?"

"I was to meet Maritha at one o'clock. We had made the arrangements by phone several days earlier. She had called me from somewhere in Europe. She was very scared. And she was worried about being followed to America. So, to ease her fears I arranged for her to travel on a false passport. She said I would understand her concern once she had the chance to present to me irrefutable proof of her allegations."

"I see. So you went to visit Ambassador Rossi, and you stayed until shortly before one. Is that right?"

"Yes."

"Then where did you go?"

"I was to meet my Maritha at the entrance to the Lincoln Memorial. The plan was that she would then come with me in my car, and we would drive while she explained and showed me everything." Kettering's voice was becoming strained, his face reflecting a building inner torment. He lowered his voice. "She had to get back home to her husband as quickly as possible. No one was to know she had even been to the States, far less learn that she had visited with me."

Mizner noticed the change in Kettering's demeanor. "Francis, everything's fine," he said in a soothing voice. "Stay calm. Nothing, and no one, can hurt you, I promise." He waited until his words took effect. "Did you get to meet Maritha as planned?"

Kettering shook his head. "I waited until after one-thirty, but she didn't show. I began to get worried, so finally I decided to backtrack to the Italian Embassy. Maybe she'd misunderstood, or had gotten lost. I had told her I'd be with Donato that night, so maybe she thought that's where we were to meet." He shrugged his thin shoulders. "I didn't know what else to do."

"You're doing fine, Francis. So you started back towards the Italian Embassy. What happened next?"

"It began to drizzle. Not hard, but enough that I knew I had to be cautious. Anyway, as I drove, a car suddenly pulled up behind me out of nowhere, and a moment later a blue flashing light was turned on inside the car. It was the police!"

Justin was enthralled at what he was hearing.

"Francis, I now want you to actually relive those next few minutes. I want events to unfold in the present as you speak. Do you understand what I'm asking, Francis? Everything is happening now. Can you do that for me?"

"Yes. It's all happening right now." Kettering's face took on a perplexed look. "Why am I being stopped? I'm not speeding."

"Look around, Francis. Do you see any other cars on the road?"

The cardinal shook his head. "No, just the two of us. It's very late, very quiet."

"What's the officer doing now?"

"He's standing beside my door. He wants me to roll down my window. He seems to be very angry. His face is pressed up to the glass. I can see his breath. He's motioning for me to roll down the window."

"Have you ever seen him before?"

"No."

"Are you rolling down your window?"

"Yes." At that moment Kettering flinched and seemed to want to turn his head. Obviously startled, he cried out.

"What's happening, Francis?"

"He just sprayed something in my face. I can't move. What is it? Wait! I can see Our Lady. It's a vision. *Our Lady is right in front of me*!"

"Francis, is it possible you're hallucinating because of the spray?"

Kettering shook his head emphatically. "No. I'm not hallucinating. It's Our Lady. She's right in front of me."

Justin was thunderstruck. But in a moment of inspiration he suddenly knew with absolute certitude what it was that Kettering had just seen. *Our Lady.* Yes! Not the Mother of God; not the Virgin Mary; not the Blessed Mother; but *Our Lady.*

Quietly, he addressed Mizner. "Doctor, could I ask Francis a question?"

If Mizner was upset by the interruption, he didn't show it. "If you think it's important," he answered.

Justin walked three short steps to the cardinal's side. "Your Eminence, did you say you can see *Notre Dame*?" He deliberately used the French pronunciation of the word *Dame*, so it came out sounding *Dahm* as he asked his question. Words, when translated into English meant *Our Lady*.

"*Yes*!" Kettering replied, still highly excited.

Look closer," Justin ordered. "It's not really Our Lady you see, but two French words. *Notre Dame*! They're written on the man's shirt. Our Lady isn't really there, Francis. It's *words* you're seeing. Words on the front of a man's shirt."

Kettering actually smiled for a second. "Why, so it is! They're big, gold letters on a black shirt. Oh, my goodness, how silly of me."

O'Bryan let out a short, involuntary gasp as he stared at Justin, his face reflecting a marveling at the man's perspicacity. Justin was nothing short of a genius.

Mizner also stared, remaining silent for several seconds. "I take it that means something to you?" he finally asked, in his quiet, unruffled manner.

"It's the answer to a prayer," replied Justin in a hushed voice. "It means everything. I'm sorry for the interruption, please continue."

Mizner turned to the cardinal. "So, we know it wasn't a vision, Francis. Tell me, what's happening now?"

"He's opening my door and pulling me out of the car. I can't talk and my legs are like rubber. Ouch! I've just hit my head on the side of the door. I can feel it starting to bleed. But I can't raise my hand to touch it. What's happening to me?" His voice was filling with genuine alarm. "Wait! There are two other men. They're opening the trunk of their car. I can see everything, but I can't move. They have a bundle in their arms. The man who grabbed me is opening the trunk of my car. Oh my God! It's my beautiful child; my Maritha. She's in a blanket, but I can see her face. Her eyes are open. She's staring at me, but she's dead." Kettering began to cry, loud wails pouring from his twisted mouth. "*Oh, Maritha*!" he screeched.

Mizner made no move to comfort the man.

"*Aagghh*!" It was a strangled cry from a tormented soul. "They've put Maritha in my trunk. One of the men has just put something else in. He's covering it with a cloth; or maybe it's a towel. Now they've slammed the lid shut. The whole car is shaking."

"What was put into the trunk with Maritha?"

"I didn't see."

"Yes you did, Francis. Tell me."

Kettering's eyes opened wide and he stared at the ceiling. He began to tremble. "I don't want to," he cried out, and turned his face to the wall.

"Francis, I want you to close your eyes. Good. Now, you must tell me. It's very important that you do. Tell me what the man just put in the trunk. You saw what it was."

"My candlestick," he finally wailed. "They deliberately killed my beautiful Maritha using one of my candlesticks as a warning to me."

"But why would they do that?" Mizner pressed. "What was so special about that candlestick? You must tell me, Francis."

Kettering seemed to resist, but somewhere in the deep recesses of his mind he found the necessary reassurance. He spoke in a hushed voice. "It was one of a pair," he began, "and my Maritha's nightmare started the day she and her husband gave me those candlesticks for my sixtieth birthday. Neither understood their significance or value at the time. It was simply a spur-of-the-moment gift to an old friend. I soon discovered their true worth, however, and when I did, I offered to return them. Of course, they refused. I never thought to question Maritha or Freddy as to where they came from. I just accepted my good fortune. A short time later, I went public with my discovery as to whose hand I thought had created such magnificence, and in the doing, signed my own child's death warrant." He paused, sniffled, wiped his eyes with the heels of both hands, but did not break down. He then lay perfectly still, eyes closed, gathering his thoughts.

"You see," he continued, "those exquisite candlesticks had been stolen from the Hermitage Museum in St. Petersburg, Russia, and given to Freddy by Archbishop Torrelli. But Torrelli was very smart. He used an intermediary. Maritha told me during a phone call that Torrelli had intended all along to use them to blackmail Freddy, and knowing what I know now, I think she was right. However, she came to this conclusion many months later, long after they had passed into my possession. There are severe penalties in Switzerland for dealing in stolen works of art. The scandal, and possible prison term would have been ruinous to them both. But now the problem was more acute, simply because I was the new owner, plus Torrelli had now discovered that Maritha was aware of what he was up to."

Justin, O'Bryan, and Mizner barely breathed as they listened, knowing that the slightest sound could break the spell. They were enthralled. The camcorder captured every word, every gesture.

Kettering sighed. "Maritha had somehow acquired a document proving the existence of a conspiracy unfolding inside the Church, and it implicated the director of the Vatican Bank along with some highly placed members of the *curia*. It also tied these priests to the top echelon of the Italian Mafia, as well as to several influential Russians. It further spoke of Archbishop Torrelli's deep involvement in black market activities inside Russia, and how he's using the Vatican Bank to launder the proceeds from the sale of plundered Russian treasures. The majority of these treasures come from the Hermitage Museum, but a many others are also being stolen every day from other museums as well. Maritha said this criminal enterprise runs to the hundreds of millions of dollars a year. Anyway, with the money the Russian oligarchs receive from selling these treasures, they're able to buy all the heroin and cocaine they want from the Italian Mafia. At the same time, they're busy setting up partnerships throughout the country to profit from every illegal activity imaginable. The Italians want to be an established presence before the Americans criminals have a chance to move in."

He took a deep breath, then hurried on. "And Maritha told me that Freddy was being blackmailed by Torrelli. You see, the Archbishop wanted Freddy's bank to begin handling most of the transfers, but Freddy had been putting him off for months. Torrelli finally gave him an ultimatum, and that's what drove Maritha to come to see me. She was in America to hand me the proof of what it is Torrelli and his clique are conspiring for the last phase of a wickedly devious scheme. You see, they expect the Holy Father to die shortly, and when he does, their plan is to seize control of the Church and move the Throne of Peter from Rome to St. Petersburg, Russia. And I'm not talking about a temporary move like when the papacy moved to Avignon, France, for most of the Thirteen Hundreds. No, this is meant to be permanent, and the mechanics for how the transfer of power are all spelled out in the document Maritha had in her possession. Torrelli, naturally, is at center stage. It seems he fully intends to become the next pope. God only knows how he plans to legitimize such an action with the College of Cardinals, but apparently he's confident that he has found a way to do just that. Maritha thought I could somehow stop the madness, but Torrelli and his murderers got to her first. Torrelli had to get that document back at all costs, no matter what." The tears began to flow. "So, you can see it was indeed a brilliant strategy to have me branded as the murderer of my mistress and unborn child. Who would ever believe me after such an abominable act if I then came forward with this story? I would be seen as simply trying to save my own skin, which would make me become more despised than I am now. And the document Maritha was carrying has vanished; a document I needed in order to show the Pope that I'm telling the truth."

Mizner sat back, and bowed his head. "Thank you for telling me. You now understand, Francis, that you deliberately blotted all memory of this from your consciousness because it was impossibly painful to bear. You erroneously thought you had failed your daughter, when in fact, you had not. But now it's all finally out in the open, and you will be able to accept what has happened, free of any hint of guilt. I repeat. You were in no way responsible for what befell Maritha. You can, and you must, take comfort in that knowledge."

Mizner waited a full minute for Kettering to digest and accept what he had been told. Then he continued in his calm, soothing voice with a gentle prompting. "Now, Francis, I want you to go back and finish telling me what's happening by your car. Alright? You just said the men have slammed down the trunk lid and that the whole car's shaking. Please go on from there."

Kettering didn't miss a beat. It was as though the interruption had never taken place.

"The man who pulled me out of my car is taking things from the glove box. He's coming around to my side again. He's taking my wallet from my pocket, and putting it in his. Now he's squirting something else in my face. I'm trying to turn away, but I can't. The stuff is all over my jacket and shirt. *It's alcohol!* I can smell it. He's spraying me with alcohol. But why? Is he going to set me on fire? Oh, my God! Why is this happening to me?" The tears rolled freely down his sunken cheeks.

"Now one of the men has jumped into my car. He's deliberately ramming it into a tree. Oh, Heavenly Father. The other two have grabbed me, one on each arm, and they're dragging me over to the car. They're leaving me holding onto the hood and fender. If I let go, I'll fall. They're doing something with my license plate. I think they're stealing it, but I can't be sure. Now they're running back to their car. One almost falls, but his friend grabs him before he does. I'm watching all three of them get in and drive away. I can see everything; but I can't move. I can't yell for help. I'm paralyzed. And my Maritha's dead!"

Mizner continued. "Is it a regular police car, Francis?"

Kettering shook his head, still weeping. "*Nooo*! There's no writing on the sides. No lights on the top. I think I can see a small antenna, but I'm not sure. Anyway, they're gone now. They didn't turn on their headlights when they left."

"How much time has passed, Francis?"

"I don't know," Kettering replied mournfully, shaking his head. "I can't lift my arm to look at my watch." A fresh flow of tears coursed in rivulets down his cheeks.

"Francis, did any of the men speak to you or to each other?"

"*Nooo*"!

"Francis, it's all right." Mizner took hold of his hand and gently squeezed. "Everything's fine, Francis. It's over. You can rest assured that soon everyone will know the truth about what happened that night. Now, I want you to relax, but keep your eyes closed. Visualize that you are standing on the shore. See the waves, Francis, notice how very peaceful everything is. Look around and bask in the beauty of God's creation. Isn't it marvelous?"

Kettering's face took on a serene look. His breathing, which had been ragged and shallow, returned to normal. His tears faded.

After a full minute passed, Mizner said, "The next time I speak your Christian name, you will become fully awake. You will no longer be troubled by what you have just told me. And you'll feel totally refreshed. Do you understand?"

"Yes."

"Good. Francis, I want you to now open your eyes."

Kettering obeyed. He smiled at the doctor, and as he struggled to sit up, spotted Justin. "So, did it go well?"

Justin answered by placing both thumbs firmly in the upward position, signaling victory. "Better than you could ever have hoped for, Your Eminence. Dr. Mizner's performed a miracle. All I can say is that when the authorities see the video, they're going to have egg all over their faces. And that goes for Cardinal Miglianico as well."

"It's that good?"

"It's a hundred times better than good," Justin replied. He turned to Mizner with a question. "Could Braddock have paralyzed the cardinal with a spray?"

Mizner nodded. "Yes, with a depolarizing neuromuscular blocking agent. Succinylcholine Chloride comes to mind. Onset is swift, but duration is short. That particular drug would not be as effective in a spray, but there are many others to choose from in the same family."

"That's all I need to know. Thanks, Doctor." Justin hooked a thumb in O'Bryan's direction. "Let's go, Jack. I've got things to do and people to meet."

* * *

Justin and two officers from Internal Affairs entered Braddock's apartment at 3:30 p.m. that afternoon. Valerie had sent the lieutenant on a wild-goose chase to Cumberland, Maryland. He wouldn't be back until well after dark, but at all times he'd be under the watchful eye of Internal Affairs officers.

All three wore business suits. The older of the two officers could have passed for Braddock, at least from a distance, and the idea to use that particular individual had been Valerie's. "Just in case any neighbors spot them entering the apartment," she had reasoned. The chief had approved.

Justin carried a new 35mm digital Nikon camera; the ranking officer, a Polaroid 600.

"Shouldn't we knock, and announce ourselves first?" whispered the Braddock look-alike.

"Say what?" Justin said, looking genuinely dumbfounded.

"You know, the Supreme Court ruling in '95. The justices said nine to zip that cops must knock and announce. We should go by the book," he pressed in a voice barely above a whisper.

"You've got to be kidding," Justin hissed back, starting to burn. "Read the damn warrant," he whispered. "It's for a *covert* entry. Do you know what the word means?"

The man nodded, suddenly feeling very much the fool in front of this retired FBI agent.

"Good. Then let's just do it. Jeez, I'm working with the Marx Brothers."

Once inside, all donned latex gloves, and paper booties.

Justin had been antsy for hours, especially after learning that Braddock had stashed a vial of blood in the apartment. They had all wondered aloud just what he had planned to do with it until Justin hit on the likely answer.

"That blood's his ace," he had reasoned to the group. "The guy's a gambler, and he's hedging his bets. Whoever hired him for this job had to have had some pretty heavy leverage to force Braddock to commit murder. My guess is he owed *beaucoup* bucks to the mob with no earthly way of ever paying it back. They in turn probably sold Braddock's services to their European brothers. He had to know that they'd have some really bad shit planned for him if he refused. The man had nowhere to turn. No one welshes on these guys. But, like I said, he hedged his bet, and that vial of blood was his insurance policy. As a last resort he figured he could take it to the police, and hopefully use it to plea-bargain his way down from a murder one charge."

None could find fault with Justin's logic. It fit. After more discussion, the decision was made to split any recovered sample, and get the FBI and *CellTest* to run independent tests.

Justin made his way to the refrigerator with the two officers a pace behind. It took him a few moments to spot the vial, but there it was, sitting in a cup all the way to the back of the middle shelf. Except it was two vials, not just the one that Valerie had told him to expect. There was a mountain of foodstuffs and a six-pack of Coors in front, but other than that, he noted that Braddock had made no real effort to hide them. No reason to. As far as Braddock was concerned no one knew they existed except Valerie, and she'd approved his keeping them.

"My money says one vial contains a clean specimen, and the other's laced with alcohol," Justin said. "He probably had a chemist associated with the mob pull it off. What a clever prick. He was definitely covering his ass."

The two officers stood back while Justin snapped photos.

"Wonder if the stuff's still good?" the younger officer remarked.

"Who in the hell cares?" growled Justin. "You think maybe it's going to be pumped into someone?"

The man reddened.

"Leave it here in the fridge till we're ready to vamoose. Now we need to try and find some money, and a woman's purse."

They began to search, making sure that as they finished with each room, everything went back to where they'd found it. They insured this by first taking color Polaroid pictures from three different angles, then they compared the room with the photos once they'd finished. The pictures went into the senior officer's inside pocket.

Braddock's apartment was a standard two-bedroom unit; a cookie-cutter floor plan found in a zillion other buildings. His was a typical bachelor's apartment, except for the fact it was spotless. Not a dish to be seen, not an item out of place. Justin mentally compared it to his own, and in comparing, found himself uncomfortably lacking. *Ain't you the regular little Betty Crocker, Braddock*, he thought, as he went about his work.

In the master bedroom they found what they were looking for. Under the bed was a large, zippered, canvas duffel bag similar to the ones SWAT teams were issued. Polaroid shots were taken to establish its exact position, so that it could be returned when they were finished examining it.

Justin moved the bag from its hiding place and photographed it again. Then, very carefully, opened the zipper. Inside, the cavity was crammed with fifty, and hundred-dollar bills, all neatly bundled and stacked.

"*Son of a bitch*!" Justin said as he snapped away.

The two officers just stared at the treasure. It was more money than they would make in a lifetime.

"Must be millions," one whispered to the other.

Justin chuckled. "Not quite. But enough." He began to probe gently with a thin, four-inch metal rod, moving the top bundles to expose a second layer beneath. He took more photos. As he worked his way to the bottom, something caught his eye. Moving stacks aside with his probe, he uncovered a small, black folder. Taking a pair of tweezers from his pocket, he slowly worked the item to the surface and placed it on the floor. More pictures were taken. Then it was time to study it. Printed in small gold letters on the *faux* leather cover were the words, *Thomas Cook & Son.*

Justin opened the snap. Inside was a sheaf of unused traveler's checks, all in American one-hundred-dollar denomination, and all signed in purple ink on the bottom left hand corner. The copperplate-perfect signature jumped out at him. Maritha von Snellenberger.

Justin sat back on his haunches. His face tightened, and his mouth became an angry slit. He stared at his find. Finally, he spoke. "You piece of scum, Braddock. You miserable, murdering prick."

"What do you want to do?" the younger officer whispered to Justin.

"Put everything back. No need to tip our hand. We've got the pictures in case he tries to move this stuff before we bust him. What a greedy pig! He probably ditched the purse, but couldn't see his way to letting the money go, the worthless scumbag. Okay, let's move."

They put the bag back under the bed and went into the kitchen. The senior officer reached into the refrigerator and took out the vials. He placed them in a small, padded case, then put the package in his pocket. "That's it. Let's get out of here."

"*That's not it, dammit*! Where the hell are the vials you're going to leave in their place? You want him to come home tonight and spot them gone? You've *got* to have brought some filled replacements. At least one."

The two officers just stared at each other, their jaws suddenly unhinged.

"No one told us to bring any vials," the older one finally blurted out.

Justin let out a deep breath. "I can see why you guys are Internal Affairs. You know jack-shit about the real world," he mocked. "God help us all. Thanks for nothing."

Neither said a word.

"Well we sure as shit aren't coming back, so we take the cup as well. Let's pray that Braddock doesn't notice that it's gone before we arrest him. Now let's get the hell out of here."

* * *

Mannix cornered Justin only seconds before he was to meet with the others. "Got a minute for an update on our walker from the park?"

Justin acted like he had all the time in the world. "Absolutely. Tell me what you've got."

"Our man was met by two thugs at Heathrow, then all three hoofed it lickety-split over to the Aeroflot counter. He didn't have to clear British customs because he was passing through, and the other two had to have come in from foreign ports as well. My tail was able to get close enough to snap some quality stills, and to hear them ask about the next flight out. It was heading for Moscow, via Helsinki, and St. Petersburg. All three booked passage to Moscow, and all three paid in cash. But you want to know the best part? We got the pictures from London just a short while ago, and made a positive ID on the other two guys. Both were in the photos you got from that Laufenburg fellow in Vienna. That, my good man, is solid proof of a connection between the Vatican, the Italian Mafia, and the Russians. These guys are all major players in the new Russian order. We've struck gold, Justin."

Justin was elated. "That's great news, Steve. Tell all your people thanks for a job well done. You guys are the best. Talk to you later."

CHAPTER 23

"I think I'll move my office over here," Chief Tuchmann joked as he made an exaggerated pretense of studying Justin's richly paneled conference room. "I could get used to this real fast."

Everybody laughed at the icebreaker remark.

"Chief, you promise to fix all our parking tickets, then you're welcome to stay for as long as you like."

"Don't tempt me, Mr. Scott."

Valerie sat to the chief's right. The rest of the small group, including the two officers from Internal Affairs, gathered around the conference table.

Justin briefed them on what he had uncovered at Braddock's apartment. He explained his theory for the two vials, and ended by blaming himself for forgetting to bring replacements.

Tuchmann just glared at his men.

"I've already split the samples, and sent them to *CellTest* and the bureau," Justin said by way of summary, "but I've also held some back for you, Chief."

"I appreciate that." Tuchmann looked around the table. "Any questions for my guys?"

There were none.

"Okay, you two are dismissed. What's next?"

Justin stood. "Chief, I want you to see a tape made earlier today at the embassy." He dimmed the lights and started the machine.

For twenty minutes the group relived with Kettering the night of Maritha von Snellenberger's murder. It was powerful stuff, and everyone felt the cardinal's anguish.

When the tape ended Justin started to speak, but Valerie jumped up, cutting him off. Her face was ashen. "Chief, I think Braddock used my staff car to transport the body," she blurted out.

"What the hell are you talking about?"

"Braddock had my unmarked Dodge the night of the murder. I was off for two days. Remember?" She stole a glance at Justin's impassive face, then continued. "You called me at Georgetown with a Red Flag. You asked if I had my police car with me and I said no, so you had the campus police drive me downtown."

"That's right, I do remember." Tuchmann drummed his fingers rapidly on the desk, weighing his possibilities. "Okay, here's what we do. Tobias, I want you to drive your car over to the FBI. I want their forensics people to go over it from top to bottom. It was their autopsy report that said the body had been in two different cars that night, and that one of the cars was definitely a Chrysler product. Well, we shall see soon enough if it was your Dodge. I'll call the director from here and ask him to expedite. Get moving, Inspector."

Valerie stood her ground. "When are we going to take Braddock down, Chief? We've got more than enough probable cause to book him right now."

"Valerie, let me make that call, okay?" said Tuchmann, deliberately using her given name. His tone was sympathetic and understanding. "Tom Braddock's not going anywhere. We've got him covered round-the-clock." The chief could see she wasn't happy with the thought of any further delay. "It'll be soon, I promise. Now go."

O'Bryan spoke up. "Chief, before the story breaks, I'd like us all to give some thought as to how much information has to be made public. Specifically, I'm referring to the fact that Maritha von Snellenberger was Cardinal Kettering's daughter. I don't think any purpose would be served by having that plastered all over the tabloids. Cardinal Kettering has suffered enough. This is something I'm guessing we'll need to coordinate with the attorney general's office and the FBI, but speaking on behalf of the Vatican, I'd very much appreciate any help you can give us."

"Monsignor, you have my word I'll do all in my power to keep the link between the cardinal and the deceased a secret. No purpose is served by having it become public knowledge, because it in no way affects the outcome of the case."

"Thank you, Chief."

Tuchmann rose. "All we can do now is wait for the reports to come back on the blood samples, and from the FBI's examination of any detritus collected from the car's interior and trunk. As soon as I hear anything, I'll get back to you. Keep your seats; I'll see myself out. Goodnight."

* * *

Two days later, at ten minutes past six in the evening Tuchmann gave the order to Internal Affairs to arrest Lieutenant Braddock. The blood samples had come back from both labs with similar results, and the fiber in the trunk of Valerie's Dodge matched the fiber strands found clinging to Maritha von Snellenberger's scalp. Officers stationed down the street from Braddock's apartment were told to pick him up. Backup was on standby.

After knocking several times and hearing nothing, they drew their weapons and kicked down the door. Thirty seconds later they were on the radio. Braddock was nowhere to be found. He had disappeared from right under their noses.

* * *

Valerie dodged the first raindrops as she entered the school and made her way to the play area next to the gym. The stifling weather had finally given way during the afternoon. The temperature had plummeted, and was now heading toward the sixty-degree mark. She ambled down the hall, listening to her footsteps echo off the walls. Dania would be tired from a long day, but happy to see her. The staff understood the problems of working parents, and kept the children until seven o'clock to accommodate those who needed the extra time.

She met Mrs. San Martin, the principal, halfway down the hall. "Hi, sorry I'm late. Busy day. You know how that goes."

The principal stopped dead in her tracks, her face creasing in a frown. "Dania's already been picked up."

"Oh, Danny got her? How sweet of him," Valerie said.

"No, Lieutenant Braddock came for her. He said you'd be too late, so he came by and said he'd drop her off at your husband's business. Dania was so happy to see her Uncle Tommy. She couldn't stop giving him hugs and kisses. He's such a nice man."

"*Noooo*!" Valerie screamed. "Tell me you've made a mistake. Tell me Dania's still here!"

The principal's hands flew up to cover her mouth. "Oh my God, what's wrong?"

Valerie began shaking the woman violently, her eyes the size of saucers. "How long ago did they leave?" she yelled.

Twen … twenty … minutes," Mrs. San Martin stammered. "But Lieutenant Braddock's picked Dania up many times. What's wrong, Mrs. Tobias?"

Valerie shoved the woman aside and dug her cellphone from her purse. She ran back to the entrance, flung open the main doors and dashed out onto the steps. She wanted to make sure the reception was perfect. She speed-dialed the stored number for central dispatch.

It was answered on the first ring.

"This is Echo Seven," she yelled into the mouthpiece. "Patch me through to Echo One, now! Break in if you have to. Tell him it's a Red Flag." She danced insanely from one foot to another, doing everything in her power to keep from falling apart. *Come on, Chief!*

"This is Echo One, do you read me, Seven? What gives, Inspector?"

"Braddock's loose and he's got my baby," she screamed into the phone. "Why didn't you listen to me and arrest the bastard two days ago when I asked you to? Now he's got Dania." She began to sob.

"Where are you, Valerie?"

"The school. Dania's school."

"How long ago did he take her?"

"Twenty minutes."

"Okay, I'm putting the entire force on alert right now. Dania's our number one priority. We'll have her back in no time. Valerie, stand by, I'm giving instructions on another line. Don't hang up on me."

He was back in less than a minute. "Valerie, don't drive. Who do you want me to send to pick you up?"

"Sergeant Maria Delgado. She knows where the school is. Send Maria."

"Done. Wait there for her. Look, I'll leave this line clear just for your use. I'll be in touch, but if you need me at any time, you've got me. Understood?"

"Roger."

"Keep the faith, Valerie. We'll get Dania back."

She jumped around in-place, not knowing what to do next. Some inner voice directed her to make another call, and she speed-dialed Justin's home number which she'd programmed into her phone only days before. "Oh, God, Justin, be there," she wailed.

He answered immediately. "That you, O'Bryan?" She heard the unmistakable mirth in his voice.

"Justin, it's Val. Braddock's gone and he's taken my baby! He's kidnapped Dania!"

"Dammit! When?"

"Twenty minutes," she sobbed. "Justin, you've got to help me. You're the only one who can help me."

Justin forced himself to remain calm. "Call Tuchmann. Tell him to mobilize everything he's got. I'll call the bureau, and get them moving on the premise that Braddock's already crossed state lines, which puts it into their jurisdiction."

"I've already spoken to Tuchmann. Oh, God, what will he do to my little girl?"

Justin had an idea. "Val, where are you? I'll come for you right now."

"No," she screamed into the receiver. "There's no time for that. I want you to go and find my baby right now. Do you hear me, Justin?" She began to sob anew.

"Val, I swear to God I'll have her in your arms before you know it."

* * *

Valerie turned off her phone, then looked up the street, and resumed her subconscious hopping from one foot to the other and breathing hard, willing Maria's speedy arrival with each ragged exhalation.

Another thought bubbled to the surface. She ran down the steps to her car and grabbed her police radio from its hiding place under the driver's seat. She toggled it on, and listened as the net came to life with instructions for every officer on duty in the District of Columbia to be on the lookout for Lieutenant Braddock. All units were cautioned against using force since he had Inspector Tobias' daughter as a possible kidnap victim. As she heard the instructions pouring out from central dispatch, she had another idea. Trying desperately to calm down, she surfed the frequencies, landing on the command net. This channel was only used by the ranking officers in metro.

"Tom, this is Valerie. Come in, Tom, I know you're listening. Please, come in, Tom." She began to sob. "Please, Tom. Please!"

"This is Echo One. Valerie, please get off the command channel."

"You heard the man, Val. Get off the net."

It was Braddock!

"Tom, speak to me. Please, Tom, let me speak to Dania."

Maria Delgado came tearing around the corner in a marked

unit and slid to a stop behind Valerie's car. She had the overhead light bar on, its flashing red, blue and white lights reflecting a kaleidoscope of color off the windows of the building. She leaned on the horn and waved to Valerie to get in.

"Valerie, stay off the goddamn net," was the first thing she said as Valerie flung herself into the car.

"He's got my child!" She pressed the transmit button on her brick. "Tom, talk to me!"

Maria reached over and yanked the radio out of Valerie's hand. She flung it on the floor and a microsecond later slapped Valerie across the side of the face. "Get your shit together, woman. If you don't grab hold right now, I'm going to cuff you and run you in. You're no use to anyone like this, least of all Dania."

Valerie's hand flew to her cheek as the tears started again. "You hit me." She began to sob uncontrollably.

"Val, I had to. You're coming unglued. We're going to find Dania. Every cop in the city is looking for her right now. It's only a matter of time. You've got to calm down. I'm sorry I hit you, Inspector. I really am."

Valerie waved her hand feebly in the air. "Oh, Maria, what am I going to tell Danny?"

"That gives me an idea. Let's go to Danny's office right now. He should hear it from us and not from some frigging news flash." She slammed the car in gear, and engaged the siren.

"No, Maria, turn it off. The noise is killing me. I can't hear myself think." Valerie began to take deep, controlled breaths, willing herself back to reality. She wiped her eyes on the back of her hand, then rummaged in her purse for a Kleenex. Blowing her nose, she looked across at her friend. "I'm sorry. I know everybody's only trying to help. I'll be okay, I promise."

Keeping her eyes on the road, Maria reached over and gave Valerie's arm a squeeze. "I know you will, boss, and I'm sorry for whacking you one."

Valerie managed a pitiful smile. "S'okay, Maria. Trust me, I've got my shit together." She looked at her friend. "He won't hurt my baby will he, Maria?"

Maria shook her head violently. "No way. Tom Braddock might be a lot of things, but he wouldn't hurt a kid. Especially not Dania. He loves that child."

"But why did he take her?" Tears started to form, but she fought to remain collected.

"He'll let her go soon, I know he will. Meanwhile, let's keep monitoring the radio, and go get Danny. While we're driving, you can tell me everything about Braddock and the murder of that woman found in the car trunk."

* * *

Dania Tobias looked over at Braddock, her face split by a huge grin. She quickly turned her focus to the radio perched between his knees. "That's my Mommy," she announced proudly. Her face turned serious. "Mommy's yelling." Then she heard her name. "*Let me speak to Dania*!"

The child jerked back in her seat. She looked at the radio, then announced in a loud voice; "I'm here, Mommy. Hi, Mommy."

No reply.

"Where's Mommy, Uncle Tommy?"

"Mommy's playing a game, Dania. That's why she's yelling. She's not angry, honey. We'll see her in a little while, okay?"

"Okay."

Braddock had a sudden flash of inspiration as he worked his way through rush hour traffic. He opened the glove box and took out a small tape recorder. He often used it to make reminders for himself. Sometimes he'd recite things as mundane as his grocery list, or matters as important as something to do with a case he was working. But now, another use had come to mind.

"Tell you, what, Dania. How would you like to play a game?"

That made her sit up. "I like games. Can we play catch?"

Before he had a chance to tell her he had another game in mind, the radio came to life.

"Attention all units. Be on the lookout for a nine-year-old white Mustang, District of Columbia tag, Foxtrot, Romeo, two, four, zero, zero. I repeat ...." And the message went out a second time over the net from central dispatch.

Braddock laughed, and thumped on the steering wheel. Ha! The idiots didn't know he'd had his car painted red three months ago. Score one for my team. That information wouldn't be updated with the Department of Motor Vehicles until his tag was renewed next August.

His smugness was short-lived.

"Central, this is Echo Seven. Put this out on all frequencies. I have an update." Valerie waited a couple of seconds, then keyed her mike. "Attention all units. This is Echo Seven. The Mustang is red. I repeat. The Mustang is red. The car was painted a couple of months ago. Target vehicle is red. Echo Seven, out."

"*Screw you, Tobias*!"

Dania became alarmed as she watched her Uncle Tommy's face contort with rage. "Mommy. That's mommy!"

"Sure is." He glanced at the child. "Go ahead and call for her, Dania," he said, fighting to bring his voice back under control. "We're going to play a game, honey. I want you to call real loud. Let's see if mommy can hear you. It might take a little while, but that's okay. Are you ready?" Then he pressed the record button, and noted that the green dot of light was blinking, confirming the tape was rolling.

"Mommy, I'm here … Mommy … talk to Dania, Mommy!" She looked at Uncle Tommy for approval.

He grinned and nodded. "Do it some more. But wait until I say go, okay?" He placed his finger to his lips.

Dania nodded that she understood, the look on her face saying this was fun.

He let the tape run for a few seconds, then nodded to the expectant child. "Go!"

"Mommy … where are you?" She paused and grinned from ear to ear. "Mommy … speak to me." She actually started to wail.

Braddock was delighted. He allowed her to continue for another ten seconds then shut off the recorder. He rewound it, muted the sound, and played it back. Fabulous! He grinned at Dania. "One more time for good luck, then let's see how long it takes mommy to find us. Isn't this fun?"

She went through her routine once more, then added at the end, "I'm hungry, Uncle Tommy."

He shut off the machine. Perfect. Especially that last bit about being hungry.

"Yeah, me, too, Dania. We'll go to McDonald's when mommy finds us, okay?" He was no longer grinning, his mind now focused on his next move. He had a new plan.

* * *

After an emergency phone call to the bureau to put their forces into action, Justin called O'Bryan. The priest answered on the second ring. Justin had made plans with O'Bryan to pick up

Mannix and Paula, then the four of them were going for a victory dinner. There was no time to tell the other two of the latest turn of events.

"Jack, Braddock's vamoosed and he's got Inspector Tobias' daughter. Meet me out front in five minutes. Dress accordingly; it might get chilly later." He slammed the phone down before O'Bryan could ask the first question.

Justin scrambled into his clothes, grabbing the first items his hands came up with. His Notre Dame sweatshirt, black pinstriped suit pants, argyle socks, and Reeboks. He secured his .38 Colt, jammed his wallet and money clip into pockets, scooped up an old portable police scanner he'd had for years, grabbed his car keys, and bolted for the garage.

Five minutes later he arrived under the portico at the main entrance where a waiting O'Bryan jumped in.

"Tell me what you know, Justin," O'Bryan said as he buckled up.

Without a wasted word Justin explained what he'd been told by Valerie. "Doesn't look good," he concluded.

"What do you think Braddock will do?" O'Bryan asked, his voice full of worry. "You think he'll hurt the child?"

"I sure hope not, but who the hell knows? The guy's run out of altitude, airspeed, and ideas all at the same time. He's heading for a flamer, but I don't think that's sunk in yet. He might have a plan, but I seriously doubt it. I think the man's winging it. The FBI has been informed so we'll cruise the streets and be ready to move as soon as the cops broadcast that they've located him." He looked at the scanner on his lap. "Sure wish I had a portable police radio with a two-way communication capability. Guarantee you, it would pay for itself before this night's over."

"I guess we should have pressed the chief to pull him in a couple of days ago like Valerie wanted to," O'Bryan said, eyes glued to the sidewalk looking at the people scooting along under a light drizzle. Then he added in a low voice, as if for his ears only, "May God protect that innocent child."

The radio crackled with the news that a uniformed officer in a marked unit had Braddock's car in sight. He had come across it abandoned in a residential area two blocks from the southwest entrance to RFK Stadium. He pinpointed the intersection. Then the officer read back the license plate for all on the net to hear. "No sign of Lieutenant Braddock or the child. And don't anyone expect much light in the area," he cautioned, seemingly as an afterthought.

CHAPTER 24

The net erupted into a cacophony of sound. Instructions went out to seal off a six square block area around Braddock's abandoned car. The SWAT team that had been placed on standby earlier was now ordered into action. Those units not directly involved in the next phase of the operation knew to stay clear of the hot zone. Every officer in the city had ears only for the drama unfolding in the east, and assignments to respond to 'domestics,' and petty crimes were answered slowly.

Archangel Four, the duty helicopter on alert that shift, was ordered into the zone to provide illumination, and the department's one rotary-wing ambulance was instructed to stand by on its home pad at Ronald Reagan National Airport.

Tuchmann confirmed that he would be on-site shortly, but emphasized that Lieutenant Hardin and his SWAT team would not be second-guessed by the command element. Commander Piper, the district commander, would be responsible for the perimeter, and would expand or contract it as needed on his own initiative.

The neighborhood was one of older homes. It was a poor section of the city, many of its buildings in a sad state of disrepair. More than a few were abandoned but had become havens for drifters, drug users, and worse.

Tuchmann's only concession to a change in procedure was to issue orders to allow Inspector Tobias inside the cordon, but with instructions to Tobias, and heard by everyone on the net, that she was not to interfere.

* * *

Braddock entered RFK Stadium by picking the lock at the ticket office entrance. Like a homing pigeon, he made his way up to the communications room, the nerve center of this behemoth. He knew this facility almost as well as his own apartment. He had spent countless hours in its stands, watching the Redskins play football when they still called the place home, and every other sport played in every season. But more importantly, he knew the layout.

A couple of years earlier, a retired metro captain had been hired as the new chief of security, and had proudly shown his old pal Braddock every nook and cranny of his kingdom. And his old pal Braddock had been duly impressed.

It was disgustingly easy to enter the communications center this chilly night; and even easier to do what he had in mind. Using his penlight, he quickly found the control panel for the speaker system. Good. He'd take care of that on the way out. Then he began a search for the one item he knew he must have if his plan was to work. Less than a minute later he found what he was looking for. There were five to choose from. To be on the safe side, he grabbed two and crammed them in his pockets. As he turned his head toward the communications console his eyes fell on another piece of equipment. He scooped it up and placed it in another pocket. Finally, he turned on the stadium speakers then tiptoed out of the room, not bothering to lock up behind himself.

His heart was pounding as he made his way down the dark corridors to the ticket entrance. There were lighted EXIT signs in the corners that would save lives if there were a fire, but otherwise their illumination value was nil.

The rain showers had followed him across the city, and as he left the stadium to return to where he'd left Dania, he heard the police helicopter noisily beating a path across the field. He instinctively flattened against a wall, and waited for it to pass. No searchlight yet, he noted, but he knew it would begin its standard illuminated grid-pattern search at any moment.

He kept to the shadows and worked his way out of, and away from, the hot zone—those several blocks cordoned off and lying inside the perimeter. His radio confirmed that he had the entire force looking for him and the kid in the wrong area. He congratulated himself for dumping the car. He was riding an adrenaline high. It should only take a couple of minutes for the finishing touches. Then, in the confusion of the moment, he'd simply vanish into the night.

* * *

Precious time was lost because the officer who found the hijack victim didn't pay attention to what the man was trying to tell him.

"Some dude stole my car, man. Do somethin'."

As the man continued to rave, the officer suddenly realized the importance of what he was saying. Five minutes later he had him repeat his story to the squad leader.

"The honky stole m' wheels, bro'. Just hauled off and whacked me with a gun butt. Lucky I ain't dead, man. An' the son of a bitch was travelin' with a young piece. What the shit she see in him?"

The sergeant came alive. He grabbed the man's arm and squeezed hard. "Cut the goddamn jive and tell me in plain English what the hell happened."

The man jerked back. "You not listenin? Man stole m'car. Jumped out of his, an' dragged me outta mine. Smacked me over the head with his gun, an' then put the lady in the car. Man, he coulda shot me." He glared at the sergeant, not in the least intimidated by the uniform. "She was kinda slow, y'know? Then he dumps a big old bag in the back seat, an' takes off. I'm lyin' on the sidewalk, y'dig? An' even though I'm seein' stars; I still know what's happenin.' The mother stole m'car."

"What make and color is it?"

"Brown, man. Don't know no make. It's my cousin's car. He let me borrow it."

"Shit." The sergeant banged his fist on the hood of his unit. "You mean *you* stole the car and *he* stole it from you. Just tell me this. Was it American? Japanese? Two doors or four?" The questions came fast and furious. "Talk to me, goddammit."

"Can't think. You shoutin' in m'face, man. My head's killin' me. I needs me a hospital. I'm hurt!"

The sergeant got on his radio.

"This is Tango One Four. Attention on the net. I have an update on Braddock. He's now in a brown car. I don't know if it's domestic or foreign, two doors or four. Braddock stole it from a dude who stole it himself. No information on where he's heading. He definitely has the girl with him." he paused for a moment then added, "Echo Seven, the man said your daughter is fine. I repeat, your daughter has not been harmed."

Tobias was back in a flash. "Thank you, Tango One Four. Thank you!"

* * *

Justin and O'Bryan heard it all. They had parked just outside the perimeter, and stood in the rain watching the helicopter sweep the area, turning night into day inside a cone of light, and the raindrops into a sea of sparkling diamonds.

"Of all the brazen bastards. He's actually dragging that bagful of money around with him. And if he stole one car, he'll sure steal another." Justin looked out at the city, oblivious of the water striking his face. "What's your plan, Braddock?" he asked the night. "Was I wrong about you? Did I underestimate you? You *do* know what you're doing, you evil piece of dirt. Give me a sign, you son of a bitch."

* * *

Dania sat quietly in the corner of the filthy room, her eyes following Braddock's every move.

He had placed the tape recorder on a window ledge, choosing this particular room because it gave him an unobstructed view of the stadium, which was critical for the success of his plan. He could just make out the flagpole through the rain, which meant his equipment should work simply because of its line-of-sight capability. He had taken two FM transmitters used by the referees during college football games, which allowed them to be heard through the stadium's speaker system. Although these radios worked fairly well most of the time, there were other times when their capability disintegrated into an ear-splitting sea of static. But they had been recently improved with the addition of a more powerful antenna. That was the second article he had snatched from the communications center.

It was time to test. He switched on the recorder, turned up the volume and toggled the transmitter.

"Mommy, I'm here, Mommy ... Talk to Dania, Mommy!"

He jumped, and a microsecond later laughed at himself.

* * *

When it came, it startled everybody.

"Mommy, I'm here, Mommy ... Talk to Dania, Mommy!"

The words boomed out over the stadium speakers, the sound carrying well beyond the confines of the facility. It was so unexpected, so loud, that a couple of the officers jumped.

"Holy shit, he's inside," an unknown voice broadcast over the net.

In an instant, the SWAT team commander was on the radio directing Archangel to fly cover over the stadium. Then he gave the word to his troops to move. "He's up in the control room. Go, go, go," Hardin commanded over the roar of the helicopter as it thundered into RFK Stadium, a metal Cyclops riding on whirling metal wings. "The lieutenant's got the kid, so no one do anything stupid. Shit, Braddock, have you lost your mind?"

Valerie heard Dania's mournful wail.

"*Ohmygod*!"

Danny Tobias grabbed his wife's shoulders and held tight. "Stay cool, hon. Don't fold, sweetheart, it's almost over."

She bit down on her tongue and nodded.

* * *

Perfect! Braddock heard the child's voice roll back from the speakers almost three city blocks away. The new antenna was more than holding its own. He shut everything off.

He walked over to Dania. It amazed him that she showed no fear, no apprehension in her dark, foreign surroundings. Most children would be in a panic, sniveling for their mothers. Not Dania. She trusted her Uncle Tommy, and anyway, he'd told her that mommy was on her way.

"Now we're going to play hide-and-seek with mommy. I bet she finds us in no time, Dania, because mommy's very smart." He knelt down and gently massaged her arm as he spoke. "But we're going to give some extra help to mommy, because we're good sports, okay?"

"How, Uncle Tommy?"

He handed her his penlight. "When I tell you to, I want you to hold it so that the light shines out the window. Can you do that for Uncle Tommy?"

"Yes." She experimented. The beam danced wildly off the walls until she got the hang of it, and was able to hold her hand steady enough to center on the target. Her face was a study of pure concentration, her tongue darting from side to side as if that was somehow crucial in directing the light.

"That's great, sweetheart. My goodness, you're a clever girl."

She gave Braddock a fleeting smile then immediately returned to the task at hand. "Where will you be, Uncle Tommy?"

"Right here," he lied. "Oh, I might have to tiptoe outside to see if mommy's hot or cold. But I'll be very close because I want to see her face when she finds her girl." He gave her a big grin. "Okay, let's begin, Dania. This is going to be lots of fun."

He turned on the recorder.

"Mommy, where are you? Mommy, speak to me!"

He left her holding the light.

* * *

Lieutenant Hardin called for two K-9 units even before his men reached the communications center. He figured that Braddock had probably abandoned the girl, and planned to get lost in the maze of tunnels while all efforts were concentrated on rescuing the child. He could just fade away into oblivion. Hardin also suggested that the perimeter be moved to encircle the stadium. "I've got you, you dumb shit," he said out loud.

The SWAT team was extremely cautious entering the booth. There was always the outside chance Braddock was still in there. Maybe he'd decide to make a stand using Dania as a shield, or a bargaining chip.

Empty! Several lights on the console winked back at the team, but their powerful flashlights revealed no Braddock, no Dania.

"There's got to be a backup transmitter somewhere else in the stadium. Dammit, we need someone who knows the layout." Hardin was speaking directly to Echo One.

"Mommy ... Mommy, where are you? Mommy, speak to me! I'm hungry, Uncle Tommy!"

Because the helicopter was making a low pass directly overhead, the last words were washed away by the noise of its turbine and the thump of its blades, important words, unheard by those directly below the flight path.

But the words were heard by people removed from the roar of the helicopter.

For several minutes there was nothing, then the child began to wail again, begging her mother to talk to her.

* * *

"What the hell are you up to, Braddock?" Justin turned to O'Bryan. "It doesn't add up. I'm telling you, something's not right." His subconscious was trying to squeeze a message out, but his brain wasn't cooperating. It was like a radio not properly tuned to a station, and all he was hearing was static.

And then he knew. The child had just finished another plea, ending with a second pronouncement to her Uncle Tommy that she was hungry. "Son of a bitch!"

O'Bryan saw the look of alarm spread over Justin's face. "What is it? What's wrong?"

Justin's eyes darted up the street. "Come on," he commanded. "We need to find a cop. We need a radio." He started up the block just as a police car came into view, lights flashing, siren whooping. Justin jumped into its path and flagged it down, holding his wallet aloft.

"Who the hell are you?" the driver yelled. "Get outta the goddam road."

Justin flashed his credentials showing him to be a retired agent. "FBI. I need to speak to Echo One. Give me your portable, now!"

The stunned officer obeyed.

"Echo One, this is Justin Scott with the FBI. Come back, One."

"What have you got, Scott?"

"Chief, we're listening to a tape on a looped playback. Braddock's transmitting on a FM gizmo. Something like the football refs use. Guarantee you, Braddock's not in the stadium. It's a line-of-sight setup, so he's in a three or four block grid to the north of the field. But chances are he's already split, or is about to, in another stolen car. Start a house-to-house search, but only in an area where your guys can see the flagpole at all times. The antenna's got to be up there because of its height. Find that tape recorder and you'll find Dania. Scott out."

Justin tossed the radio back to its owner and started running down the street towards his car. "Come on, move it," he yelled over his shoulder to O'Bryan.

* * *

Valerie heard Justin's explanation along with her husband and Maria Delgado.

"He's right. Let's go, Maria, the chief needs every available pair of eyes. Go, go, go!" At last, something positive, something concrete. She was going to find her baby. "Thank you, Justin," she whispered to herself.

* * *

The helicopter pilot thundered out of the stadium and began to stalk the surrounding streets. People were pouring out of their houses and making their way into the middle of the pavement, heads turned upward, scores of eyes fixated on the low flying chopper. The pilot radioed the problem to the command center.

"Echo One to all units. Get on your loudspeakers and order the civilians off the streets. I want these streets cleared, now!" Despite his earlier promise not to interfere, Echo One was in command.

* * *

Justin told O'Bryan to be on the lookout for Braddock moving alone. If he was still on the streets, he'd be dragging his bag of booty along, too.

"What's that?" O'Bryan suddenly asked a minute later. "Justin, stop the car."

"What?"

"Over there," O'Bryan pointed. "Look. On the other side of the street. The guy next to the pickup truck. He just tossed a bag into it. But look at the window, Justin. It's broken."

"Sweet Jesus."

The man heard the car approaching and instinctively jerked

upright. He looked squarely into its headlights as Justin sharply wheeled his Jaguar across the centerline.

No doubt about it. It was Braddock.

In an instant Justin was out of the car, gun already in hand. "Freeze, Braddock. FBI."

"Screw you, asshole!" Braddock fired as the figure darted toward the safe haven afforded by the line of parked cars.

At that moment the helicopter came roaring over the rooftops and illuminated the scene. The pilot and observer witnessed the drama unfolding less than seventy feet below as night turned into day. Archangel Four radioed to all available units to converge on their position.

Maria Delgado saw the helicopter go immediately into a hover, and realized she was only seconds away. She tore up the street for half a block and flew around the corner. She went into a skid on the rain-slickened blacktop, fishtailed out of control and slammed sideways into an illegally parked car. It catapulted into the car in front of it, which in turn ricocheted into another. But she had no time to worry about that. She could see the two men clearly in the beam of light from the helicopter. They were firing at each other.

She leaped from the car, her Glock automatic firmly grasped in both hands, and took up a combat stance.

Suddenly, the man with his back to her was hit, the violent impact lifting him off his feet, then throwing him to the ground. She realized no one could live through that. Had to be a rifle, but who in the hell was the shooter? Her mind was a whirlwind.

The second man, caught in the glare of the helicopter's searchlight, was suddenly blinded. He raised his gun hand as he turned full face toward Maria. She let loose a fusillade, aiming carefully for the center of the Notre Dame sweatshirt. Braddock went down.

"No, Maria. Hold your fire. That's Justin. Maria! *Noooo*!" Valerie had seen the man's face.

What the hell was Valerie yelling about? Delgado darted to the side of the street, her weapon still trained on the fallen form.

And then she saw his face. It wasn't Braddock! She wheeled in the direction of the other figure, lying on his back, limbs akimbo, with half his head missing. But even with only half a face, she recognized Tom Braddock.

She raced to the man she'd shot and threw herself down. Valerie was beside her in a flash, joined a second later by O'Bryan. The three of them encircled Justin. He didn't move. Danny joined them.

Maria went into shock. "But he's wearing a Notre Dame shirt. It has to be Braddock, Val. He's wearing the shirt you told me he always wears!"

Justin had been hit twice. Blood seeped from his upper right chest and his left thigh. Valerie bent close to his mouth, and felt more than heard a faint exhale. He was still alive. There was not yet that horrible gurgle that signaled imminent death, but she knew it could come at any moment. She jumped up and ran back to the car.

"Echo One, get the chopper down, stat. We have a badly injured FBI agent. It's Justin Scott. No time for the medevac. Get Archangel on the ground, now!"

The pilot heard it all and began to rise, backing away so that he could get a better view of the terrain. No room. Too many cars parked on the street, and utility lines on both sides. He swung the craft to face the stadium. *The parking lot.* There were only a dozen police cars there.

"Echo One, we're going down in the stadium parking lot. We'll be ready to transport as soon as they get the patient to us. Archangel Four, out."

Valerie directed O'Bryan and Danny to put Justin into his own car. With O'Bryan ensconced in the driver's seat, she scrunched down on the rear floorboards, cradling Justin's head in her arms. "Hang in there, Justin, hang in there," she sobbed into his ear. "You'll be in the hospital before you know it, I promise."

Maria and Danny led the way in a commandeered marked unit which had arrived while they were carrying Justin to his car.

As the caravan of two started out, O'Bryan spotted a motorcyclist astride a huge Harley Davidson at the side of the road. The rider, his face hidden behind a blue and purple futuristic plastic helmet, saluted as the Jaguar passed. Then he gunned his engine and tore away in the opposite direction in search of a pay phone to make a final, untraceable, coded report to his European masters.

As Justin was lifted onto the helicopter, O'Bryan yelled at Valerie. "I'm going with him. I've got to give him the last rites. Give him absolution." Hot tears were forming, clouding his vision. His friend was either dying, or already dead. He couldn't tell.

Valerie nodded and O'Bryan jumped in.

Archangel Four lifted off, forcing those in its wash to turn their backs and hunch their shoulders as it rapidly gained altitude and headed toward downtown.

"Attention on the net. This is Tango Two Five. I have the child. I repeat, I have Dania. She's fine. Dania is safe." He paused for a second to allow the information to be understood by all units, then came back on the net. "Echo Seven, I'm one minute from your position. Stay there. I have a young lady who really wants to be with her mother. Tango Two Five, out."

Valerie sank to the ground and began to sob anew. For Dania. For Justin.

CHAPTER 25

Four days had passed since Braddock's death. Four busy days with new events seemingly unfolding on an hourly basis.

On the afternoon following the shoot-out, The FBI director read a prepared statement to the press, one that had taken fifteen hours to draft. It was a masterpiece of misinformation.

Judge MacAllister told the world that his agency had set a snare weeks ago to trap the real murderer of Maritha von Snellenberger. At every phase of the operation the bureau had enjoyed the full cooperation of the Vatican; the Metropolitan Police Department; and most importantly, Francis Cardinal Kettering. The judge emphasized that at no time was Kettering a suspect, but that he had agreed to be publicly vilified to help the many law enforcement agencies involved ensnare the real murderer. All evidence against the cardinal had been fabricated, some even by the murderer himself, a brilliant homicide detective, but also some by the bureau in an attempt to lull the man into a state of complacency. But always with the full approval of the Justice Department. Time was needed to build the case, and to uncover accomplices. And if there existed a true hero in all of this, it was Cardinal Kettering. The bureau would be forever in his debt. In closing, the director noted that the murderer had been killed by a retired FBI agent who had been brought back on active duty to work this one case. Because the investigation was incomplete, the judge stated that he would be unable to answer any questions.

It was a slick piece of work, allowing the bureau to wriggle out of a potentially embarrassing situation, one caused solely by its own rush to judgment.

The Vatican Press Office politely referred all questions back to the FBI. The wall of silence was not to be breached.

The media moguls went berserk. Editors pontificated how their publications had been blatantly used to report falsehoods, with no mention made of the fact their sales had jumped fifty percent in the corresponding period. They expressed indignation at the Vatican's allowing the reputation of one of its princes to be sullied in the process.

The final bombshell for O'Bryan came at two o'clock in the morning, ninety-six hours after Braddock's demise, and Justin's near- fatal shooting.

Justin had been in surgery seven hours that night. Four days later, his doctors still didn't know if he'd make it. His estranged wife had been holding a bedside vigil in the critical care unit. So had Paula. Everyone prayed.

The ringing of the phone startled O'Bryan, leaving him momentarily confused. He peered at his watch while reaching for the receiver, noting through the fog that he had been asleep for less than twenty minutes. As he identified himself, he was overcome with a feeling of dread. *Dies Irae*. It would be a messenger from the Four Horsemen saying that Justin was gone. The seventh seal could now be opened.

"Jack, it's Cardinal Kettering."

"Justin's dead, isn't he?"

Kettering paused for a second, obviously taken off guard. "No, Justin's okay. At least I think he is. It's Cardinal Miglianico. I just hung up from speaking with the Holy Father. Cardinal Miglianico died less than an hour ago, may his soul rest in peace with God."

All vestiges of sleep vanished. "*The Mig is dead*? Was he murdered?"

"No. According to the Holy Father he died in the middle of saying mass. A heart attack, maybe a stroke. He just collapsed at the altar and was gone within seconds. No one's suggesting foul play. Jack, the man was close to eighty."

"I know, but it does make one wonder just the same. Thanks for telling me."

"Wait, there's more. It seems that Cardinal Miglianico briefed the Pope last night for over an hour, and told him what really happened that frightful night here in Washington. He also told the Holy Father of the strong possibility that something terrible was afoot inside the Church. And he named names. Needless to say, the Holy Father is very distressed. But then the Holy Father told me something truly incredible. It seems that my dear friend Cardinal Miglianico was the mysterious person that you and Justin referred to as *Deep Throat*. He revealed to the Holy Father that he had faxed several messages to Mr. Scott over the last several weeks, messages insisting that I was innocent; messages pleading with the detective not to give up the hunt for the real murderer. Even the Pope was unaware of just how much Rafael truly believed in me, in spite of his having to distance himself for the good of the papacy and the Church. And to think that I doubted my friend. May God forgive me."

Jack was spellbound.

"Are you still there, Monsignor?"

"So Cardinal Miglianico was our *Deep Throat*," O'Bryan finally whispered. "Who in a million years would have ever suspected him? No wonder he was such a good secretary of state."

"Which leads nicely to my last bit of information. The Holy Father will announce in the morning that I'm to become the Vatican's next secretary of state."

"My congratulations, Your Eminence."

"Thank you, Monsignor," Kettering answered formally. He paused for a moment then continued in a more relaxed voice. "Jack, I would be honored if you would agree to become my personal assistant. I need someone I can trust; someone I can count on. You are that person. Please say yes."

"I accept, Your Eminence."

* * *

Two weeks passed. Kettering and O'Bryan had refused to leave for Rome until they knew Justin would live. For a while, it was a daily struggle just to survive, but once his mind told the body to speed up the healing process, the body responded. Soon Justin was on his way to being the Justin of old.

Seated now in an airline terminal golf-cart, Justin and Paula were accompanying Kettering and O'Bryan to the *Alitalia* boarding area. The clerics were going home.

"Still no word who really shot Lieutenant Braddock, Justin?" Kettering asked, as he draped his coat over a chair in the VIP lounge.

"None, Your Eminence," Justin replied, "and I suspect we'll never know. However, one can make a strong case based on the tape we have of him in the park that he was done in by his European friends. He botched both his assignments, and it could be they decided to take advantage of the moment and dispose of him. Or he could have been shot by someone he owed a great deal of money to. It's no secret that half the people in this city listen in on police calls, so when Braddock's name went out over the airwaves as being wanted for murder, it's possible certain people listening in decided to stalk him themselves. But like I said, we'll probably never know, and I suspect the authorities aren't going to lose a lot of sleep trying to solve that case either. Just as well, really."

"You know, there is one other possibility," Paula said, quietly. "One that none of you has thought about."

All three pair of eyes turned to her.

"The shooter could have really been stalking Justin and not Braddock. We know now that he did indeed use a high-powered rifle, probably one outfitted with a starlight scope. So, maybe in the limited light, the slight drizzle, and amid all the confusion of the moment, he simply saw a Notre Dame shirt in his cross-hairs and said to himself; *uh-uh, that's got to be Braddock*. So then he immediately turned and shot the man he thought was Justin. How ironic. Because if that indeed is was what happened, then Braddock paid the ultimate price for the simple mistake of *not* wearing his Notre Dame shirt the one night it really counted. Then, moments later, Maria Delgado came on the scene, made the same mistake, only she shot Justin, convinced she was shooting Braddock. Those damn university shirts have caused nothing but grief from day one." She gave an embarrassed little shrug. "Anyway, it's a thought."

Justin took a long moment to digest what she had said. Finally, he nodded, a look of admiration crossing his face. "You know, Paula, you could very well be right. And if you are, it's not a comforting thought to know there could be a guy with a grudge still out there gunning for me."

Kettering patted Justin's arm. "No, Justin, I still like to think the sniper made sure the right man was killed that awful night." He really wasn't convinced by his own words. "And speaking of the dead, I've come to the sad conclusion that Maritha's mother, Catherine, and my son-in-law, Freddy, have also been murdered. Most likely about the same time my Maritha was killed. I suspect Freddy was lured into Russia and eliminated because, like Maritha, he knew too much. I only pray that someday I can recover his body so as to be able to lay it to rest beside that of his wife and unborn child."

Justin studied Kettering's sad face. "They're all constantly in my thoughts and prayers."

Kettering managed a weak smile. "Thank you." He looked quickly to O'Bryan, to Paula, then back to Justin. "I make the following vow to all of you. I shall ferret out those responsible for corrupting God's house on earth, starting with Archbishop Torrelli and Monsignor Caffarone, and I'll not rest until I've brought them to account. I know it won't be easy, and I understand it will take time, but it will be done. Maritha, Freddy, the child, and Catherine, will not be allowed to have died in vain."

The flight to Rome was called.

Kettering and O'Bryan said their good-byes to Paula with kisses on both cheeks and a heartfelt hug. After O'Bryan had shaken hands with Justin, Kettering stood close and offered his. "Thank you for everything, Justin. You saved my life, and in the doing renewed my will to live. There is nothing more I can add, other than my promise of prayers for your continued speedy recovery." Tears glistened.

Justin flushed with embarrassment. "Thank you, Francis, and you're welcome," he said, deliberately using Kettering's Christian name. "I'm just glad I was able to help."

He waited until the plane was airborne before allowing Paula to flag down a passing mover to take them back to the main terminal.

Justin allowed a smile of satisfaction to spread across his face. He caught Paula's eye and winked. Paula winked back.

THE END

AUTHOR'S BIOGRAPHY

Ian A. O'Connor is the author of *Point Option – A Time-Travel Military Thriller* which was the 2022 winner of the prestigious Silver Falchion Award for the year's "Best Thriller". It was presented to Ian at the 15th Annual Nashville Writers Conference. His recent thriller, *The Pegasus Directive – The Top Secret Kennedy Assassination File* features the same Andrew St. James who was re-introduced to readers in *The Twilight of the Day.* It is a chilling tale of what happened to U.S. pilot-POWs during—and after—the Vietnam War. It was awarded a bronze medal by the Military Writers Society of America for its "totally believable story."

Ian is a retired USAF colonel. He is a recognized expert in the field of national security management, a background that serves him well as the foundation for all of his novels. His other thrillers include: *The Seventh Seal* and *The Barbarossa Covenant*, both "Justin Scott Thrillers". *Kirkus Reviews* wrote in high praise of his work: "The end result fits nicely into the Tom Clancy-meets-Dan Brown canon." His co-authored book: *SCRAPPY: A Memoir of a Fighter Pilot in Korea and Vietnam*, published by McFarland Publishing Company, remains a favorite of the international military aviation community. It recounts the amazing career of USAF Colonel Howard "Scrappy" Johnson, recipient of the 1958 Collier Trophy the year's most meritorious flight.

Colonel O'Connor holds a commercial pilot certificate with single engine, and multi-engine ratings. He is a member of The Air Commando Association; an associate member of The Red River Valley Fighter Pilots Association; the VFW; and the Mystery Writers of America. He lives on Florida's Treasure Coast with his wife, Candice.

www.ingramcontent.com/pod-product-compliance
Lightning Source LLC
Chambersburg PA
CBHW030422310726
48979CB00009B/1579/J